"Gene, I don't think you should do this."

Ross edged closer to Gene and the skittish horse. The glint in Gene's eyes and the eager tilt to her chin worried him. She seemed to vibrate with excitement. "I don't want you to get hurt," he added.

"I won't," Gene said just as a whistle blew. "That's for us." She smiled down at Ross. "Aren't you going to wish us luck?"

He would much rather have hauled her off the horse and wrapped her in his arms. But he could just imagine what her reaction to *that* would be. So he said, "Good luck. And remember, if things aren't going well out there, just pull out. I promise you none of us will think anything of it."

"You might not, but I will." She reached down and touched Ross's face. "I appreciate your concern, but you worry too much." Then, her eyes sparkling in that way he was beginning to distrust, she saluted and said, "We'll see you later."

I hope so, he muttered under his breath. *And I hope you're still in one piece.*

Dear Reader,

I've always admired those hardy—some would say foolhardy—men and women who compete for the love of the sport and the sheer thrill of riding.

In writing *Rivals and Lovers,* I was able to experience the excitement vicariously through my heroine, Gene Logan, who truly is a *woman who dares.* Even better, I created a hero worthy of her—an ex-Formula One driver who knows all about high-voltage competition. And I brought them together through a greathearted horse, based on one I once knew. I hope you enjoy reading their story as much as I enjoyed writing it....

Now I'm on to my next Superromance project—a three-book family saga set in Kentucky. Centered on an aging matriarch anxious to rectify past mistakes, these stories will explore the conflicting emotions that often run rampant in powerful families: jealousy, intrigue, betrayal, loyalty, love and pride. And, of course, each story will feature an unforgettable romance. I am very excited about this trilogy, for it takes place in the thrilling world of Thoroughbred racing—a setting close to my heart. I can hardly wait to present it to you in late 1995 or early 1996!

Till then,
Risa Kirk

Risa Kirk

RIVALS AND
LOVERS

Harlequin Books

TORONTO • NEW YORK • LONDON
AMSTERDAM • PARIS • SYDNEY • HAMBURG
STOCKHOLM • ATHENS • TOKYO • MILAN
MADRID • WARSAW • BUDAPEST • AUCKLAND

ISBN 0-373-70607-3

RIVALS AND LOVERS

This edition published by arrangement with Harlequin Enterprises B. V.

® and TM are trademarks of the publisher. Trademarks indicated with
® are registered in the United States Patent and Trademark Office, the
Canadian Trade Marks Office and in other countries.

Printed in U.S.A.

RIVALS AND
LOVERS

CHAPTER ONE

UNTIL DISASTER GALLOPED in late that Friday afternoon, Geneva Logan was having a fairly ordinary day. She was at her desk reviewing the latest designs for her company's "Warm Fuzzies" greeting card collection. She had just about decided that the artwork was a little too cutesy when her friend and assistant, Wally Tanker, buzzed her on the intercom.

"Uh... Gene, there's a call for you on line one," Wally said, sounding odd. "I know you said you didn't want to be interrupted, but I think you should take this. It's someone named Kenny Fielding, and he seems... a little hysterical."

Gene looked up with a frown. Kenny Fielding was the owner of Fielding Stables, where her sister Shelley rode and trained horses. The only reason she could think for him to call was...

"Oh, my God!" she exclaimed. She snatched the phone. "Kenny? This is Gene. Has something happened to Shelley?"

When all she heard at the other end was a gasping sound, she feared the worst. *I knew it!* she thought, her fingers whitening on the receiver. Her sister was an outstanding equestrienne, as she had been herself years ago, but Shelley was involved in the arduous sport of three-day eventing now, and she had recently been contacted by a new sponsor who expected her to ride an untrained horse named—what was it? Some ancient Roman name. Archimedes, or Attila, or...

She caught her breath. What difference did the *name* make? The horse had probably just killed her sister!

"Kenny?" she said again.

Kenny still sounded choked when he answered. "Oh, Gene, I'm sorry, but...can you come right away? We're at the hospital, and Shelley needs you. She wanted to call herself, but—"

"Is she all right? She's not—" Gene couldn't bring herself to say the words.

"Well, she's not exactly all *right,*" Kenny said. "I mean, her leg is broken, but they're not sure that's all."

Gene leaned back against her chair with a gasp. It was only a broken leg, she thought, relieved. Then she bolted upright again. "What do you mean, they're not sure that's *all?*"

"Well," Kenny said, "she wouldn't let anyone touch her until I agreed to call you."

"What? Why not? What's the matter with her? I want someone to examine her immediately! You tell her that right now!"

"I'd like to, Gene, but I can't. She insists no one is going to do anything until she talks to you. I'm sorry, I tried, I really did. But you know how she is."

Gene did know. One of the reasons no one thought they were sisters was that Shelley was blond and blue-eyed and sturdy, while Gene had dark hair and green eyes and looked deceptively fragile. But, as much as she hated to admit it, they'd each inherited the family traits of stubbornness and temper—both of which *she* had learned to control long ago.

Wondering why she was thinking about such trivialities, she said, "I'll leave immediately. Where are you?"

Kenny named the hospital, and said they were all still in the emergency room. She was going to ask who he meant by "all," but she was anxious to be on her way. "I'll get there as soon as I can," she said. "In the meantime, I want you to insist that a doctor examine her."

"I'll try," Kenny said before they hung up. "But you'll probably have better luck at that than I will."

Gene doubted it. Shelley could very obstinate when she was in one of her moods. She was just replacing the receiver when Wally appeared in the doorway.

"Shelley's had some kind of accident," she told him. "She's at the hospital."

He looked shocked. "Is it serious?"

"I don't know. I'm leaving now to find out."

"Is there anything I can do?"

Gene glanced down at her desk. The drawings caught her eye, but she couldn't think about them now. She had to let her boss know she had an emergency. As she flipped the file closed, she said, "Yes, there is. Please let Mason know that I had to leave. I'll make a decision about these tomorrow."

"Will do. What else?"

"I don't know, but if something comes up, you handle it. I'll call you later and let you know what happened."

"Good luck."

"Let's hope we don't need it," she said. She grabbed her purse and ran out, in such a hurry that she didn't remember her suit jacket until she reached the parking lot. It wasn't important enough to retrieve, so she climbed into the car and tried to insert the key. Her hand was shaking so badly she couldn't do it.

"Easy," she muttered as she forced herself to sit back and take a deep breath. It wouldn't help anyone if she got into an accident on the way. If she didn't calm down, she'd end up in the emergency room herself.

Suddenly, she wondered if this was how her parents had felt about the times she'd been injured during her riding career. As a teenager, she had competed in three-day eventing as well as jumping classes, and while she hadn't fallen often, it *had* happened. She'd accepted the occasional broken bones and the scrapes and strains and sprains as part of competition, but when she looked back, she wondered how her mother and father had survived it. She was thirty-five now, Shelley five years younger. Even though they were both adults, Gene was practically beside herself with worry.

The thought reminded her she'd better get going, and this time when she tried to insert the key, she had better luck. Seconds later, she was zooming onto the freeway.

For once, the traffic was light; the hospital mercifully just minutes away. She found a parking space near the emergency-room entrance, but as she hurried up the walk toward the door, she could feel her heart pounding again. Her first sight of Kenny standing by the admissions desk wasn't reassuring. He looked white as paste.

"Kenny!" she called. As she started toward him, she had a vague impression of two other men hovering nearby, but she didn't pay attention to them.

The stable owner's face flooded with relief when he saw her. "Gene! I'm so glad you're here. I've been so worried, I think I'm going to be sick."

Gene could see that he did look ill. But her sister was undoubtedly in worse shape, so she didn't have time to coddle him. She had to find out her sister's condition before she collapsed from sheer anxiety herself.

"Here, sit down and tell me about it," she said, half dragging him over to a group of chairs. She pushed him into one, then sat down beside him. "What did the doctor say?"

"Nothing yet. Shelley's still insisting that she has to talk to you first."

Gene's expression turned grim. "Where is she?"

He pointed to a closed door opposite. "In there. But you can't go in. They told us to wait out here."

Waiting was the last thing Gene planned to do. A red sign on the door said, No Admittance Unless Authorized, but that wasn't going to stop her. She wanted to know what had happened to Shelley, and she wanted to know *now*. She stood, and Kenny looked up at her.

"Maybe you'd better ask a nurse or someone," he said.

There was no one to ask. The admissions desk was empty, and as Gene looked around, she didn't see anyone who seemed to be in charge. She was about to start toward the forbidden door when one of the two men standing to the side caught her attention. He was tall and good-looking, and he was leaning heavily on a cane. He had the most piercing blue eyes she'd ever seen, and as their gaze held for a few seconds, she had the unsettling feeling that she knew him. She jerked her eyes away and said to Kenny, "I'm going to find out what's going on."

"But you're not supposed—"

"I know. But I'm going to, anyway."

When Gene pushed the door open and walked in, two women who were bending over a hospital chart by a desk looked up. One was wearing a lab coat; the other had on a nurse's uniform, and they both appeared irritated at the interruption. The nurse started to speak. "I'm sorry, but you can't—"

"I already have," Gene said. Ahead of her were five compartments, each marked off by curtains hanging from ceiling tracks, fabric walls meant to give the illusion of privacy, and yet allow quick access. Three of the cubicles were empty, their complicated arrays of machinery standing idle. But the curtains on the remaining two were closed, and as she hesitated, wondering if one of them held Shelley, the woman in the lab coat came forward. Her name tag identified her as Victoria Martin, M.D., but before she could say anything, someone shouted from behind one of the curtains. The doctor came to a halt and glanced over her shoulder.

"Damned motorcycles, anyway," she muttered. She started toward the shouter, but before she disappeared behind the curtain, she said to the nurse, "Take care of her, will you, Mary?"

Gene didn't want to be taken care of; she wanted to see Shelley. "My name is Geneva Logan," she said crisply, "and I understand that my sister is—"

"Gene? Is that you?" a familiar voice called from behind one of the closed curtains. "What took you so long? I asked Kenny to call you ages ago!"

Gene looked at the nurse, "Would you mind? Shelley is my sister, and—"

The nurse looked resigned. "Go ahead. Maybe now that you're here, she'll let us do our jobs."

Gene was almost afraid to ask. "How bad is it?"

"I can't tell you. We haven't been allowed to take X rays."

"Well, we'll see about *that*," Gene declared. She turned and headed toward the cubicle.

Shelley was propped up on the hospital bed, her right leg resting on a pillow. It was encased in an air-filled plastic bubble that paramedics use when they suspect a patient may have a broken bone. As soon as Gene saw the cast, she forgot about giving her sister a piece of her mind, and hugged her instead.

"Oh, Shel, what *happened?*" she asked.

Shelley gingerly returned the embrace before she lay back again. With a grimace, she said, "He stopped. I didn't. End of story."

Despite the bravado, Gene saw how pale Shelley's face was and she took her sister's hand. "I'm sure there's a little more to it than that, but I'm going to let it go for now. The important thing is to let the doctors take a look at you. You have to let them examine you, Shel. They need to do tests—"

Shelley's fingers tightened on hers. Her expression fierce, she said, "Not until you promise me something."

"Now, Shel—"

"No, I mean it. We've both had broken bones before, and I know that this one is bad enough that they'll have to put me under to set it. I won't let them do it until I'm sure I have everything settled."

Gene was beginning to think that Shelley had suffered a concussion along with the break in her leg, so she tried to assume a soothing tone. "Whatever you say...."

"You mean that?"

"Of course, I do. You know I'd do anything for you."

Shelley's face flooded with relief. "Great! Now, here's the plan—"

"Plan?" Gene repeated suspiciously. "I didn't agree to a plan! I just said—"

"You said you'd help. Now, this is about Achilles—"

"Who's Achilles?"

"For heaven's sake! He's the horse that put me here!"

Gene's mouth tightened. "What about him?"

"Don't look like that. If you'll listen, I'll tell you. I'm not going to let this go, Gene. I mean it. Achilles is going to be the best eventing horse I've ever ridden...." Shelley hesitated a moment, then added reluctantly, "At least he will be, when I get him trained. Right now he's a little green, I admit. But after you ride him for a while, I know he'll—"

"Wait a minute. What do you mean, after *I* ride him for a while? I'm not going to—"

Shelley sat up. The sudden movement made her wince, but she grabbed Gene's arm, anyway. "You said you'd do anything for me!"

Gene tried to free herself. "Yes, but that doesn't mean I'm going to start riding again! I haven't been on a horse in years!"

"That's not true, and you know it. But even if it were, it's all the more reason for you to do it now. You used to be good, sis. You know you were."

"Yes, and... *used to be*... are the... operative words," Gene declared. She jerked her arm from Shelley's tight grip and gave her sister an appalled look. "You can't seriously be suggesting that I, who haven't been on a horse in longer than I can remember, try to ride an animal that put you in the hospital! Look at yourself, Shelley! Riding is what you do for a living, and Achilles threw you. What do you think he'd do to *me* if I was foolish enough to try to mount him?"

Shelley looked at her exasperatedly. "I'm not asking you to *compete* him! I just want you to... to exercise him. You know, get him ready for competition. You can do it, I know you can. Kenny has that big cross-country course for you to practice on, and if I ask him, he'll help to train you both. All you have to do is take Achilles out there and work him for me. Come on, Gene, you were once one of the best junior riders in the world. You can do it, I know you can."

Gene didn't even have to think about it. "No, I can't," she said firmly, shaking her head. "I won't. It's crazy even to try. If I don't get killed myself, I might hurt the horse, and then what?'' She shook her head again. ''It's out of the question. If it means so much to you, you'll just have to get someone else.''

''I don't trust anyone else!'' Shelley exclaimed. She looked down at the cast on her leg and burst into tears.

It was so seldom that Shelley cried, even as a child, that Gene was taken aback. It made her realize just how much this horse meant to her sister, and for an instant she was tempted... But only for an instant. The situation might have been different if the horse was fully trained and all she had to do was exercise him until Shelley could ride again herself. But to expect her to take on a horse who had little or no training at all was too much to ask. She couldn't do it, not even for Shelley.

''I'm sorry, Shel,'' she said, steeling herself for her sister's reaction. ''I just can't. I see how important this is to you, but—''

Shelley looked up. ''You don't know, Gene. This is my big chance! I've waited all these years for a horse like Achilles, and now that he's being offered to me, *this* has to happen! It isn't fair! If you don't agree to do this, the sponsors will give him to someone else!''

''But they'll understand. They'll wait.''

''They won't, I know it! Oh, please! I've never asked anything of you before in my entire life, and if you agree to do this one thing for me, I swear I'll never ask anything else!''

Gene knew that wasn't true, but this wasn't the time to argue about it—not with Shelley's blue eyes filling once more with tears.

''Even if I did agree, what makes you think the sponsors will allow it?'' she asked. ''They want *you* to train the horse, not some has-been junior rider who hasn't been in the saddle in years!''

"Will you do it if they say yes?"

"Well, I—"

"Can we ask them?"

Hoping this was all some pain-induced fantasy of her sister's, Gene said, "Yes, yes. But first we're going to get this leg taken care of, and anything else that was broken, including," she added pointedly, "your head."

She reached for the button to call the nurse, but Shelley was faster than her sister was. She grabbed the control hanging by the side of the bed and stabbed a button. When someone answered, she said, "Would you ask Ross Malone to come in here?"

"Shelley, what are you doing?" Gene asked. "Who's Ross Malone?"

"I am," a deep male voice answered.

Startled, Gene turned around. The man with the cane who had been in the waiting room was coming up behind her. As soon as Shelley saw him, she held out her hand. "Thanks for sticking around, Ross."

Ross Malone limped around the bed and took Shelley's hand. "I told you. I feel responsible," he said. "We couldn't leave until we found out what the doctors said."

Shelley dismissed the medical staff with a wave. "Who cares what they say? I haven't seen anyone yet, and besides, I had more important things on my mind."

"But what could be—"

"You'll see," Shelley said. "Ross, this is my sister, Gene Logan. Gene, this is Ross Malone, the owner of

Outdoor Outfitters, the company that's sponsoring Achilles.''

Gene did her best to hide her annoyance. Later, she would speak to Shelley for not warning her first, but right now, all she could do was shake Ross Malone's hand and mutter, "Pleased to meet you."

"Likewise, Ms. Logan."

Shelley looked from one to the other with a satisfied expression and said, "Gene has agreed to ride Achilles until I can get up on him again, Ross. I hope that's okay with you."

"I didn't exactly *agree* to ride the horse, Mr. Malone," Gene said hastily with a glare in her sister's direction. "I just said I'd think about it."

"But—" Shelley said.

Gene managed to silence her with another grim look before she turned to Ross Malone again. He seemed startled by Shelley's idea—as well he should, she thought. If she'd been in his position, she would have politely told them they were both out of their minds.

She started to say something, but Shelley interrupted. "I know what you're thinking, Ross, but Gene can handle Achilles. You don't know what a good rider she used to be."

"Used to be," he repeated. He was obviously trying to decide how to handle the situation. To Gene, he said, "No offense, but Achilles *is* a powerful horse."

Illogically, Gene felt a prick of annoyance. Where did he get off implying that she might not be up to the task? Her chin came up a fraction, and before she knew it, she was saying, "The *horse* isn't the problem, Mr. Malone. I may not have ridden for a while, but I'm not exactly a beginner."

"I should think not. Gene started riding when she was a child and competed at an international level," Shelley contributed eagerly.

Gene glared at her again. "That's beside the point," she said. Ross was staring at her with a strange expression, as if trying not to laugh. Stiffly, she said, "Do I amuse you, Mr. Malone?"

"No, of course not," he denied with twinkling eyes. "I was just trying to... to picture you riding that horse."

Gene's face darkened. Shelley apparently noticed, and sank back into her pillow when Gene said, "And the picture you see is funny, Mr. Malone?"

"No, no, of course not," he said. "It's just that, as I said, Achilles is a big horse, and you... well, you look much too delicate to manage him."

"Is that so?" At five foot four and a hundred and five pounds, Gene knew she looked much more fragile than she actually was. Her size had always been a curse. "Is that your polite way of saying that you don't want me to exercise your horse? Because if it is—"

Their eyes met, and she saw that she had annoyed him. But her satisfaction was short-lived when he had the gall to say, "Well, now that you mention it, I—"

Shelley sat up quickly. "Wait a minute! Gene, what are you saying? Ross, you can't mean—"

Gene didn't pay any attention. She was too busy trying to outstare the man to whom she'd taken a great dislike. At the back of her mind, a frantic little voice was shouting, *What are you doing?* while at the same time, another part of her was whispering persuasively, *You know you want to do it. You've always been sorry you gave up riding.*

Across from her, several emotions flickered across Ross Malone's handsome face, irritating her even more. But just as the tension rose another notch, Shelley figuratively elbowed her way in again.

"Ross, please!" Shelley begged. "We both know Achilles isn't anywhere *near* ready for competition. Gene can't possibly ruin him before I'm able to ride him again—"

Gene turned to her. "Well, thanks a lot for the vote of confidence!"

"Oh, you know what I mean!" Shelley said. She looked at Ross again and continued passionately, "He *can't* stand around in a stall until my leg heals! It wouldn't be good for him, or you, or anyone!"

Ross tried to reason with her. "I know how important this is to you, Shelley—"

"No, you don't!" Shelley insisted. "You couldn't possibly!"

"Shelley, there will be other horses," Gene intervened.

"Not like Achilles! Even if you're lucky, a horse like him comes along only once in a lifetime!"

Ross winced a little at the naked pain in Shelley's voice, but he continued, "If you can't ride him, I'll *have* to get someone else."

"But that's just the point, don't you see?" Shelley cried. "I won't be sidelined forever, and in the meantime, you'll have Gene!"

Gene wasn't going to be forced on anyone, especially not on Mr. Ross Don't-Think-You-Can-Do-It Malone. "Shelley, if he doesn't want me to—"

"But he will, after he sees you ride!" Shelley said shrilly. "It's just that he's never seen you on a horse, so he doesn't know how good you are. Once he realizes—'' She broke off and turned to her sponsor again. "Don't say no until you've seen her ride, okay? After that, you can decide."

"Now, wait a minute," Gene said. "I never agreed to—''

Shelley turned to her. "You promised!"

"Be reasonable, Shelley," Ross pleaded.

Shelley looked from one to the other, her expression tragic. "I don't understand you!" she almost wept. "It's the perfect solution, don't you see? Oh, if you don't agree, I'll just *die!*"

Gene's green eyes met Ross's blue over the pitiful figure in the bed. What would it hurt? she wondered. If he agreed to try, she could, too—for a while. Then at least they could say they'd done everything they could to make things right. Not even Shelley could be unhappy with that.

"If it's all right with—" she said reluctantly.

"If it's all right with—" he said with an equal lack of enthusiasm at the same time.

They both looked down at the injured rider, who examined each of their faces before she sat back with a sigh.

"Thanks," Shelley said happily. "I knew you wouldn't let me down." Then, before Gene could remind her that this was a trial—and only that—Shelley closed her eyes. As if the delay was all their fault, she added, "Now I think you'd better call the doctor. Whatever they gave me before is wearing off, and this leg hurts like hell. If you don't mind, I should probably get it set now before I pass out from the pain."

CHAPTER TWO

WHEN ROSS CAME OUT OF the emergency room, his partner, James Daughtry, was hovering nearby. With his conservative suit, his short brown hair and his brown eyes magnified behind strong glasses, James didn't look like the excitable sort, but Ross knew better.

"What happened?" James demanded before Ross could say anything. "Is Shelley all right?"

"Oh, yes, she's just fine," Ross said wryly. "In fact, for a woman with so much on her mind, a broken leg hardly seems to matter."

"What do you mean?"

Kenny rushed up to them, his expression anxious. "What did you find out?"

Ross answered, "I think they're about to take Shelley down to X ray."

"Finally!"

"Yes, well, she's directing things now, and apparently she's decided to get the show on the road."

Kenny eyed the No Admittance sign on the door. "Do you think I could see her?"

"I don't see why not," Ross replied. "Everybody else has. By now, I think they're resigned to a parade through there."

As Kenny disappeared through the door, James grabbed Ross's arm. "So what happened?" James demanded. "What did the doctor say? Will Shelley be able to ride the horse?"

Ross glanced back over his shoulder. Through the window in the door, he could see Gene Logan talking to the nurse. He watched her a moment before he said, "Well, it's kind of complicated."

"Complicated?" James's voice rose. "How much more complicated can it get?" He slapped a hand to his forehead. "Oh, I knew right from the beginning this whole thing was a mistake! We should have behaved like normal businesspeople and hired a public relations firm. Or better yet, gone with a simple ad campaign to generate more sales. Why did we have to sponsor a horse? This is all my fault!"

Ross tried not to smile at his partner's melodramatics. "We both agreed to do this, don't forget."

"Yes, but I—"

"Everything is going to be okay. Trust me."

"But I feel responsible!"

"You always do, but you're overreacting," Ross said calmly. "You couldn't predict this would happen."

"No, but I could have prevented it. After all, it was my idea, wasn't it? Now we've spent all this money for the horse and we have no rider!"

"Not exactly," Ross said, beginning to head for the exit.

"Not exactly?" James echoed, following on his partner's heels. "What do you mean?" Hope dawned in his eyes. "Will Shelley be able to ride the horse, after all?"

"Oh, she'll be able to ride," Ross said.

James raised his eyes heavenward in grateful thanks. "Praise the Lord!"

"Eventually."

James halted in midstride. "Eventually? What does that mean?"

The doors opened automatically as Ross approached. When he went through them, James followed. Even with his cane, Ross walked fast; his legs were so much longer than his friend's, James almost had to trot to keep up.

"Ross, what aren't you telling me?" James panted as they headed into the parking lot.

Ross finally stopped, because they had reached the car. He was driving, but as always, it took him a few extra seconds to maneuver his left leg into place as he got behind the wheel. By then, James had climbed in on the passenger side.

"Ross," James said as he reached for his seat belt, "why do I have the feeling that I'm not going to like what you have to tell me?"

"Probably because I'm not sure I like it myself," Ross said. He backed carefully out of the parking space before he added, "I have to give them one thing, though—they're quite a team."

"Who?"

"Shelley and her sister."

James looked at him uncomprehendingly. "That was Shelley's *sister?* They don't look anything alike!"

"Well, there's a family resemblance all the same. They both have wills of iron and a stubborn streak to match."

"I don't like the sound of that. What happened?"

Ross didn't know how to tell him. He still couldn't understand his reaction to Gene Logan. For one thing, she didn't look like a "Gene" to him; the name was too forceful, too strong and no-nonsense for a woman as lovely and delicate as she was.

Was it her looks that had thrown him off? he wondered. He'd been so preoccupied with her appearance that he had missed the stubborn set of her chin and the challenge in her green eyes. He hadn't realized he'd underestimated her until he'd been maneuvered into agreeing to something he didn't want to do and still wasn't sure was right. How had that happened? Even now, he couldn't put his finger on it.

"Well?" James asked anxiously.

Ross knew he couldn't put it off any longer, so he said, "Shelley asked if her sister could exercise the horse until her leg heals."

"And you said what?"

"I said we might give it a try."

James looked at him as though Ross were out of his mind. "A *try?* I don't believe it! Does she even know how to ride? Ross, this is awful! What were you thinking?"

"What else could I do?"

James sat there for a moment, his mouth opening and closing like a fish. Then he declared, "You could have told her you were sorry, but that we had to find someone else to ride the horse. *That's* what you could have done."

"Yes, I could have, but I didn't. Besides, I figured, why go out and start looking for another rider when one was right there offering her services? Remember what a hard time we had finding Shelley?"

"Yes, but—"

"Maybe *you* want to ride the horse until Shelley's fit."

"*Me!* Good grief, no!"

"Well, then?"

James was silent. Ross knew from experience it wouldn't last long, and it didn't. Two seconds later, James was demanding, "How do you know she can even ride?"

"Shelley told me she could," he said. Then before James could erupt again, he added quickly, "She says Gene used to be a junior champion."

"A *junior* champion? And how long ago was that? Oh, God," James exclaimed suddenly, clutching his thinning hair in dismay, "we're going to be ruined! All that money for the horse—not to mention an expensive promotion campaign, and for what? Before we even sign up for the first competition, our rider breaks a leg!"

"Yes, but no one could have—"

James didn't hear him. He rushed on, "And now her sister, whose entire equestrian experience probably consists of bouncing around on a fat little pony somewhere, is going to get killed trying to ride our horse! Instead of generating sales, we'll go broke paying for all the lawsuits!"

"James, will you calm down?"

Wild-eyed, James looked at him. "I *am* calm! If you think I'm not, wait for my breakdown when the company goes bankrupt."

"It won't be as bad as you think."

"And just how do you figure that?"

"Well, Shelley isn't going to be out of action forever, you know. And in the meantime, if her sister can't handle the horse, we'll just get someone else to ride him until Shelley can take over. I'm sure Kenny will know someone who wants to exercise Achilles. After all, say what you like about the horse, he is a beautiful animal."

"For someone on a suicide mission!" James fell back against the seat. "Oh, why did I give up smoking? I could use a cigarette now—an entire pack!"

"You worry too much. Everything will be okay."

James closed his eyes. "I hope you're right. We've invested a lot in this project, much more than we should have," he repeated. "If it doesn't work out..."

He didn't finish the thought, but Ross knew they were both thinking the same thing. James hadn't exaggerated his earlier claims about bankruptcy by much. The promotion campaign they'd designed— sponsoring a three-day-event horse to increase sales and publicity—was an effort to save their company. If they couldn't stem what was rapidly becoming a tide of red ink, Ross didn't know what they'd do. They'd tried everything else, it seemed, but the recession had affected everyone. People who were worried about jobs and bills and paying their mortgages weren't all that interested in the latest outdoor equipment—unless it was buying a tent in case they lost their house.

He and James had known from the beginning that this horse thing was a gamble, but they'd taken the risk, anyway. James had been nervous enough about the venture, so Ross hadn't mentioned his own misgivings. Even after they bought the horse and made the riding arrangements with Shelley, he'd still been

uneasy at the thought that the fate of the company
might be in her hands.

And now?

How did he feel now, when the future of Outdoor
Outfitters seemed to depend on how well Shelley's
fragile-looking sister could ride a mountain of an untrained horse—appropriately named, Ross thought
with a grimace—Achilles.

"YOU'RE GOING to *what?*" Wally said incredulously
the next morning at the office when Gene told him
what had transpired at the hospital the day before.

"I know it sounds crazy—"

"Crazy! It sounds insane! Were you out of your
mind or what?"

Wearily, Gene sat down behind her desk. The Warm
Fuzzies file was still there, but she brushed it aside, in
no mood to deal with anything warm and fuzzy right
now.

"I don't know what happened," she said, sitting
back and rubbing her temples. "One minute I was
telling Shelley it was out of the question, and the next,
I was agreeing to do it."

Wally still looked stunned—as well he might, Gene
thought. She'd had an entire night to think about it,
and she still couldn't believe what she'd done. What
had possessed her to say she'd ride that horse? Aside
from the fact that she hadn't ridden in years, she
didn't have the time or the energy to exercise a horse.
Riding him would take too much from her already-
tight schedule. She could just imagine Mason's reaction if she told him she had to leave early every day
because she had to get to the stables.

It was especially difficult now in the middle of trying to launch this new line of greeting cards. It had been Mason's idea, but as vice president of the Greetings card company, she was responsible for it, and now that she was committed, she didn't have a minute to herself. In fact, before Shelley's accident yesterday, she'd been contemplating bringing a cot into the office.

Obviously she hadn't been thinking clearly when she'd agreed to her sister's outrageous scheme. The minute Ross Malone had intimated that she didn't have the ability to ride the horse, pride had reared its ugly head and before she knew it, she was practically daring him not to give her the chance.

How had it happened? she wondered dismally. It wasn't because he was so good-looking—even if he was. She'd known handsome men before. What was it about Ross Malone that had made her want to prove herself to him?

"Well," Wally said, interrupting her reverie. "What are you going to do?"

She'd already decided. Crisply, she said, "I'm going to call Shelley and tell her I've changed my mind, that's what. She'll understand."

Wally didn't try to hide the skepticism in his voice. He knew Shelley, too. "She will?" he asked.

"She'll have to, that's all," Gene stated. "Shelley knows a lot of people in the horse world. Someone will exercise that horse for her. Most of them practically live at the stable, anyway. One of them can take time out from their schedules to work Achilles until Shelley can do it herself."

"I don't know," Wally said dubiously. "If that's true, why did she ask you?"

Gene looked at him in exasperation. "How do I know? Maybe before she broke her leg, she fell on her head. I just know I can't do this, not even for her. I've got a life, too, you know," she added defensively. "I can't just put everything on hold because she's afraid she's going to lose the horse to a competitor. It wasn't fair of her to ask me."

Wally studied her for a moment. Then he said, "You know, I think, deep down, you really want to do this."

She was outraged. "That's ridiculous!"

"Is it? You used to compete, Gene. You told me so yourself."

"I was a kid then!"

"Yes, but even now, whenever you talk about horses, your face sort of lights up...." He hesitated, then he added, "Maybe you miss it more than you realize."

"Miss it? Are you kidding?" Gene said, her voice rising. "I'm happy here. I love my work!"

Wally rolled his eyes. "Methinks the lady doth protest too much."

"And *I* think *you* don't have enough to think about," Gene retorted. "Don't you have some work to do—in your *own* office?"

He grinned. "I can take a hint. But you know," he added innocently as he headed toward the door, "now that I think about it, maybe you're right. It wasn't fair of Shelley. You've got too much work here. You just can't do it."

"Damn right," Gene muttered as he went out.

She looked at the phone. Should she call now and get it over with? Shelley was still in the hospital. When Gene had talked to her this morning, she'd learned that the fracture was worse than the doctor expected, and Shelley had to stay over a couple of days to make sure the leg didn't swell. Gene could tell that hadn't gone over well with her active sister, who had already been climbing the walls and badgering everyone about how soon she could get out. It was probably cruel to give her more bad news now, Gene thought, but the longer she waited, the harder it would be.

Resigned to a big scene, she was just reaching for the phone when it rang. She glanced through the open door, saw that Wally wasn't at his desk and answered it herself.

"Greetings," she said. "Gene Logan here."

"Good morning," said a voice that made her feel instantly tense. "This is Ross Malone—you remember, we met yesterday at the hospital?"

She wasn't likely to forget, she thought. "I remember. What can I do for you, Mr. Malone?"

When he hesitated, she realized she'd sounded a little cool. Well, so what? she thought rudely. She wanted him to keep his distance, especially since, much to her annoyance, her heart had started racing at the sound of his voice. Wondering what *that* was about, she bit back an apology.

"Is this a bad time?" Ross asked. "If it is, I can call back."

"No, it's fine," she said, deciding to get this conversation over with as quickly as possible. "How can I help you, Mr. Malone?"

"Why don't you call me Ross? After all, we might be working together."

"Might?"

"Well, I'm calling to find out if you've changed your mind about riding Achilles."

He'd given her the perfect opening; all she had to do was walk through it. Instead, she asked perversely, "Why would you think that?"

"Look," he said, an edge in his voice, "I know we promised Shelley that we'd give this a try. And I don't want to influence you, but... have you seen Achilles?"

Suddenly, she felt like being difficult. "No, I haven't," she said. "Why?"

"Well... um... he's pretty big."

Was he actually implying that she couldn't ride a *big* horse? She felt her hackles rising. "Well, 'big' is relative in the horse world," she said coolly. "As I recall, Shelley mentioned that Achilles was just under seventeen hands. I've ridden Warmbloods bigger than that."

She'd expected him to be impressed—or at least think twice about what a formidable rider she must be. To her irritation, he persisted, "Yes, but were they as intractable as this horse? When we bought him, it was with the understanding that he needed training. *Much* more training. Shelley knew that, but I wonder if you do."

She couldn't hold back the sarcasm. "Yes, that had occurred to me," she said. "Shelley's one of the best, most capable riders I know, and if Achilles succeeded in throwing her, I imagine the horse needs a little work."

He sounded relieved that she understood. "Exactly. So in that case, I'm sure you realize our reluctance to—"

Gene didn't know what was wrong with her. He was giving her a perfect out—all she needed to say was that she thought her sister's plan was even more ill advised than he obviously did. Instead, what she *said* was, "Look, Mr. Malone, if you didn't want me to exercise the horse until Shelley could ride him herself, you should have said so. If you felt this way, why did you promise her we could give it a try?"

He was irritated by the question; she could hear it in his voice when he said, "Maybe you're right." He paused fractionally. "Look...why don't we just start over and set up a convenient time to meet at Kenny's stables. You can ride the horse, and *then* we'll decide if this is going to work or not. How does that sound?"

It sounded as though he were doing her a favor. Through her teeth, she answered, "That's fine with me, Mr. Malone. What time would you like to meet?"

They agreed on Saturday morning. Early, Gene suggested coolly, not telling him that she wanted to get the trial over with before all the stable groupies arrived. She hung up the phone and saw Wally in the doorway.

"I thought you weren't going to do it," he said.

"You were listening!"

"I couldn't help it, you were shouting."

"I was not shouting!" she said loudly. She lowered her voice. "And besides, he implied that I couldn't ride the damned horse."

"I hate to ask you this, Gene, but...*can* you ride it?"

She wasn't even going to think about that. "I'm going to look pretty stupid if I can't, aren't I?"

"Is that a yes or a no?"

"Never mind." She reached for the phone again. "And before you ask, I'm going to call Kenny and throw myself on his mercy. He has all those schooling horses. I'm sure he'll let me practice on one of them."

"And what about Achilles?"

"Achilles," she said, looking up Kenny's number before she dialed, "is just going to have to wait."

ACHILLES WAITED until that same night after work, when Gene went out to the stables to have a look at the horse that was causing all this turmoil. Kenny had said he'd meet her, but she found the stall by herself and was standing there when he rushed up.

"Sorry I'm late," he panted. He took off his hat and brushed a hand through his curly brown hair. He was in his mid-thirties, but had the kind of face that seemed ageless. Short of stature, but lean and wiry, he smiled at her, his blue eyes crinkling at the corners. "Got a call at the last minute. Important biz, you know. Money owed—to me, not the other way around."

"The best kind," Gene agreed. "But don't worry, I just got here myself."

Kenny saw her looking at the horse. "He's a beauty, isn't he?"

It took her a moment to answer. Kenny had known she was coming so he hadn't put the horse's blanket on yet. As Achilles wandered around the stall, his pure white coat glistened under the lights, and she had to swallow before she said, "Yes, he is."

She'd tried to hide it, but Kenny must have heard something in her voice. ''He reminds you of someone, doesn't he?''

And just like that, out of the past cantered a memory of another white horse who had taken her to her junior national championship—and who she knew would have won her the worlds, if he'd been able to. It had been years ago, but as memory claimed her, she left Kenny Fielding's barn and was suddenly astride that other white horse at the Forum in Los Angeles.

The stands were packed that night, she remembered; the lights like a thousand suns. It had been raining outside, but the air in the arena was cool and moist. But all she'd felt, or seen, or heard, was her horse as they went around the course in the final jump-off round at the World Show Jumping Championships. They'd made it around the entire course; all that was left was the wall looming at the end. It seemed impossibly high, but she had confidence in her horse, and as they thundered down the last few yards, she gave him the signal with her hands and her heels and he instantly obeyed her, as he always had.

Even now, she could feel him engage his powerful hindquarters, and then suddenly, they were surging into the air, flying over the wall as though it weren't even there. At the apex of the jump, she'd felt so exhilarated that, if it hadn't been a breech of protocol, she would have shouted aloud with sheer joy. All they had to do was come down cleanly and get over the finish line and the championship was theirs. After years of preparation and hard work, the trophy was practically in the palm of her hand.

To this day, she didn't know what had happened. One instant she and the horse were coming safely down on the other side of the wall; the next minute she heard a sound she would remember to her dying day: the *crack!* as the bone in his front leg shattered.

She still recalled her sense of utter disbelief that this could be happening. Desperately, she had tried to gather him up again, frantically telling herself that if she could get him going, this would all prove to have been just a nightmare. A champion to the last, her horse tried valiantly, but even he, with his formidable will, couldn't obey her last command. Momentum carried them inexorably forward, and before she could stop him, she was thrown violently to one side as he went down.

People came running into the arena from every direction to see if she was hurt, but all she cared about was her horse on the ground. Screaming, as the tears streamed down her face, she clawed her way to his side and froze in despair. Even now, she could still see the blood. It seemed to be everywhere—on her, on him, on his beautiful white coat she'd been so proud of—

"Gene, are you all right?"

Gene started violently, coming back from the past to see Kenny looking at her with concern. It was a moment before she could answer. Finally, she managed to say, "Yes, I'm...fine."

He searched her face. "Shelley didn't tell you, did she?"

She had to make herself say it. "What? That he looked so much like...High Cotton?"

Kenny shook his head. "I told her she ought to warn you, and she said she would. I'm sorry, Gene. I should have thought of it when we talked on the phone."

"It's not your fault. Besides, it was years ago." She tried a smile that slipped off her face when she glanced at the horse again. Even she could hear the quiver in her voice. "I didn't think it would hurt so much after all this time."

He put a sympathetic hand on her arm. "It always hurts, when you lose a horse as good as I heard that one was."

"Thanks." Gratefully, she put her hand over his and tried to get a grip on herself. Forcing another smile, she said, "Besides, they don't really look that much alike. High Cotton was a little smaller and more compact. And he had a much better head."

"He did, did he?"

He smiled, too, and the awkward moment passed.

SHE FELT BETTER the next night when she went out to the stable—until she rode one of the schooling horses Kenny graciously offered her. At the end of the first practice, he had to assist her out of the saddle; on the second night, he had to help her take off her boots because she didn't have the strength to get them off herself. By the third ride, her knees were scraped raw on the inside; on the fourth night, she fell asleep in the bathtub after she'd dragged herself home. But on Friday night—when everyone else was out having fun, she thought, feeling sorry for herself—she managed to climb onto the school horse, ride creditably around the practice jump ring and then get out of the saddle by herself.

But Saturday morning still loomed, and when she realized that she still hadn't gotten any nearer to Achilles than the bars of his stall, she began to have second thoughts again. To hell with pride. She'd just call the whole thing off. What was she trying to prove, anyway? And to whom? She didn't even know Ross Malone; she wasn't sure she wanted to. And, she had to admit, it didn't add to her confidence to hear stories about how Achilles terrorized the stall cleaners, or fought the groom who tried to lead him out for free exercise in one of the big paddocks. Kenny was the only one who could handle the white horse, it seemed—and even he had trouble at times.

"But don't worry," Kenny had told her kindly that Friday night after he'd given her a lesson. "You'll be okay."

"You think so?" she groaned. She had planned on riding Achilles for the first time tonight, but after being on the school horse for two hours, she was too tired and sore even to think of getting up on Ross Malone's white beast. "Every bone in my body hurts. Muscles that I didn't even know were there are sore. I have to sit down."

"Here," he said sympathetically, helping her along as though she were a doddering old woman who couldn't maneuver on her own. "Let's go to the office. You can put your feet up and rest for a while."

"How about forever?" she moaned.

"You're doing just fine," he said when they reached the office. He helped her collapse onto the sagging couch in the corner and then gave her a cup of what passed for coffee from the ancient automatic coffee-maker.

"I don't want to do *fine*," she said, taking a sip and trying not to grimace. "I want to do a good job when I ride that horse."

Wisely, Kenny didn't ask her why she was putting herself through all this agony. Maybe he already knew she was trying to prove a point. But the answer to what the point had been, or for whom she was trying to make it eluded her as she rested her head and closed her eyes. She felt utterly exhausted.

"You'll be able to ride him," Kenny said, taking a seat behind his cluttered desk. As he did, several invoices for his customers' board bills fluttered to the floor. Absently, he picked them up and stuck them in a drawer.

"How can you be so sure?" she asked. At the moment, she doubted she could even climb onto the horse tomorrow, much less control him enough to take him around the jump course.

"I'm sure because I've seen how you ride," Kenny said.

She opened one eye. "Don't judge me by what you've seen this week. I've felt like a sack of potatoes up there, going every which way."

"You might have felt that way, but you sure didn't look it," he said, smiling. "In fact, the way you took Persia around the indoor course tonight, I'd say you were almost ready for competition again." He paused. "It's a good thing Shelley wasn't here. She might have been a little jealous."

"Of me? I doubt it. Shelley's a wonderful rider."

"She is. But she complains all the time that she's not as good as you were. She told me you were a natural, and now that I've seen you in action, I can see what she meant."

"You're being kind, and I thank you. But Shelley can more than hold her own."

"That's true. You're two different kinds of riders. But... here, look at this. Maybe you've forgotten." Swiveling the chair, he reached for something in the bookcase behind him and handed it to her.

"What's this?" she asked.

"Open it and see."

It was a photo album of pictures that had been taken during Gene's days of competition. In front were shots of her astride the first horse she had ever owned, a Welsh pony-mustang cross named Angel that she had ridden from the time she was five until she retired him when she turned ten. Next was the Appaloosa who had taught her so much—in patience, she remembered with a smile, thinking of how stubborn the gelding had been. That horse had loved going over jumps, but only when *he* wanted to—not necessarily when Gene did. She almost laughed, thinking of the arguments they'd had.

On the following pages were shots of Thunder Roll, the big bay who would have tried anything for her, even jumping through fire. And finally, she saw with a lump in her throat, there was High Cotton. When she saw her favorite picture of him—them—rising in perfect form up over a five-foot vertical, she thought wistfully of the courage he'd had, as well as that indefinable something that horse people prized because it was so rare, the quality called "heart."

She closed the book when tears began to fill her eyes. "Where did you get this?" she asked.

"Shelley brought it out one day to show me. She really is proud of you, Gene."

"I'm proud of her, too."

He smiled. "So am I."

That's when she knew that Kenny Fielding loved her sister. The look on his face told the whole story and she wondered if Shelley realized it. She doubted it. Gene loved her sister, but Shelley was oblivious at times, especially when she was preoccupied with something, as she was now, with Achilles.

The thought reminded her abruptly about her date with destiny tomorrow morning. Yawning, she levered herself up off the couch before she said, "Kenny, you've already done so much for me that I hate to ask anything else. But would you do me another favor?"

He walked her out of the office to her car. "Anything you want. Just name it."

She searched for her car keys and found them at the bottom of her purse. "I'm supposed to meet Ross Malone here tomorrow morning about eight, but since I haven't even ridden Achilles yet, would you mind if I came here a bit earlier to try him out?"

"Sure, no problem. What time?"

"About seven?"

"Seven, it is. And I'll tell you what. I'll even have him tacked and warmed up for you."

"You don't have to do that."

"Yes, I do," he said with a grin. "Shelley figured you'd want to come out early, so she already gave me my orders. She wants this test to be perfect, just like you do."

Gene looked wry. "She probably wants it more than I do. At this point, I'd just like to live through it."

Kenny opened her car door. After she had slowly and painfully climbed inside, he leaned down to wish her good luck. "Not that you'll need it," he said confidently. "I just know everything will go off without a hitch."

HITCH WASN'T the word for it. Gene had barely climbed into the saddle the next morning before Achilles humped his back. She was still trying to find the stirrup irons and gather up the reins when he began hopping down the aisle. Faintly, she heard Kenny say something, but she didn't have time to look back. A strange thing was happening to her, and for a few seconds, she didn't know what to make of it.

Then she knew. High Cotton had pulled the same trick when she first got on him in the mornings. It had been a game to him, a way to let her know that, while he might soon have to do her bidding, he would be doing it on his own terms. The hop established his independence, and she never tried to cure him of it. It was a pact between them, a gesture of mutual respect.

And now Achilles was doing the same thing. Suddenly, she stopped worrying about her ability to ride him. She laughed aloud. As they always did, the horse felt her relax, and he stopped abruptly, as though he couldn't figure out why she wasn't scared of him.

"You big fake," she scolded, her confidence growing. "I don't think this is going to be so bad, after all."

Feeling much better about the situation, she guided Achilles out of the barn and into the warm-up arena, where she quickly discovered that, despite the physical resemblance, Achilles was no High Cotton. Her horse had been a smooth mover with a mouth like silk; Achilles felt like a Mixmaster, going every which way under her. They hadn't gone two circuits of the arena before she was panting from exertion.

"How did Shelley even *ride* this creature?" she gasped to Kenny as they lurched by the spot where he was standing at the rail, watching.

He grinned. "She said he needed a little work."

"A *little!* He—" Whatever she was about to say was lost when Achilles suddenly shied violently at something only he could see. Before she knew it, they were halfway across the arena and he was trying to get his head down so he could buck her off.

"Oh, no, you don't!" she cried, gritting her teeth and pulling back as hard as she could to keep his head up. She knew she had to keep him moving forward, so she gave him a nudge with her heels. He responded by taking off at a gallop.

"You need any help?" Kenny shouted, grinning again as they flew by him, clods of arena dirt spouting up in their wake.

Gene didn't have breath to answer. Ahead was the open gate that led to the jump arena, and Achilles charged through it as though the hounds of hell were after him. As he headed for the first obstacle, she blanched. It was a four-foot oxer, a two-fence combination with a spread between, and as they thundered down the line toward it, there was no time to turn away. Fighting the urge to close her eyes, she tried to adjust Achilles's stride, but for all the attention the horse paid her, she might as well not have even have been there. With a surge of power that astounded her, he lifted them high into the air...and cleared the fence with a foot and a half to spare.

Gene was so amazed that, as they landed on the other side with a jar that shook her teeth, she practically fell off from sheer surprise. Achilles seemed just as awed at what he'd done, for he actually slowed—momentarily—from a dead run into a more gentlemanly canter.

"Did you see that?" she cried over her shoulder to Kenny.

"Yes, I—watch out!"

At the sight of Kenny's face, she turned forward—just in time to see a second fence dead ahead. This one was an upright which looked immense, no doubt because Achilles had increased his speed again and was charging it like an out-of-control locomotive. This time, she was determined to take control. Verbal commands were useless when she was out of breath, so she tightened her jaw, took hold of the right rein and tried to turn Achilles away from the jump. Once again, she might as well not have been aboard for all the heed he paid her. They were up and over before she knew it, but this time there wasn't a moment to gloat. Heady with success, Achilles charged toward the next jump.

"Gene, watch out...!"

Kenny's voice floated out from somewhere behind them, but she couldn't take a second to look back. The fence ahead had a six-foot spread, and right behind it was a pool of water. Gene had no idea how Achilles would react to water, so she tried to collect him, shorten his stride, straighten him out...all to no avail. Achilles was so proud of himself that he charged full out no matter what she tried to do. They were coming up much too fast, and Gene knew that if he didn't slow down, it would be disaster. Redoubling her efforts to control him, she gathered the reins and put her weight back.

For a moment, nothing happened. Then, before she was prepared, he slowed down. In fact, he came to a dead halt before she realized that's what he intended to do. One instant, she was readying herself to fly into the air with the horse; the next, she was soaring up there all by herself while he stayed behind and watched—no doubt with a satisfied smirk on his face.

He's good, she thought giddily as she flew high over the jump. She hadn't even guessed that he was going to stop. It had been a long time since a horse had fooled her like that. But then, it had been a long time since she'd given one the opportunity, especially to toss her off... right into the water.

"Damn!" she sputtered as she landed. Green, brackish liquid sprayed up around her, and by the time she fought her way to the surface, coughing and choking and vowing to smite that horse where he stood, three men were running toward her.

Three? she thought. She'd heard of seeing double, but... triple? Maybe she'd landed on her head without realizing it, she thought, pushing her dripping hair out of her eyes just as the figures separated themselves. When she saw Kenny in the lead, closely followed by one of the men she had seen at the hospital, with Ross Malone right behind them, she blinked. What was *he* doing here? she wondered frantically. It couldn't be eight o'clock already!

CHAPTER THREE

IT WASN'T eight o'clock. In fact, it was barely seven-thirty. Ross had been wrestling with his conscience all week and had finally decided that he couldn't let Gene Logan ride Achilles. Pride, stubbornness and whatever else drove her, be damned, he'd thought, and told a relieved James they were going to get there early and tell her they'd changed their minds. Achilles was too much horse for someone who hadn't ridden in so long, he'd say. Outdoor Outfitters couldn't be responsible for another injury; they'd have to work something else out.

But, despite their early arrival, they were too late. By the time they reached the jumping arena, Gene and Achilles were there working. At least, that's what Ross thought they were doing. It was difficult to tell—they were going around so fast. Ross was about to shout for them to stop when he saw Achilles head for the first jump. His heart lurched. The obstacle was too big and too high. They'd never in a million years make it over safely.

But then Achilles launched himself into the air, and before Ross knew it, horse and rider were over and down. The incredible sight stopped him in his tracks.

I didn't know it could be like that, he thought, awed. Even when it was over, the picture stayed in his mind. He'd never seen anything as beautiful as Gene on that white horse, horse and horsewoman flying over that jump.

"Did you see that?" James asked. He sounded as stunned as Ross felt.

Ross started to answer, but Gene and the horse were galloping on. It seemed to him that this time she was fighting Achilles. Was she trying to slow him down, or turn him, or...what? He knew something was wrong, and his hand tightened on his cane in dread. But then, when the pair thundered up and over the jump in that same spectacular way, he relaxed. He'd been mistaken, he told himself. Obviously, Gene had control of the horse.

Or had she?

James said something to him again, and again he was about to answer when he realized that Achilles was heading toward the next obstacle. Horse and rider were going at such a speed they were almost a blur, and Ross was assuring himself again that Gene knew what she was doing when Achilles just...stopped.

Right before Ross's horrified eyes, Gene left the saddle and flew over the jump all by herself. Ross couldn't believe it. For a horrifying instant, he couldn't breathe. The only thing he could think was that it was happening again. Achilles had done the same thing to Shelley, and—

And then, Gene landed. Hard—right in the middle of the water jump. When water sprayed up, obscuring her, the sight broke Ross's trance. Shouting her name, he ducked under the fence rails and started running. Kenny and James were already ahead of him. He hurried as fast as he could, but the tip of his cane sank maddeningly into the soft dirt with every step, slowing him even more. It had been a long time since he'd felt so frustrated by his handicap; if he could have made it without the cane, he would have flung it away in fury. But he needed the damned thing, especially in this heavy going, so all he could do was head as fast as he was able toward Gene and hope that she wasn't hurt.

If Gene was hurt, she was too furious to know it. Long before Ross reached her, she was on her feet. Still dripping, she ignored Kenny's outstretched hand and James's apprehensive offer of help, then she gave Ross a look, too, when he finally came lurching up. She jerked off her protective hat and glared at them as if this were their fault. And maybe, Ross thought guiltily, it was.

"Are you all right?" Kenny asked her anxiously.

"Is there anything we can do?" James asked.

Ross didn't say anything for a few seconds; he was too distracted by how beautiful she looked. Tendrils of hair curled around her flushed face, and her drenched clothes clung to her body....

Abruptly, he realized he was staring and jerked his eyes quickly up to her face. "Maybe we should call a doctor," he said.

"I don't need a doctor," Gene snapped. She'd caught him staring, and her eyes narrowed. Angrily, she brushed her hair back with both hands. It stood up in points, but Ross didn't even think of laughing. Before he could say anything more, she turned to Kenny. "Just get me that damned horse."

The damned horse had run off to the other end of the arena. Achilles was prancing back and forth along the fence, showing off for two mares who happened to be in paddocks on the other side. Gene's mouth tightened when she saw what the horse was doing and Ross felt almost sorry for Achilles, especially when he realized she intended to climb into the saddle again.

"You're not going to—" he started to say.

She silenced him with a look. Her voice glacial, she said, "I certainly am, Mr. Malone. And if you try to stop me, I'll break your arm."

Kenny obviously decided that compliance was the better part of valor, at least in this situation, so he sped off to fetch the unrepentant Achilles. Ross wanted to object, but changed his mind when Gene gave him another look that dared him to contradict her. Without another word, she sloshed after Kenny, and seconds later, she was in the saddle again. As she reached for the reins, James said worriedly to Ross, "Do you think this is a good idea?"

He couldn't take his eyes off Gene. "No. But I don't think any of us has much to say about it."

"But what if he throws her again?"

Ross recalled the light of battle in those green eyes and said, "Somehow, I don't think even Achilles is fool enough to try that a second time."

He was wrong. Clearly buoyed by success, Achilles tried to sidestep when Gene started him out, but she jabbed him sharply with her heel to get him back on course. Annoyed, the horse pinned his ears and tried to rear, but she brought him down again. His feet had barely hit the ground before he attempted to rub her off against the fence, and when she smacked him smartly with the reins to show him who was boss, he leapt forward and broke into a run, as though trying to scare her off.

Ross watched with both trepidation and admiration. The horse obviously believed he could get the upper hand if he was stubborn enough. *Too bad for him,* Ross thought. Gene was undeterred. She just sat there and let Achilles race around until he finally began to slow of his own accord.

"Oh, no, you don't," she said grimly as they went past the three men who had hurriedly regrouped outside the fence. "You wanted to run, now you're going to run."

Gene made Achilles go around the entire arena several times at a gallop before she started him on the real work. By this time, a little crowd had gathered to watch. But as though a spell had been cast, no one dared venture inside the riding ring. People stood with their horses by the fence while Gene made the horse take the jump course three times.

Ross could see that not even the powerful Achilles could keep up that breakneck pace forever. He was right. The horse was tired long before Gene relented, but things did seem to go a little more smoothly each time. By the fourth go-around, Ross was relieved to see that there was no sign of the reckless abandon of that wild first ride. Finally, guided by a rider every bit as obstinate as he was, Achilles was starting to behave like a civilized horse.

Even now, Gene wasn't finished. She made the tired white horse go around one final time, prodding him with her heels, forcing him up and over the jumps whether he wanted to go or not. She didn't beat him; she didn't yell or scream or threaten. All she did, as far

as the fascinated Ross could see, was *compel* the horse
to do her will. He'd never seen anything like it. By the
time Gene finally reined Achilles to a halt by the fence,
her clothes were almost dry, but the horse was soaking wet.

"Well?" she challenged, looking directly at Ross.
"What do you think now?"

Ross didn't know what he thought. He still felt
dazed by what he had just seen—or maybe he was just
overwhelmed by the lady herself. Whatever the reason, he completely forgot what he'd come here to tell
her. He could feel James giving him a curious look
when he said, "Well, I think that, if you want to, we
could give it a try."

Her chin lifted in that gesture he was already coming to know only too well. "I want to," she said.

After that, what could he say?

"WHY DID you *say* that?" James asked as they left the
stables. "Why did you ever agree to let her ride that
horse? It's going to be a disaster, I just know it!"

"So you've said before," Ross said, but he was
preoccupied. He couldn't stop thinking about what
he'd just seen. Gene Logan had certainly proved herself today, and he knew that they couldn't deny her the
chance to ride the horse.

But that wasn't really why he'd changed his mind,
was it? Uncomfortably, he had to admit that the real
reason was much less admirable and a lot more self-
ish. The truth was that he'd never seen anyone ride like
that, not even Shelley. Gene's sister was an accomplished rider, but she didn't have the . . . the *charisma*
that Gene had on a horse. Seeing them together had

given him a thrill he couldn't explain. He couldn't get it out of his mind. He knew they had something here, something unexpected and rare. If they played it right, he thought, everyone might win.

"Well?" James asked.

Ross rarely felt impatient with his partner, but as they headed back to the car, he said curtly, "If you're so worried about this, maybe we should sell the horse and get out now. Is that what you want?"

"Sell him?" James brightened, then he slumped again. "I only wish we could. But we put up all this money, remember? The campaign is set and we can't back out now."

"All right. I'm open to suggestion."

"I don't know what to suggest," James said woefully. "But we have to do something, don't you agree? I almost had a heart attack when I saw Gene fall. And when she landed in the water..." He made a terrible face. "How can people ride horses, anyway? It's got to be the most dangerous, idiotic thing to do on the entire planet."

"More dangerous than racing cars for a living?"

Involuntarily, James glanced down at Ross's leg. "Well, no, I guess not," he admitted. Then he said accusingly, "But you can't tell me that you weren't worried when she took that spill. I saw your face. You went white as a sheet."

"I was worried. I admit it. In fact, I was so relieved that she wasn't hurt, it took me a minute or two to realize how mad she was. If the sparks from her eyes had been real, I'm sure the three of us would have been singed and the entire place set ablaze. Not to mention what would have happened to the horse, of course."

"How can you think this is funny?"

Ross hadn't realized he'd laughed aloud. "Well, you have to admit—" He stopped midsentence when he saw James's face. "You're right. It wasn't funny," he said soberly.

"Damn right," James muttered. "So now what?"

"I don't know. If she'd told us to go to hell and take the horse with us, it would have been easy. But she didn't, and it's not. I don't know about you, but I wasn't about to tell her she couldn't ride Achilles. Not after she'd gotten up from that fall and climbed back into the saddle. And you can't deny it, she did put the horse through his paces. By the time she finished with him, I think even *I* could have ridden him. And I've never been on a horse in my life."

"Yes, well, neither have I," James admitted. "Furthermore, I have to say I don't care to try. But do you *really* think this is a good idea? First, it was Shelley, then Gene takes a spill. Maybe the horse is some kind of outlaw, or something."

"Now, James—"

"No, I mean it. We could get publicity, all right, but the wrong kind. We can't have customers boycotting the company because our horse does his damnedest to kill everyone who comes near him!"

They'd reached the car. "Fine," Ross said. "You tell her, then."

"Me?" James looked horrified. "Oh, no, not me! I saw her face, too, before she got on the horse again. If I'd been Achilles, I would have been shaking in my shoes. And if she felt that way about *him,* what would she do to *me* if I tell her she can't ride him?"

"Then I guess we're going to have to let her try it for a while. As we said before, if the arrangement doesn't work out, we can always change our minds."

"You won't be so complacent when we're being pilloried in the press."

"You know what they say about publicity. Even bad press is good."

"You make jokes now, but you won't be laughing if this blows up in our faces."

"I'll be the first to admit you were right," Ross promised. He tossed James the keys. "Do you mind driving?"

Surprised, James caught the key ring. "No, I don't mind," he said. He hesitated, then he asked, "Why? Is your leg bothering you?"

"A little bit, not much." Ross didn't want to admit that a fiery ache had started with the first running step he'd taken. Even now, years after the accident, he wasn't supposed to walk fast, much less run. If he tried, he inevitably paid for it with pain that could last through the night.

"You shouldn't have run like that," James commented as they got into the car.

Ross rubbed his knee. "I know. But sometimes I forget."

As they drove away, Ross looked back at the stables and caught a glimpse of a tired white horse going on the automatic walker. He smiled. He didn't know much about horses, but he suspected that it would be a while before Achilles tried to get the best of Gene Logan again. His smile turned wry. After what he had seen this morning, he thought, it would be a while before *he* tried to cross her.

His leg suddenly throbbed again, and without intending to, he thought about the accident. It had been years now, but he could still smell the burning rubber and hear the ear-splitting shriek of metal being torn apart. Without even trying, he could feel the force that had hurtled him—and what moments before had been a powerful Formula One car—relentlessly toward the wall. At the time, he knew the crowd was screaming and that other drivers were frantically trying to maneuver around him as he careened out of control, but things happened so fast, it was all a blur.

All except the fire, he thought, closing his eyes at the memory of a tower of flame roaring up right in front of his face when he hit the wall. His suit protected him until the foamtrucks came and snuffed out the blaze, but nothing could save his left leg from being shattered when he crashed headfirst into the barrier.

They'd had to cut him out. To this day, the last thing he remembered about that time was James standing over him, clutching Ross's hand. James had been one of the owners of the car, as close to him as any friend could be, and in those last moments before they took him away, he extracted a tough promise from James. After the rescue workers pulled him gingerly out of the wreckage and laid him on a gurney, he looked up into James's eyes.

"I don't want to wake up and find out that they've amputated my leg—"

James clung tightly to his friend's hand. By then, Ross was going into shock; he could feel it. He knew the sight of tears in James's eyes should scare him, but he was starting to drift away, and it didn't.

"You're getting a little ahead of yourself, buddy," James said hoarsely. "Right now, I wouldn't worry about the leg."

He found out later that they were all wondering if he'd wake up at all, but as he felt himself slipping into unconsciousness, all he could think about was making James promise.

"I mean it," he whispered. "No matter what they say, you won't let them take my leg." He tried to smile, but it hurt too much. Grimacing, instead, he added, "If you do, I'll come back and haunt you until you die, I swear it. Now, give me your word. I want to hear it."

Tears made two streaks down the dirt and soot on James's face, but he finally said in a choked voice, "I . . . promise."

He'd let go then, knowing James wouldn't let him down. But when he woke up again the evening of the following day, he was almost sorry he'd made James promise. By then, he'd had two surgeries he wasn't even aware of, and more were scheduled—just in an effort to save the leg, not to fix all the things that were wrong with it. Even with massive doses of drugs, the pain was so intense that he blacked out. When he woke up a second time, his soon-to-be ex-wife, Marilyn, was sitting by the bed.

As soon as he saw Marilyn's worried expression, the sarcastic remark he'd been about to make—their usual form of communication in those days—went unsaid. He was doubly glad he hadn't tried to be smart when he saw her expression. He figured he must be in bad shape when she smiled tenderly and reached for his hand.

"Hi," she said softly, still his wife for the moment. "You gave us all quite a scare, boss."

Trussed up as he was, with his leg in traction and wrapped in thick bandages from hip to toe, he couldn't move. Not that he was eager to try; a slight experimental shift in position immediately sent up howls of agony from every part of his body. Still, he tried to be his cocky self because he thought Marilyn expected it.

"It looks like I really did it this time, didn't I?" he said.

She blinked, obviously trying to hold the tears back, but they filled her eyes, anyway. "You sure did. For a while, it looked—" She stopped, biting her lip.

He'd never seen her this way, not in the six years they'd been married. In those early days when he'd been an apprentice driver, working his way up the circuit, trying hard to get good enough to attract a sponsor's attention, Marilyn had married him knowing all he'd ever wanted to do was race. It hadn't taken long for him to realize she had deliberately blinded herself to the very real dangers of the sport. But by then, it was too late.

Even so, she'd handled the first injury well, a flip into the wall from which he had emerged with only a sprained ankle and a dislocated shoulder. She'd also been pretty good about the second accident, and the third and the fourth and the fifth. She didn't like to see him hurt, of course, but if it wasn't serious, she could deal with it—or so she claimed.

But long before he'd earned a position as one of the top ten drivers in the standings, Marilyn started talking about his doing something else for a living. She wanted him to get a normal job, whatever that was. Something nine-to-five. Work that would have bored him to death in the first five seconds.

He'd tried to explain, but soon their conversations were turning into arguments, the arguments into ultimatums. Divorce loomed even before Ross was involved in a six-car pileup at Indianapolis, and he was sure that only the fact that he'd lost his spleen and cracked a kneecap had stopped her from serving him with the papers right there at the track.

She hadn't been so considerate when he got out of the hospital, but by then he was glad she was divorcing him. He didn't want her to worry so much, and he hated the constant arguing and angry feelings between them. He loved Marilyn, but he couldn't give up racing. It was like life to him and he couldn't imagine living without it. The very elements that frightened her—the excitement, the unpredictability, the danger—elated him. He couldn't get enough of it.

And then came the crack-up that shattered his leg and his future, too. As he looked at Marilyn sitting by the hospital bed that day, he'd suddenly realized that, even though he hadn't had enough of racing, it had had enough of him—at least for a while.

"Oh, Ross," Marilyn had said mournfully to him. "I'm so sorry."

So was he, but he had only himself to blame. The fact that he hadn't killed anyone was the one thing that made it bearable. James and several others had tried to talk him out of entering that race. The knee he'd cracked in the last pileup was still weak, and they wanted to put him on the injured list. But *no*, he thought bitterly, he'd been too obsessed and arrogant, too sure he was invincible. He'd wanted to win so much, he'd ignored all the warning signs—the sharp pain in his knee when he downshifted during the practice runs, the way the leg gave way a little too much on the turns. Everyone connected with the car had noticed him drifting out during one lap and James had asked him about it when he got back to the pit. Avoiding their eyes, he'd insisted that nothing was wrong and that they all worried too much.

It turned out they hadn't been wrong. He had, and he was going to pay for his mistake. Just how high the price was to be, he hadn't guessed that day. It was a good thing, too, he'd often reflected during the following months, when one operation followed another with a frustrating lack of progress. Self-obsessed as he was, he didn't realize for a long time that the doctors weren't worried about whether he would ever race again; their concern was whether he would ever *walk* again.

It had taken four operations and months of grueling physical therapy, during which the only thing that kept him going sometimes was sheer determination not to give in to the pain, before he had finally walked out on his own. With Marilyn on one side, and the therapist behind him, he'd left the hospital leaning heavily on a cane. It had been a slow, torturous trip, but no win he'd ever enjoyed in racing had ever been so sweet.

It was too bad that his triumph had been so short-lived, he reflected. As though he'd already sensed what the answer would be, he hadn't asked about the possibility of his driving again the entire time he'd been in the hospital. He'd told himself he wasn't afraid of the answer, he was too preoccupied with getting back on his feet. But then came the day, almost a year after the accident, when he had to ask. He'd done it during a checkup.

His doctor, Ben Denver, was one of the most prominent orthopedic surgeons in the country. Ross knew by then how lucky he was that Ben had been at the hospital when he was brought in. During all those months of surgeries and recoveries, Ben had been right there encouraging him. But that day, when he'd asked how soon he could return to racing, the doctor had looked at him in such a way that Ross knew, beyond any doubt, that his career had come to an end.

"Racing?" Ben repeated. "Ross, you aren't serious."

"I was, until now," he said, trying to save face by being flippant. But he'd been thinking—in real panic—that if he couldn't race, what was left for him? Driving cars wasn't just his passion; it was the way he made his living. He didn't know anything else. He'd looked at the doctor again. "Come on, Ben, don't kid me about this. You know what racing means to me."

When Ben pulled up a stool and sat down beside him, Ross wanted to get up and run out of the room, but of course, he couldn't do that. Bitterly, he'd realized that he couldn't run anywhere. He'd left that ability behind forever that day on the track.

"Ross," Ben said quietly, "I thought you knew that you were never going to race again."

Even then, childishly, he'd tried to deny the facts. "You told me I'd be able to drive," he protested.

"*Drive,* yes. But like the rest of us, in a regular car, not in a souped-up, high-speed, Formula One death machine. And even that," Ben added, "is a while off.

You'll need more range of motion before I let you get behind the wheel. As it is, we can be thankful it's your left leg—"

"We?" he said angrily.

"Yes, *we,*" Ben repeated, his voice sharp. "You think you're alone in this? My team and I agonized over how to *save* that leg. Oh, yes, I think I've earned the right to say *we.*"

He'd been ashamed of himself. "You're right," he mumbled. "I didn't mean to act like a jerk. I'm grateful. It's just—"

Ben stood and put a hand on Ross's shoulder. Quietly, he said, "I've never been where you are, but I think I can understand how angry and frustrated you must feel. I don't know what I'd do if someone told me I had to leave orthopedic surgery and try something else. It's tough."

That's an understatement, Ross had thought bitterly. Ben had a wife, a job, work, a future. What did he have? A bum leg, an empty apartment and a cane to keep him company.

But things had gotten better. Excitable James, who had decided racing was too dangerous a sport for his equanimity, approached him not long after that. He'd been waiting for the right time, he'd said, and now that Ross was well enough to listen, he had a plan. He had the backing and business acumen; Ross had the abilities and the name. They could put the two together and open an outdoor clothing and gear chain.

And so, Outdoor Outfitters—"All you need to add is fresh air"—was born. At the time, it seemed a stroke of genius. In the fitness-conscious eighties, sales boomed. They started with one store; soon they had two. Before long, they had expanded to six and were planning more across the country. But then, just as they were riding high, the economy soured, people lost jobs, and despite a frantic retooling toward simpler, less exotic equipment and more down-to-earth clothing, sales fell off. When the situation started to look really bleak, they knew they had to do something, and when James suggested sponsoring an eventing horse for the publicity value, Ross seized the idea. He was desperate enough to try anything. With James starting to backpedal every step of the way, they'd found the horse and someone to ride it. It had all been going according to plan until the day Achilles balked at a jump and sent Shelley to the hospital. And then, of course, he'd met Gene Logan, and somehow he knew nothing would ever be the same.

"What are you thinking about?" James asked.

Ross had been so deep in thought that he hadn't realized they were almost back at the office. He didn't want to admit what he'd really been thinking, so he said, "I don't know. I guess I was thinking about Shelley."

"What about her?" James asked as he parked the car.

Now he had to make up a story. "Uh . . . well, I was thinking that we should call Shelley and tell her the good news."

"The good news? Oh, you mean that Gene is going to be riding the horse. I guess you're right, we should. Do you want to do it, or shall I?"

"I will," Ross said as they headed into the building. "I'll call her right now."

James stopped. "Ross, are you all right?"

"I'm fine. Why?"

"You seem so preoccupied."

He forced a smile. "We've got a lot to be preoccupied about, don't we?"

James looked alarmed. "You don't think this is going to work, do you?"

"Did I say that? I've just got a lot on my mind."

"You're sure."

"I'm positive. Now, let me go call Shelley. I'm sure she's eager to find out what happened today."

"Tell her I said hello."

"Will do," he said cheerfully. He could feel James watching him as he headed toward his office and he couldn't blame the man for wondering if something was wrong. He'd never felt like this. For one thing, he hadn't thought about cars in days. He'd long ago accepted the fact that he'd never race again, but still, he...dreamed. Now, he was shocked to realize that ever since he'd seen Gene Logan walking into the hospital, she'd been the only thing on his mind.

As Gene drove home, she berated herself. What had she done? All she'd wanted to do was prove she could ride that horse. But because of stubborn pride and some ridiculous need to save face, she was in deeper than ever. Why had she shown off like that? She'd been thrown before. Instead of getting into a lather about it this time, she should have gotten up, dusted herself off—or in this case, wrung herself out—and told Mr. Ross Malone that she'd changed her mind. Promises were one thing, but getting herself killed trying to keep them was beyond even the call of sisterly duty.

It was maddening, but whatever point she'd been trying to make was lost now. The thing to do was to figure out the best way to tell Shelley she'd decided against being part of this insane plan. Her riding career was behind her. She had a good job that she enjoyed, a home, a schedule, roots. She'd made peace with her decision long before.

Even more aggravated, she pulled into the driveway and cut the engine. Shelley would just have to understand, she told herself as she got out of the car. She wasn't going to stir up all the old longings she thought she'd dealt with years ago, not when she had so many other things to look forward to. Her life was going in the *responsible* direction she'd planned, and no one, not even a horse with a mind of his own was going to distract her.

Not even, she thought before she could stop herself, if that horse did remind her of an old friend.

The light on the answering machine was blinking when she went inside, and when she saw it, she groaned. The last thing she wanted was to talk to *anyone*. She had already decided that after she called Shelley, she was going to take a long, hot bath and fall into bed for about a week.

But she couldn't just let that hypnotic red light blink, so she limped over to the phone and punched the playback button. As soon as she heard Shelley's voice, she winced. She should have known that her sister wouldn't wait to be contacted.

"Gene," Shelley gushed into the tape, "Ross just called to tell me that you're going to ride Achilles until I'm in shape again. I don't know how to thank you. You're the best sister in the whole world, and when I get out of here, I'm going to do something really special for you. You don't know how much this means to me. I'll never forget it, as long as I live. As *soon* as you get home, call me and tell me what happened. I can hardly wait to hear. You must have ridden the socks off that horse, Ross was so impressed. He couldn't say enough about you—how you handled the horse, how well Achilles responded to you—"

Shelley was so pleased, she actually giggled. "If I didn't want you to do this so much, I might be jealous, kiddo. It sounds like the same story all over again. You know, 'Shelley's a good rider, but Gene . . . Gene is brilliant.'"

Shelley laughed again, obviously too thrilled to dwell on past hurts. "Well, never mind, that doesn't matter anymore. All I care about is that we get to keep the horse until I can take over. Oh, Gene, I'm so proud of you! Call me right away, okay? I'll be waiting. . . ."

The message ended with a beep, but Gene just stood there. As the tape reset itself, she knew that she couldn't call her sister now and say she'd changed her mind. Shelley sounded so happy, so relieved that everything was going to turn out. How could she take that away when Shelley was lying in the hospital with her leg in a cast? It would be too cruel.

It wasn't until Gene was upstairs soaking in a hot bath with bubbles up to her chin that she wondered about her own motives. Was she concerned about Shelley's feelings . . . or did she have something far less altruistic in mind? If she'd been serious about keeping her promise not to ride, would she have been so easily swayed by the message she'd just played?

And what had Shelley meant when she'd said Ross was so impressed? she wondered impatiently. He hadn't sounded so overwhelmed to *her*. In fact, when he'd told her they could give this a try, he'd sounded as if he was doing her a favor.

The bathwater suddenly seemed too cool. She'd soaked long enough, and she reached for a towel. But as she dried herself, she wondered again what she was really trying to prove—that she could still ride as well as she ever had? That she could train a difficult horse even after all these years? Or was it, she thought with a squirm, that she was just trying to impress Ross Malone?

"Ridiculous," she muttered. She was doing her sister a favor, and that was all there was to it.

She was heading out of the bathroom to get dressed when she happened to catch sight of her reflection in the mirror. She stopped and stared. She'd been so preoccupied with...*that man*...that she had completely forgotten to rinse the shampoo out of her hair.

CHAPTER FOUR

SHELLEY LOOKED at her watch for what seemed like the fiftieth time since she had clumped into Kenny's stable office on crutches at six o'clock this morning.

"Where *is* she?" she asked fretfully.

Kenny was sitting behind the desk, calmly reading a horse publication and drinking a cup of coffee. Since Shelley had asked this question about a dozen times already, he didn't look up from his magazine when he said, "Don't worry. She'll be here."

"But *when?*" Shelley persisted. "It's almost six-thirty, and there's still no sign of her. If she doesn't get here soon, she won't have time to give Achilles a proper workout before she has to leave for the office."

"She knows what she's doing."

"Oh, really? If that's true, why isn't she here?" She looked at him a moment, then added, "And stop reading that damned magazine for a minute and pay attention to me!"

Obligingly, Kenny looked up. "Why don't you sit down and have some coffee?"

"I don't *want* any coffee. And I don't want to sit down, either, so stop suggesting it."

With a sigh, Kenny put aside the magazine. "What do you want, then?"

"What I *want*," she said childishly, "is to go out and ride the damn horse myself, since Gene obviously has better things to do!"

Kenny had been sitting with his boots propped up on the cluttered desk. It seemed clear he wasn't getting through to Shelley, so he put his feet on the floor, stood and tried again. "I don't think you're being fair," he said. "Gene has been out here every morning at six for the past week. It can't be easy for her, trying to exercise that horse and work at the same time."

She looked at him indignantly. "Why are you taking her side?"

"I'm not taking anyone's side. I just think you're frustrated—"

"Wouldn't you be?"

"Yes, I would. But you can't take your frustration out on your sister. She's doing everything she can."

"She's not here to ride!"

Kenny gave up and grabbed his hat. "I'm going to check the horses."

"Well, you'd better saddle Achilles," she snapped, "because if Gene isn't here in the next five minutes, I'm going to ride him myself!"

Wisely, Kenny didn't reply to that. Shaking his head, he went out, leaving the door open behind him. Shelley debated about following and giving him a piece of her mind for deserting her, but a scrap of common sense told her she had to rein in her temper, so she stomped over to the desk and jerked Kenny's vacated chair toward her with one of her crutches. She wasn't prepared for the movement and nearly lost her balance.

"Damn it to *hell!*" she cried. She hated these stupid crutches. She wanted to throw the damned things against the wall. The only thing that stopped her was the knowledge that she wouldn't be able to retrieve them if she did, so she clenched her teeth, hopped around and gingerly sat down. The chair moved out from under her, and when she had to grab it quickly or fall off, she almost burst into tears from pure aggravation. The crowded desk top caught her eye, and for an instant she was tempted to vent her frustration by sweeping everything off into one giant heap onto the floor.

"What's the matter with that man?" she muttered furiously as she glared at the disorder. "Hasn't he ever heard of a filing system?"

Apparently, Kenny hadn't. As she stared down at the mess, she saw old invoices for saddles and bridles, outdated bills for feed and other supplies, orders from various people for who-knew-what, and most significant of all, unpaid board bills that seemed to be collecting dust and coffee rings instead of money.

"No wonder he's always broke!" she exclaimed. Before she knew it, she was riffling through the stack. What she saw appalled her. Some of the outstanding bills were months old, and when she recognized the names of the horse owners, all of whom were keeping their horses at the stable—free, it seemed—she threw the papers down in disgust.

"It's amazing the man is still in business," she muttered. "Why is he giving all these *deadbeats* a free ride?"

She always paid her board and training bills religiously, exactly the first of the month, but she knew a lot of people let things slide. It wasn't uncommon for a horse to be repossessed by a boarding facility because the owners hadn't paid. And it wasn't unheard of for miscreants to sneak horses out in the dead of night to avoid paying.

Well, it wasn't any of her business. If Kenny Fielding wanted to gallop down the path to grief and ruin, it was his affair. Right now, she had problems of her own—one of which, she thought grimly, was the tardy Gene. Where was she?

She loved Gene. But it was hard living up to a perfect sister. Shelley had adored horses from the time she was small—but unlike Gene, to whom riding seemed to come effortlessly—*she'd* had to work at horsemanship. She'd always been secretly thankful that Gene had gotten away from horses, but even now, after all this time, it was galling to admit that her sister could probably still ride better than she.

And the proof, Shelley thought grumpily as she sat back in the creaky chair, was what Gene had accomplished with Achilles, and in such a short time. She had watched this entire week as Gene put the horse through his paces, and even though the big white horse had fought her every step of the way, inch by inch, he'd started bending to her will—something Shelley wasn't sure now he'd ever do for her.

Without warning, she felt close to tears. *It wasn't fair,* she thought. She was a *good* rider. But manufactured competence wasn't the same as natural ability, and she knew it. She had always dreamed of being the best of the best, and even with his lack of training, she had seen immediately the great potential Achilles had.

She knew this was the horse that could finally take her to the top, like High Cotton could have taken Gene—

She frowned. She didn't want to think about High Cotton and the career that had ended so tragically. It didn't do to dwell on such things. Falls were part of every competitor's life. If she let it get to her, she'd never climb back into a saddle again. *Which* she intended to do as soon as she could get this damned cast off. As she looked down at the cumbersome plaster encasing her leg, she wondered again why she'd taken that stupid spill. Why hadn't she bounced, or rolled? Why hadn't she done *anything* but land awkwardly like some stupid, graceless oaf? She knew how to fall. She'd done it more times than she could count. Why had things gone wrong *this* time, when she so badly needed to be healthy and sound?

Aggravated once more, she glanced toward the door. It was six forty-five. If her sister was coming, she should have been here long before now.

I've waited long enough, Shelley decided, and reached for the phone. She dialed Gene's number, and listened impatiently while it rang three times at the other end. When Gene finally picked up, Shelley knew she wasn't going to see her sister at the stable this morning.

"Hello?" Gene mumbled, her voice heavy with sleep.

Shelley couldn't help herself. "Gee, I'm sorry I woke you," she said sarcastically. "But I've been sitting here waiting, and I thought we should be in touch before noon."

"Noon?" Gene sounded confused. "What time is it?"

"Almost seven."

"Seven!" Gene groaned. "I had the alarm set for five. I must have turned it off and gone back to sleep."

"Really? Well, then, I guess this means that you won't be coming in to ride before you go to work, doesn't it?"

Suddenly sounding alert, Gene said, "Yes, I guess it does. Do you have a problem with that?"

"As a matter of fact, I do. When *are* you going to work Achilles?"

"When I have time. Now, look—"

"But the horse needs at *least* an hour of work a day, Gene. You know that!"

"Look, Shelley, I know how anxious you are—"

"I've got a right to be anxious. He has to be ready!"

"He will be!" Gene said sharply. "Now give it a rest."

"But—"

"Do *you* want to exercise this horse?"

"You know I can't do that."

"Then do you want someone else to exercise him until you can?"

"No!"

"All right, then, I hate to remind you, but I am doing you a favor, remember? I've got a million things to do at work, but I'm still trying to ride the horse for you. You're just going to have to relax and let me do things my way for a while."

"I can't relax!" Shelley wailed. "You know how important this is to me!"

Sounding ready to lose her temper, Gene said, "I know I'm not doing as good a job as you would, or doing it the way you like, Shelley, but—"

"I'm sorry, I don't mean to be a pest. I'm just so frustrated. It's so hard for me to see anyone but me riding Achilles—even you!"

Gene paused. Then she said, "It won't be forever, Shelley."

"It seems like it!"

"I suppose it does. Maybe you just need something to do to occupy your time."

"What? The only thing I know how to do is ride!"

"Well, you can't do that right now. Why don't you look for a temporary office job? You've always been good with numbers. Maybe you could help out in an accountant's office for a while."

Involuntarily, Shelley looked down at Kenny's chaotic desk. Grimacing, she glanced away again. "That's a fine idea," she said impatiently. "Assuming someone would be dim enough to let me try, I'd go out of my mind in five minutes. You know how I feel about clerical work, about being inside."

"Well, for a while, it looks like you don't have much choice, doesn't it?"

"I know you want to help, Gene, but I just want to ride!"

"No one wants you back in the saddle more than I," Gene assured her. "But until that leg heals, you'd better find something to do, or you'll drive us all crazy with your many demands."

"Have I really been that bad?"

"Yes," Gene said flatly. "In fact, the way you've been acting, you'd think I'd never been on a horse before."

"But I didn't mean it like that."

"Well, that's nice to know. Look, I'm sorry to cut short such a stimulating conversation, but I've really got to go. And before you push the panic button again, I promise to come out to the stable after work tonight and ride Achilles. Will that make you happy?"

"That'll be fine. Thanks, Gene," Shelley said, suddenly meek.

"You're welcome. Now goodbye—and for all our sakes, please find something productive to do!"

Shelley hung up, too. She would give some thought to what Gene had said . . . later . . . maybe. She glanced at her watch again. It was still early, but there was no reason she couldn't call Ross's office and leave a message. On that thought, she picked up the phone again and dialed.

"Outdoor Outfitters, Ross Malone speaking."

She hadn't expected Ross to answer, and for a moment she forgot what she had intended to say. "Ross? This is Shelley. I . . . um . . . didn't think you'd be in at this hour. I was going to leave a message for you."

"That's okay. I came in to get some work done."

"You sound like Gene. She's always doing that, too."

"What's that?"

"Going in early to work."

He was elaborately casual. "Really? You know, you never mentioned what kind of work she does."

"She's a vice president at a greeting card company. I thought you knew."

"No, I didn't. I guess I never thought to ask."

"What you mean is that you assumed she was someone's assistant, or something."

"I did not. Not that there's anything wrong with being an assistant," he added hastily. "It's just that, well, Gene doesn't seem to be—"

"The assistant type? That's true. For one thing, she's too bossy."

He laughed. "I can't deny that. So, what can I do for you, Shelley?"

"Nothing, really. I thought I'd call and give you a progress report on your horse. He's doing just fine, you know. Gene is really putting him through his paces."

He was casual again. "Well, that's good to know. I'm glad things are working out."

"Oh, they are. In fact, things couldn't be better."

"I hope you're right."

What did that mean? She tensed. She didn't want anyone changing their minds. "I am right," she assured him. "In fact, the way things are going, I think that by the time my leg heals, Achilles is going to be ready for his first competition."

"Really?"

She wasn't sure of anything at this point. But she wasn't going to tell him that. "Yes, of course. In fact, maybe one of these days you can come out and see just how well he's doing."

"I think that might be a good idea. How often does Gene ride him?"

"Oh, every day, of course."

"When will she ride him today?"

He wasn't thinking of coming *today*, was he? For a moment, Shelley felt sheer panic. Gene was going to have a fit if Ross came to watch her ride Achilles at this stage. The horse wasn't ready for a demonstration and no one knew that better than she did. She tried to think of a reason to keep him away, but all she could think of was a weak, "I don't know, Ross. I thought she was coming this morning, but—"

"Then she'll be there tonight?"

What had she done? She couldn't lie to him, so she had to say, "I think so. But Ross—remember what I said before about Achilles doing so well? What I meant was…well, we're starting with a green horse— a *really* green horse. I…I don't want you to be disappointed when he doesn't seem fully trained."

"I understand," he assured her. "Don't worry. I'll see you after work."

What could she say? "All right. I'll look forward to it."

Wishing she'd never called, she replaced the receiver. When she looked up, Kenny was standing in the doorway. He'd obviously overheard at least part of the conversation, because he had that *look* on his face. His scrutiny made her nervous and she stared back defiantly.

"I didn't do anything," she said guiltily. "Besides, how was I supposed to know that Ross would want to come tonight to see the horse work?"

Kenny pushed his hat back with one finger. "Are you going to tell Gene?"

She tried to look indignant. "Of course I'm going to tell her. It's not a secret, or anything."

"When?" he asked.

That was a good question, she thought. She knew Gene was going to hate being watched as she worked Achilles. But it was done now; she'd just have to accept it. And it might not be so bad, she tried to tell herself. After all, Gene *had* been working hard with the horse. Maybe Achilles would surprise them all and behave himself tonight.

"Shelley?"

"I'll *call* her," she said. She happened to glance down at the desk. The disorder caught her eye again, and she used it as an excuse to change the subject. "And when are you going to attend to all this paperwork?" she demanded. She grabbed a handful of unpaid bills. "It's no wonder you say you never have any money. Half these people owe you for back board, and the other half have never paid you at all!"

Kenny took the bills from her hand. "Since when are you so interested in my business?"

"Since I realized that some of your customers are taking you to the cleaners, that's when. Honestly, Kenny Fielding, if you don't—"

She didn't get a chance to finish the sentence. Before she realized what he was about to do—almost before he realized it himself, it seemed—he tossed the papers down on the desk, grabbed her by the shoulders and planted a kiss on her lips. She was so shocked at first that she didn't do anything. Then, to her surprise, she kissed him right back.

"Why...Kenny," she said, flustered and flushed, when they finally pulled apart.

He straightened and hitched up his pants. A little red-faced himself, he looked at her and said, "I've been wanting to do that a long time, Shelley Logan. And now that I have—"

She still felt a little breathless. "What?" she asked.

"Now that I have," he said, reaching for her again, "I have to say that it was definitely worth the wait."

ACROSS TOWN, Gene pulled into her parking space at work. Shelley's call had interrupted what almost felt like a drugged sleep, and she still felt tired and edgy. The sight of her reflection even after applying makeup this morning made her wince. She had circles under her eyes and her hair looked listless. It didn't help that Wally was waiting for her when she walked into the office. She took one look at his face and she knew something was wrong.

"What is it now?" she asked resignedly.

"Which problem do you want first?" Wally asked. He glanced at the notebook he was holding. "The one where the paper we ordered for the new designs isn't going to be available until next year? Or the one where the artist decided she couldn't handle such a big project at this point in her life and left for the Bahamas this morning?"

Gene couldn't believe he was serious. "You'd better be kidding, Wally. And if you are, I'll tell you right now, it's not a good time."

"I'm afraid it's all too true. The paper company sent a fax last night, but Stella didn't even have the decency to do that. When I called to see how things were progressing at her end, all I got was a recorded message saying she needed some space."

"Swell," Gene said, heading into her office. She threw her briefcase on top of the desk and asked the dreaded question. "Does Mason know?"

"He does about the paper, but not about Stella. I thought maybe you'd like to tell him."

"Oh, thanks."

He grinned. "Hey, that's what vice presidents get to do, isn't it? Smooth things over with the boss. What can I do? I'm just a lowly assistant."

He was a lot more to her than that and they both knew it. But she said, "In that case, lowly assistant, would you mind getting me a cup of coffee? And make it strong. I need something bracing before I face Mason."

Wally reached behind him and produced a steaming cup. "Here. I *thought* you might want this. Anything else I can do?"

Gene sipped the welcome coffee and thought. The paper problem she could handle, but finding another illustrator at this late date was going to be more difficult. She was not going to dwell on how much work had gone down the drain. Somehow, she'd have to deal with it.

After a moment, she said, "Please bring in the file of illustrators and start going through it. In the meantime, I'll tell Mason the bad news."

As she anticipated, her boss wasn't pleased. But then, neither was she. She'd have to start all over again with a new artist for the Warm Fuzzies collection.

"So," Mason said, settling his considerable bulk back into his desk chair. He was a balding man in his fifties who, with his paunch, sagging jawline and fringe of gray hair, could have passed for a warm fuzzy character himself. But he was a businessman through and through, and the steely glint in his blue eyes proved it. As he regarded her over the rims of his glasses, he asked, "What are you going to do now?"

"Find another illustrator, of course," she said. She deliberately made it sound easy, even though she knew it was not. "We have the concept nailed down, so it's a matter of finding someone to carry it through."

"Do you have anyone in mind?"

At the moment, she didn't. But she wasn't going to admit that, either. She didn't want Mason thinking she might not be up to managing the project. Mentally cursing all artistic temperaments, she said, "I've got a few possibilities in mind. I'll keep you posted."

She turned to go, but he said, "Just a minute, Gene."

She looked back. "What is it?"

"Is everything all right? I've noticed that for the past week or so, you haven't been yourself. You seem preoccupied and distracted—and if you don't mind my saying so, you look a little tired. Is this new division too much for you? If it is, I can bring in someone else to help."

Was he asking if she could handle her job? "No, it's not too much. I have been working hard, I admit. But I can manage."

"Don't get upset. I didn't mean to imply that you couldn't. I put it badly because I was concerned. I've never seen you this way."

She knew she should have told him before about the riding arrangement she had with her sister, but it was too late now. Besides, it wasn't his problem that Achilles was consuming too much of her time and energy, she thought. With all she'd taken on, sometimes she felt she was meeting herself coming and going.

"I didn't mean to snap," she said. "I guess I am a little more stressed than I realized."

"Understandable, considering this setback with the artist. I'm glad that's all it is. Take the weekend off and get some rest. Things will look better next week."

Gene hoped he was right as she went back to her office. Wally was waiting anxiously when she got there, and he asked, "How'd it go?"

"Better than expected, but we'd better find another illustrator immediately. What about Susan Cauthen, or..." She stopped. "Do I seem different to you?"

He regarded her warily. "Different? In what way?"

"I don't know. Preoccupied, distracted, that sort of thing. Don't worry, you can tell me."

"Well, you have seemed a little tired these past few weeks, since you started riding again. Is that what you mean?"

She wasn't sure what she meant, but Mason's comment still rankled. Until today, she thought she'd been juggling her job and Achilles quite well. Now she couldn't help wondering if maybe she wasn't doing as well as she'd thought. Was that why she'd missed noticing signs of the problems that had suddenly cropped up? She always had her finger on the pulse of things. Why hadn't she sensed that Stella was turning out to be a flake? What had Gene been thinking of, if it hadn't been work?

"Hey, are you still here?"

Gene blinked. Embarrassed that Wally had caught her woolgathering, she said, "Never mind. Maybe I've got the blues. I'll be better next week, I'm sure. In the meantime, I'll take over the search for a new illustrator, while you begin calling around for another paper supplier. I'd like to have something to work from by the end of the day. I think we can do it by five, if we try."

When five o'clock came, Gene realized she'd been too optimistic. She and Wally had worked through lunch, but by quitting time they were no closer to solving their problem. Available artists and agents were either out of town, busy with other projects, or not interested in her Warm Fuzzies concept. Estimates on new paper stock ranged from the suspicious to the ridiculous. After a last futile call, she slammed down the receiver.

"Doesn't anyone want work anymore?" she said irritably. Wally was sitting opposite her, poring over past contracts, and he looked up.

"I guess not. I've called almost a dozen companies about the paper. You know what results I got."

Gene glanced at the clock. "We've wasted the entire day. Now it's after five, and we still don't have anything settled. I think it's time we went home."

"This early?"

She reached for her purse. She knew she'd probably be sorry, but right now, she'd had it. "Everybody else has closed up shop. We won't get anything more done today, so let's go."

"You don't have to twist my arm," Wally said. He stood and stretched. "The way I feel now, I'll probably crash on the sofa as soon as I walk in the door."

"I know what you mean. I'm going home and—" She stopped midsentence. How could she have forgotten? She couldn't go home. She had promised to ride tonight. For a few seconds, she considered not showing up, but she knew what Shelley's reaction would be to that. It would be easier to go to the barn and get the thing done than to explain to her sister why she'd changed her mind. Sighing heavily, she said good-night to Wally and drove out to the stables.

GENE HOPED that Achilles would give her a break and behave himself tonight, but he proved once again that he was no gentleman as soon as she saddled him. As though the evil-minded horse had sensed how much it would annoy her, he was particularly difficult during the training session. By the time she put him in the cross-ties to groom him before returning him to his stall, she was feeling a little evil-minded herself. Shelley's sudden appearance didn't help. She was just reaching to unhook the girth when her sister came down the passageway, shouting at her.

Irritated anew, Gene turned to look. At first she felt a tinge of sympathy for Shelley, who was still trying to get used to her crutches. But then, as she came closer and Gene saw her sister's aggressive expression, her sympathy vanished. Wasn't it enough that she'd dragged herself down here to ride? she wondered. Was she going to have to listen to a minute-by-minute critique of the training session, too?

Apparently so, for Shelley's first words were, "What are you doing?"

"What does it look like?" she said, turning back to Achilles. "I'm untacking the horse."

"So soon? You only rode him half an hour."

"Not that it matters, but it was at least forty-five minutes. What are you doing here, anyway? Aren't you supposed to be home with your leg up?"

"I've been home, and it's boring."

"I see. So you decided to come down here and annoy me."

"I only came to tell you—"

When Shelley stopped, Gene slowly straightened and turned to look at her again. "Tell me what?"

Shelley flushed—not a good sign. "It wasn't my fault, honest," she said, while Gene tensed. "I didn't mean to, but it just came out. If I'd thought he'd actually come to watch, I never would have said—"

"What are you talking about?"

Shelley looked everywhere but at Gene's face. "I talked to Ross Malone this morning—"

"And?"

"And, well, naturally I had to tell him how well you and Achilles were doing...."

Gene's face clouded. "And?" she repeated.

"Now, Gene, don't be upset. But when we were talking, I must have been a little more enthusiastic than I realized, because before I knew it, Ross was saying he'd like to come out again and watch you ride. And so... and so—"

"When?" Gene asked flatly.

"I... What? What do you mean, when?"

"You know damned well what I mean!" Gene exclaimed. "When did you tell him he could watch me ride?"

"Well, I... I tried to get you out of it, I did! But I mean, he *is* sponsoring the horse." Shelley laughed nervously. "Well, actually, the horse belongs to him, doesn't it? So if he wants to come and see Achilles, I couldn't tell him not to, could I?"

"Shelley—"

"Oh, all right, all right. The truth is that he wanted to come tonight—"

"*Tonight?*"

"Yes, tonight," Shelley said defiantly. "Look, I didn't want to tell you before because I thought you'd be nervous, but really, I think things went pretty well, don't you? I mean, Achilles could have run *me* through those bushes down on the lower part of the cross-country course, just like he did to you. And when he went *around* that tree jump instead of over it, we all admired how well you stayed in the saddle—"

Gene advanced on her sister. "Are you trying to tell me that Ross Malone was here tonight, *watching* me ride this horse? Why didn't you tell me before? Why didn't you warn me? Oh, Shelley, how could you do this? Don't you ever think of anyone but yourself?"

"I'm sorry, Gene, really I am! But what could I say?"

"You *could* have said—"

"Hey!" called a new voice behind them. "What's all the shouting about?"

Startled, they both turned to see Kenny walking down the aisle. With him was Ross Malone. Gene had been so involved, she hadn't heard them coming. She was mortified at the thought of how she and Shelley had been yelling at each other. She was still holding the saddle, and she quickly shoved it onto a nearby rack. Then, her cheeks burning, she hid her face by bending down to take off the protective leg wraps Achilles was wearing.

As the two men approached, Shelley glared at Kenny and said, "We weren't shouting."

"You could have fooled me," he said. "We could hear you all the way down at the office." He paused. "Anything wrong?"

Gene knew she looked foolish lurking behind the horse, so she straightened with the wraps in her hand. "Nothing's wrong, Kenny," she said. She had to force herself to give a cool nod to Ross. "Hello, Mr. Malone. I didn't expect to see you here tonight."

"So it seems."

Gene flashed an irate glance at Shelley before saying, "I'm sorry you had to hear that. But if Shelley had told me you planned to be here—"

"I should have called you and asked."

Yes, you should have, she thought. If she had known he intended coming tonight, she would have come down even earlier and worked the horse so he didn't dare misbehave—as he had. As galling as it was to admit, it seemed she'd made a fool of herself in front of Ross once again.

"Achilles is your horse," she said stiffly. "You have every right to watch him work."

"And now that I've seen him—"

"Yes?" Her chin lifted a fraction.

"Er...Shelley," Kenny said, "could I see you in the office for a minute, please?"

For once, Shelley seemed only too pleased to let older sister handle things. "Sure," she said. "Let's go."

Thinking dire thoughts about what she'd have to say to Shelley about leaving her alone with Ross Malone, Gene didn't wait until the cowardly pair disappeared. Instead, she grabbed a brush and started in on Achilles's gleaming white coat. Ross's silence unnerved her, and to fill it, she asked, "So, what do you think of your horse?"

When he didn't answer right away, she steeled herself and looked at him. He was staring at her, and his scrutiny made her even more nervous. Quickly, she turned to Achilles, but she had to ask, "Is something wrong?"

"No. I was just wondering..."

She abandoned the pretense. Dropping the brush into the nearby basket, she dusted off her hands. "What?"

Ross glanced at the horse, then to her. Finally, he said, "Are you sure you want to do this? When I was watching you tonight, Achilles seemed such a handful. Not that you can't handle him," he added quickly. "I've seen that you can. But Shelley has told me how dedicated you are to your career, and we both know how much work this horse is going to need before he's ready to compete. I'm just wondering if it might not be a good idea to find someone else to ride him until Shelley can do it again herself."

Earlier tonight—especially after the hard day she'd had—when Achilles was taking her on that wild ride through the shrubbery down in the pasture, Gene had wondered the same thing. But when Ross voiced the identical concern now, she was surprised by her reaction. Without warning, she felt such a fierce wave of possessiveness toward the horse that she put a hand on the animal's neck.

"I can do it," she said. "I know how it looked tonight, but he'll get better—"

"I know he will. I'm just not sure—"

Achilles was still tied in the aisle. As though he were following the conversation, he began to nod his head up and down. One huge foot pawed the floor, then pawed it again. Distracted, Ross asked, "What's he doing?"

"I don't know. Maybe he's telling you he doesn't want another rider."

"That's ridiculous."

"Is it? Horses understand more than we think."

"I don't believe this. The horse can't possibly know what we're talking about."

"Are you sure?" Ross's earlier comment made her feel perverse, and she said flippantly, "Maybe you should ask him."

"I'm not going to ask him anything! This whole thing is—"

He never finished the sentence, because just then, as though he *had* been following the conversation, Achilles shook his head and snorted out a mighty, contemptuous breath. Alfalfa-colored particles sprayed everywhere, catching Ross in a full blast, all the way down the front of his suit and white shirt.

Gene was appalled. Quickly, she searched her pockets for a tissue, but Ross had already taken out his handkerchief. She expected him to be furious—he certainly had every right to be—but as he wiped his face, she was certain she saw a twinkle in his eye. It redeemed him on the spot—or spots, in this case, she thought, and stifled a giggle by biting her lip.

"Well," Ross said calmly, "it seems you have a supporter."

"I can't believe he did that."

Ross looked with distaste at the used handkerchief before dropping it in a nearby trash can. Then, to her surprise, he actually grinned. "I can. Look, maybe we should just start over and pretend this didn't happen. I'll tell you what...you ride the horse, and I'll stay out of it." He glanced at Achilles, and when there wasn't another dissenting blast from the big equine nostrils, he looked relieved. "I guess that means he approves," Ross said. "So, what do you say, Gene?"

Once more she knew what she should say, but she didn't. What was it about this man? she wondered. She hardly knew him, and yet, right from the first, she'd felt this inexorable pull in his direction. Was it the look in his eyes? His wry self-expression? Maybe it was because he could stand there with alfalfa bits covering his shirt and still look so handsome he took her breath away.

Suddenly, she knew they both had a stake in this now, and it wasn't just because of the horse. Something was happening here, and she couldn't turn her back and walk away. She had to find out what it was.

So, ignoring the small voice that kept telling her to get out while she could, she said, "After what he just did to you, do you think I'm going to argue with this horse?"

CHAPTER FIVE

GENE AND ROSS WENT OUT to dinner the next night. When he rang the bell exactly on time and Gene went to the door, she attributed her nervousness to the fact that she hadn't been out on a date in longer than she could remember. Clearly, she was out of practice.

She hadn't even been able to decide what to wear. A suit seemed too businesslike, pants too casual. Finally, when she remembered that she'd never seen Ross in anything but a jacket and tie, she chose a simple silk dress in shades of green...and then didn't know whether to add a blazer or sweater to it. Her indecisiveness irritated her, and she grabbed a shawl and went downstairs just as the bell rang.

"Hi," she said, opening the door. She was about to make a comment about his being on time when she saw that he was holding a huge bouquet of carnations, daisies and white and yellow roses, all enveloped in clouds of baby's breath. For a second or two, she was speechless. It had been a long time since a man had brought her flowers, and she was touched.

"Hi, yourself," Ross said. He gestured. "I didn't know what kind you liked."

"I like them all," she said, finding her voice. "They're beautiful, Ross. Please, come in while I put them in water. Then we'll go."

She always forgot that he used a cane. As she took the flowers from him and stood aside so he could enter, she wondered if she overlooked it because, despite his pronounced limp, he appeared so athletic and fit. Or maybe, she thought, as he smiled at her before carefully maneuvering his way past, it was because of his eyes. She'd never met a man with such a compelling gaze.

"Go ahead and have a seat if you like," she said. "I won't be long."

She left him in the living room, while she hurried into the kitchen. In record time, she found a vase tucked into the rear of a cupboard, but as she filled it and started to put the flowers in, she realized that her hands were shaking.

For heaven's sake, she thought. *Stop acting as though you've never gone out with a man before. You'll never get through the evening if you don't get a grip.* She took a couple of deep breaths to calm down. Then, carrying the vase, she went into the living room and put it in the place of honor on the coffee table.

Ross had been looking at her framed caricature collection. He was still chuckling over one particular drawing, and when she came in, he said, "These are wonderful. I recognized that one of Shelley right away."

She joined him by the picture wall. The caricature he'd indicated was one of her favorites, too. It depicted a beetle-browed, fuming Shelley with her hands on her hips and what looked like smoke coming out her ears. She was standing eyeball to eyeball with an equally belligerent steed. Clouds of dust were flying up around them, and it was obvious from the horse's stance—hooves on *his* hips, *his* ears flattened—that they'd had a major difference of opinion. As in all good caricatures, the distinctive features of both subjects had been exaggerated—although not by much in Shelley's case—to produce a comic effect. Gene was pleased that Ross liked it, and she smiled.

"Thanks, but don't tell Shelley," she said. "She hated that one from the moment I sketched it. I think it's because she recognized herself all too well."

"You drew this?"

He looked so surprised that she laughed. "I did all of them. It's not a big deal. Anyone can do it."

Ross looked back at the drawings and shook his head. "I don't think so. I can't draw a straight line, myself."

"It's not a matter of drawing straight lines," she teased. Then, because he was looking at her so strangely, she added, "I can't really take any credit. It's just something I took up when I was younger. The show circuit can be exciting when you're in the ring, but before and after that, it's hours of boredom. I had to amuse myself somehow, and this was it."

He seemed fascinated by her ability. "They're all so good. Do you draw your own line of greeting cards, too?"

Genuinely amused, she shook her head. "Thanks for the thought, but I wouldn't have the time or the patience to do that. I just do this for my own pleasure."

"I think you're being modest. I don't know much about things like this, but these are—look, there's one of Kenny! At least, I think it's Kenny. Isn't that his hat peeking up from behind all that office clutter?"

She laughed again. "How did you guess? I drew that one the first day I saw his office. I couldn't resist all those teetering stacks of books and magazines and heaven knows what else he collects."

"Has he seen it?"

"Oh, yes."

"What did he think?"

"He thought it was funny." Her eyes sparkled. "But then, he has a better sense of humor than my sister."

They left for the restaurant soon after that, and by the time they arrived and were seated, Gene had forgotten her earlier nervousness. Ross was absolutely charming and Gene found herself relaxing and enjoying his company. It wasn't difficult, she had to admit. Now that they weren't trying to prove something to each other, neither of them was quite so tense. Ross even ordered a bottle of champagne.

"This is lovely," she said after the waiter had poured them both a flute. "But what are we celebrating?"

He touched his glass to hers. "How about . . . a new partnership?"

She didn't want to ruin the moment, but she had to say, "A temporary one, you mean. As soon as Shelley is fit to ride, I'll go back to my cubbyhole of an office, never more to be seen again."

He held her eyes. "I hope not," he said softly. "Oh, I hope not."

And just like that, the atmosphere changed. Incredibly, she felt herself blushing, and she took a quick sip of the excellent champagne. The waiter saved her from the problem of a response by returning for her order, and before Ross could send him away again, she began quizzing the poor man about every fish dish on the menu. She hadn't realized that Ross was amused until she finally selected something and the relieved waiter turned to him.

"I'll have whatever the lady is having," Ross said, his eyes laughing.

"Excellent choice, sir, excellent," the waiter murmured. He collected the menus and asked, "Will there be wine tonight?"

Ross tipped his head in Gene's direction. "You decide."

Something more to drink was the last thing she needed. "Champagne will be enough for me. But you go ahead."

"No, I think I'll stay with this, too."

The waiter nodded. "Another bottle, then, sir?"

Ross wouldn't take his eyes off her. "We'll see how it goes," he said.

"Very good, sir."

The instant the waiter left, she leaned forward. "Why are you staring at me like that?"

"Was I?"

"Yes, you were." She glanced covertly around at the other tables, and added in a lower voice, "You're embarrassing me."

"I'm sorry. It's just..." He paused and shook his head. "Never mind. I didn't mean to be rude. I guess I was just wondering why you didn't have any pictures at home of yourself riding. From what Shelley says, you were once quite a competitor."

Was that really what he'd been thinking? She had the feeling that it wasn't, but she let it go. This new subject seemed safe enough, and she sat back. "I did love it one time," she said. Then she smiled. "But what did I know? I was a child, a young girl."

"You must have enjoyed it. Competing is a lot of work."

"I didn't think of it as work. In fact, I couldn't wait to get out to the stable and ride every day." She had to laugh. "I did well in school, but only because I knew that my parents wouldn't let me ride if I didn't. But to be honest, I have to say that there were many times when I felt classes definitely got in the way of what I *really* wanted to do. Back then, I couldn't imagine doing anything else but riding for the rest of my life."

"But you quit."

Her smile faltered a bit. "Yes, I did." She didn't know how much he knew, but she didn't want to go into details about High Cotton, so she said, "My horse had a bad accident during a competition and had to be put down. After that, I couldn't seem to regain either my enthusiasm, or my competitive edge. And then, too, reality began to rear its ugly head. I realized I had to make a living someday, so I thought I'd better get started before it was too late. I went to college, got my business degree and . . . well, I finally ended up at Greetings."

"It seems a natural place for you to be, given your artistic talent. Still, it must have been quite a wrench to give up riding. Shelley said you were good enough to compete on an international level."

As she answered, Gene made a mental note to tell Shelley she was talking much too much. "It was my horse who was good enough. High Cotton was one in a million, I think. He—"

Without warning, she began to feel emotional, and she broke off. As though he understood, Ross took another sip of champagne and waited. After a moment, she was able to go on. "I'm sorry," she said. "It's been years, but sometimes it's still difficult to talk about him. He was such a good horse. I don't think there was anything he wouldn't do for me."

He was staring at her again. "I've been told he was a white Thoroughbred, just like Achilles."

What *more* had Shelley told him? Gene wondered. Her entire life story?

"He was," she said. "But don't worry," she added, anticipating him. "At first Achilles did remind me of High Cotton, I admit. But it was only his color. They have very different personalities."

She didn't say it, but her tone implied that she was grateful for the distinction. With a slight smile, Ross said, "I understand. Shelley told me what happened to High Cotton." Startling her, he put a sympathetic hand over hers as he added, "I know we're all taught to anticipate such things, especially in such highly competitive sports, but I don't think you can ever prepare yourself for a loss like that...."

It took her a moment to notice that his voice had trailed off. His simple gesture of putting a hand over hers had been a comforting one, and yet it also seemed fraught with something she couldn't quite identify. Fighting a crazy impulse to turn her palm up and lace her fingers in his, she pretended she wanted more champagne and grabbed her glass.

"You sound as though you're talking from experience," she said a little unsteadily, after she'd taken a sip.

"Well, I am. How do you think I got this bum leg?"

She looked at him in astonishment. "You rode, too?"

He laughed. "Good grief, no! Or at least, not in the way you mean." His eyes twinkled. "I used to race cars for a living."

"You were a race car driver?"

"Well, that's another way of putting it—yes. You didn't know?"

She was embarrassed to admit it. "No, I... I never thought to ask." She reddened, remembering something. "I don't follow car racing, but maybe that's why I thought you looked familiar when I first saw you at the hospital." Her blush deepened. "Did you have your picture in the papers? Was that where I saw you?"

"Probably," he said, making light of his previous fame. "But that was a long time ago."

"I guess that's why I assumed that you'd always been in business."

"Outdoor Outfitters was something I got involved in after I hit the wall for the last time. By the time I came to, it was pretty clear that the only way I'd ever get around an Indy track again would be in a pace car with an automatic gearshift."

His attempt at nonchalance wasn't quite successful. She could hear the pain and regret in his voice, and she had to stifle her own sympathetic impulse to reach for his hand. "What happened?" she asked. Then she added quickly, "I'm sorry. I shouldn't have asked. It's none of my business."

"No, it's all right. The simple truth is that one day I did a stupid thing and... crashed."

"How awful!"

He smiled faintly. "Well, it wasn't pleasant, I'll tell you that. In fact, it was a doozy, all right. I smashed in the whole front of the car. The only reason I've still got my leg is that I refused to leave it behind when they cut me out. I made James promise—"

"James was there? James Daughtry?"

He laughed at her stunned expression. "I know it seems hard to believe, given his...um...excitable personality, but James was one of the owners of the car."

"James was involved in such a dangerous sport?"

Ross smiled again. "He didn't drive the car," he said. "He just stood on the sidelines, or down in the pit, and fainted a lot. And what do you mean, dangerous? You should talk. What's more hazardous than jumping a horse over all those impossible fences on some wild cross-country course?"

"Oh, but that's different!"

He looked genuinely amused. "Tell me how."

"Well, for one thing, we're not hurtling around at five hundred miles an hour—"

"We never went that fast. Just a little over two-twenty."

"Oh, *just* two-twenty. That's practically dawdling down a country lane."

"Well, not even I could say *that*. I admit, when I crashed that last time at Indy, I was going pretty fast."

"How can you make jokes about it?"

He started to say something glib, but when he saw her expression, he answered seriously, instead. "It's not that I'm making light of what happened. But in the hospital, when I was going through all those operations and all that therapy afterward, I learned that if you can't laugh, sometimes all you'll do is cry.''

"Oh, Ross. You must have had a terrible time."

He looked away from her sympathetic gaze. "It wasn't easy," he said gruffly. He met her glance. "But what was even more difficult for me was learning to ignore the looks I still sometimes get when people think I'm not watching. And then there are those who come right up to me and ask what happened—as if curiosity alone gives them a right to know. I don't mind the kids, but when adults do it—" He broke off, embarrassed. "I'm sorry. I didn't mean to get into all that."

"It's all right. I understand. I've never been involved in such a serious accident as you were, but I had my share of injuries and broken bones during the years I was riding. I didn't like it when some stranger came up to me and demanded to know what stupid thing I'd done to hurt myself. It always made me feel as if it were my fault." She paused. "Maybe it was, but they didn't have to point that out."

"I know what you mean," Ross said wryly.

Gene knew that he did, and she looked away, discomforted by the strong effect he was having on her. She knew that if she wasn't careful, she'd start telling him things she'd never told anyone, not even her talkative sister. He seemed to inspire the sharing of confidences, and she wasn't sure she liked his seemingly effortless ability to touch on her deepest feelings. She hardly knew him, she reminded herself. It was much too soon to share such personal experiences.

"Were you married when you were racing?" she asked. As soon as the words were out of her mouth, she was mortified. What had she just been telling herself? Her cheeks pink, she added hastily, "I'm sorry, Ross. I don't know why I'm asking such personal questions." She pushed her glass away. "I'll blame it on the champagne."

He smiled and pushed the glass toward her again. "I don't mind. And to answer your question, yes, I was married when I was driving. For part of the time, at least."

She couldn't seem to stop asking questions. "What did your wife think about your profession?"

He looked rueful. "That's why we're not married anymore. She held on as long as she could, through all the flameouts and spins and minor fender benders, but it got to be too much for her even before the big crash. She said she couldn't stand by, wondering which race was going to finish me."

Gene shuddered at the thought. "I can't blame her for that. I don't think I could have done it, either."

"I didn't blame her, either. Still, it's a funny thing. Marilyn—that's her name—and I have a better relationship now than we did when we were married."

"You're still friends?"

"Don't look so surprised. It can happen. In fact, I think that part of the problem—if you want to know the truth—was that Marilyn and I were friends who tried to make something more of our relationship than it was meant to be. I was glad that when it was all over, we were able to go back to being friends again."

"I think you're lucky. Not many people can do that."

"I know. And I hope you get to meet her sometime. You'd like her, I think. She comes into the office now and then, to give me advice. Or, as she puts it, to keep me on the straight and narrow. And now, turnabout is fair play. What about you?"

"Me? You mean have I ever been married?" Gene looked down and was surprised to see that her entrée had arrived. She didn't remember finishing her salad. She picked up her fork and held it poised over her plate. "I've come close a couple of times, but...it didn't work out."

"That's too bad."

"I guess," she said, stabbing a piece of miniature carrot. "But I've finally accepted that maybe I'm—"

"Difficult?" he said with an evil grin. "Stubborn and opinionated and set in your ways?"

She gave him a mock glare. "I *was* going to say, that I'm married to my work."

He laughed. "That makes two of us, then. It seems that we have more in common than we thought."

She knew what he said was true. But it was too dangerous a topic to pursue, so she said, "Well, I do enjoy my work. It's always a challenge. For instance, right now, I'm involved in setting up a new card division called—" She pointed a finger at him. "Promise you won't laugh?"

He crossed his heart. "I swear."

"All right, then, it's called Warm Fuzzies."

He laughed, after all. Then, when he saw her expression, he quickly sobered, although his eyes continued to sparkle. "I'm sorry. It's just the way you said it."

"I knew you'd think it was too cutesy."

"It *is* cutesy, but so what? You're in the business to make people feel good, aren't you? Warm Fuzzies seems to be a perfect concept for that."

"You really think so?"

"You're asking me?" he said with another grin. "Remember, our motto is, 'All you need to add is fresh air.'"

She laughed. "I see what you mean."

"Still, back to the original subject, I think one *can* get too involved in work."

"Has that happened to you?"

"Or maybe to you?" he countered.

She didn't want to answer that. "You know, now that I think about it, I don't believe that *was* the original subject. And how do you know all these things about me? No, don't tell me. Obviously, my sister delights in gossip. What *else* has she told you?"

He tried to appear solemn—a look that failed when his eyes began to shine in that intriguing way again. Innocently, he said, "All she said was that you were so involved with work that you didn't have time for any personal . . . relationships."

"Shelley loves to hear herself talk. A pity she doesn't know what she's talking about."

"Then you are seeing someone?"

Was that dismay she saw in his eyes? She found she was pleased at the thought. "No, I'm not seeing anyone," she admitted. She paused a fraction before adding casually, "Are you?"

"A workaholic like me? No, I have as much as I can handle in my life right now. What with Achilles and all the problems at the office, I don't have much personal time."

"I guess we *do* have more in common than we realized."

"Yes," he said. "I guess we do."

There was a short silence, while Gene wondered if she'd made the right move. She thought she'd be relieved that they had safely negotiated the relationship mine field and come out unscathed on the other side, but if that was so, why did she feel she'd missed an opportunity?

"So," Ross said after a moment. "Tell me why you decided to ride Achilles. You've said how busy you are at work, and that horse takes a lot of time."

"He does take a lot of time, that's true," she said. "But I couldn't refuse Shelley. The horse means a lot to her, and as we've mentioned tonight, it won't be forever. Just until she gets back on her own two feet."

By this time, the waiter had come and gone again, and coffee had arrived. Gene realized that she must have eaten her dinner, but all she could remember was one tiny bite of carrot. Where had the time gone?

And, although she thought that they'd established the ground rules, she found him staring at her. Unnerved again, she reached for the sugar bowl and added two lumps to her cup before she remembered she didn't sugar her coffee. She felt too foolish to ask for a fresh cup, so she tried not to grimace as she took a sip of the sweet stuff. Ross reached for his own coffee. "You said you agreed to ride for Shelley, but I wonder if you also had another reason."

"And what might that be?"

"Maybe after all these years away from it, you missed riding."

She *had* missed riding; she couldn't deny it. But it was disconcerting that he'd guessed. The man seemed to know far too much about her. And she couldn't blame it all on Shelley. Was *she* that transparent, or was he just a good judge of character? Feeling even more confused about him, she countered with, "Do you miss racing?"

"Every day of my life," he said fervently. Then he caught himself and added, "But it doesn't do any good to wish for things that might have been, so I try not to think about it too much. Things are different for you, though. That's why I asked."

"And that's why I told you. I'm riding Achilles for Shelley, no other reason. The instant she's able to ride again, she'll have the horse back."

"But you'll ride him until then?"

"I promised, didn't I?"

Ross looked at her strangely for a moment, then he looked down at his coffee cup. "Yes, you did."

"You sound like you're having doubts again."

"No, no. I was just wondering..."

She waited, but when he didn't finish the sentence, she prodded, "What?"

He'd obviously decided not to pursue his line of thought. "Let's talk about the horse," he said. "Is it too soon to judge what kind of ability Achilles has?"

She knew he hadn't been wondering about his horse's potential, but she couldn't accuse him of deliberately changing the subject. Besides, she could feel the faint tension that had sprung up between them, and it made her nervous. Something in his eyes made her feel ... she didn't know what.

Keep your mind on business, she told herself. *Answer his question.* "I think that Achilles could be the best."

He looked at her askance. "You don't have to say that."

"I'm not just saying it. I realize that he doesn't look it now, but if someone keeps up with him, he could go all the way to the top."

"I'm not so sure. Don't forget, I've seen him at his worst—"

Gene remembered a night last week when Achilles could have easily earned the horse from hell title, and she laughed. "You think you have, but take it from me—you definitely haven't seen him at his worst."

"Oh? You mean all those little temper tantrums of his, and the bucking exhibitions, and the grand finales of throwing his riders over fences don't count?"

"I know it's hard to believe, but those qualities are exactly what make me think he could be the best. All the top eventing horses have courage, stamina, determination—and just a touch of wildness. Otherwise, they'd never risk going full speed over all kinds of terrain, jumping obstacles that hide what's on the other side."

"And the riders are the same, aren't they?" he teased. "In other words, you *both* have to be a little crazy."

"Yes, just like I imagine what all those Formula One drivers have to be," she shot back.

"Oh, now—"

"No, don't try to deny it," she said loftily. "Who else but a lunatic would go roaring around an oval track at those speeds, with only a metal shell as protection from disaster?"

They laughed together, and then, the check paid, they left the restaurant. As Ross drove her home, she felt such a glow that she let down her guard. "You know, when I first saw you, I wondered—"

"What?"

Already she regretted having started this. "Well, I wondered why a man like you would even consider sponsoring an eventing horse. I mean, it just didn't figure. But now I think I know why."

He looked at her in amusement. "You do, do you? And just why is that?"

"It's the competition," she said promptly. "It might not be as exciting as car racing, but there's a thrill to it all the same."

"Yes, but I'm not the one who's riding—"

"I know. But I still think a part of you responds to a challenge like that. You want to be in on the excitement."

"Vicarious excitement?" He made a face. "That makes me sound a little pitiful, don't you think?"

They had reached her address, and as he stopped the car, Gene looked at him and thought that no one in a million years could ever describe Ross Malone as pitiful.

"No," she said. The words were out before she could stop them. "I think it makes you sound quite wonderful."

The interior of the car was dark, but the streetlight down the block made his eyes glimmer as he looked at her. "You really think that?"

She'd said it. She had to stand by it. Holding his gaze, she said, "Yes, I do."

For several moments, the only sound to be heard was the creaking of the car engine as it started to cool. Still gazing at her, Ross sat back on the seat. The movement made the upholstery squeak and Gene realized that she was holding her breath. It was the way he was looking at her, she thought.

Ross leaned toward her...it was as if he were drawn toward her, and she knew he was going to kiss her. Did she want him to? she wondered. Yes, she did. She definitely did. Then an unwelcome thought struck. If she allowed it, it might lead to...something she wasn't sure she was ready for.

Ross seemed to think the same thing. When Gene didn't move—didn't dare move, the moment spun itself out, and he sat back. The tenuous connection between them shattered, and for an awful moment, she felt as though she were teetering on the edge of an abyss. The disorienting sensation made her close her eyes briefly, and when she opened them again, the world was settling back into place. As though nothing had happened, Ross reached to open his door.

"You found me out," he said.

"I... did?" she stammered. She was having a hard time thinking straight.

His grin seemed a little forced. "Yes, you did. I agreed to go ahead with the horse, but only because I knew I'd never get James to sponsor a car. Don't tell him about the vicarious pleasure business, will you? He'll only get nervous, and we both know he's already anxious enough."

Gene didn't know why he was putting on this act until she looked deep into his eyes. The smile on his face wasn't in them. Did he feel the same way she did—that something was happening between them? Or had she just imagined this whole thing? She'd had all that champagne. Maybe this was just some wine-induced fantasy.

Maybe she was just overtired. She might be seeing things that just weren't there. Relieved at the idea, she said, "I won't tell him. It will be our secret."

He looked as though he wanted to say more, but changed his mind and got out. By the time he'd walked around to her side of the car, she'd regained her composure, and when they reached the door, she was able to say, "Thanks for dinner. I enjoyed it."

"I did, too. We'll have to do it again sometime—when our busy schedules mesh, that is."

"I'd like that." She was searching for her keys.

"Thanks for coming tonight. And also for everything you're doing. James and I really appreciate it."

"I'm glad to do it."

"Well . . . good night."

"Good night."

She found the keys at last, at the bottom of her purse. He waited until she had the door open, then he turned and started back down the walk.

It's better this way, she told herself as she watched him go. But just when Ross's car turned the corner, a little voice in her head said plaintively, *No, it's not.*

CHAPTER SIX

"I CAN'T BELIEVE we're doing this," James said for the third time as he and Ross were driving to Rancho Caballero, a horse park some miles north of San Diego. It was Sunday, just after six in the morning, and they were heading out to watch Gene ride Achilles in something they'd learned was a schooling event. The sun was already up, but James looked as though he should still be in bed. His face was pinched, there were bags under his eyes, and because he kept running a hand through it, his hair was standing on end.

Ross raised his eyes heavenward, seeking strength, before he handed across the thermos he'd brought. James had been complaining from the instant Ross had picked him up, and he was tired of it. "Here," he said, "make yourself useful and pour me some coffee, will you? You're making me nervous."

"I'm making you *nervous!*" James took the thermos and wrestled the cap off. "You could have fooled me. If you looked any calmer, I'd think you were asleep."

"What are you so worried about? You're acting as if this was your first horse show."

"It *is* my first!" James looked around for the other cup and finally spied it on the floor. He snatched it up, saying, "And how you can just sit there is beyond me.

Not even you can believe that horse is ready to compete."

"As we've been told, it's not really a competition," Ross reminded him calmly. "It's a session to give horses and riders some experience on a cross-country course."

"I don't care what you call it. Oh, this is crazy! Why did we ever let Shelley talk us into this? Something awful is going to happen, I just know it."

While Ross hid a smile at these melodramatics, James threw himself back against the seat. Then Ross's smile faded. It wasn't really funny, he knew. When Shelley had first brought up the subject of taking Achilles to a schooling show, he hadn't exactly been thrilled by the idea, either. In fact, privately, he agreed with James. In his opinion, Achilles wasn't ready for a test like this. But then, to be fair, he didn't know that much about it, so he'd called Gene to ask what she thought.

He should have guessed what her response would be. After pondering for about two seconds, she said breezily, "There's really no other way to tell how Achilles is going to react under pressure, you know. It's one thing to work him out at the stable, where he knows the routine and what to expect. It'll be another to see what he does in a strange environment. I think Shelley's right. It's a good opportunity to find out."

"What do you think he'll do?" he asked cautiously.

"That's hard to say."

She seemed to relish the idea that something exciting would happen.

"Try," he commanded.

"Well, he could take it completely in stride, or he could come unglued. We'll just have to see."

"And given those alternatives, you think it's a good idea?"

"Yes, I do." She seemed to realize he wasn't quite as enthusiastic about the plan as she was. "Don't you?"

He didn't know what he thought. Until this horse trial business had come up, he believed he was handling things just fine. But now that it was time to see just what Achilles could do in public, so to speak, Ross had suddenly realized he wasn't handling this well at all. It was one thing for Gene to ride the horse in a controlled environment—or as controlled as it was going to get, he thought with a wince. It was another for her to risk life and limb on a strange cross-country course.

And for what? he thought guiltily. So that Outdoor Outfitters could generate some publicity. James had been right. They should have just hired an agency to make a commercial. If they'd acted like normal businessmen, he wouldn't be worrying about strong-willed women who seemed determined to prove something by putting themselves in danger.

Like he had done when he was racing?

He squirmed at the thought before telling himself that riding and racing weren't the same thing.

Weren't they?

Abruptly, he realized that Gene was still waiting for his answer. "I'm not sure what I think. I know that you and Shelley are the experts, but it seems to me that this is asking too much from a horse that you've admitted is still untrained."

"Oh, at this stage, we certainly wouldn't expect him to be perfect, Ross," she assured him. "In fact, that's why Shelley wants to take him to this small trial first. It will be a miracle if we get around the course in one piece. Anything could happen the first time out."

How could she sound so casual? "What do you mean, it will be a miracle if you get around in one piece? Aren't you worried?"

"If I was worried, I wouldn't do it, would I?"

He couldn't tell if she was teasing him, or not. "I don't know, maybe you would. In fact," he went on more firmly, "now that I think about it, I'm positive you would."

"I'm not crazy, Ross. If I didn't think the horse could do it, I wouldn't try. After all—" she was definitely teasing him at this point "—he's too valuable an animal to take chances with."

Ross had a sudden image of Gene, pale and lifeless on the ground, while Achilles galloped unconcernedly away. Sharply, he said, "I'm not worried about the damn horse. I'm worried about *you!*"

"Why, Ross," she said, sounding surprised, "I was just joking."

"I don't like that kind of kidding around." Annoyed that he might have betrayed his feelings a little too much, he went on stiffly, "This is serious business. We've all—pardon the pun—got a lot riding on this. I, for one, don't take it lightly."

There was a short silence. Then, sounding a little stiff herself, Gene said, "I realize we don't know each other very well, Ross, but you should be aware that neither Shelley nor I take this lightly, either. If we didn't think Achilles was ready for this, we wouldn't recommend it. Of course, it's your decision. After all, Achilles is your horse.''

He felt like a fool. Before this conversation, he'd been wondering when he could ask her out again, but now it seemed a pointless question. He seemed to have a genius for offending her, he thought. Maybe he should consider himself lucky that she hadn't told him exactly what he could do with his horse.

"I'm sorry," he said. "I didn't mean to make you angry. I admit that James and I don't know much about this process, so if you think Achilles is ready for this, we'll defer to your judgment."

He could tell that his attempt at apology was only partially successful. Her voice still cool, she'd said, "Thank you. Was there anything else?"

There had been, but he decided to let well enough alone—that time, anyway. He still wanted to take her out, but obviously that hadn't been the time to ask for a date. And there were other considerations, he thought after he'd said goodbye and hung up. It had been a long time since he'd been so instantly attracted to a woman, and while he wanted to believe that Gene felt something for him, too, he couldn't forget that she hadn't asked him to come in the other night after dinner. Ever since, he'd been driving himself crazy wondering why not. Had he been imagining that their feelings were mutual? If she *had* been interested, wouldn't she at least have offered him coffee?

All this introspection made him feel even more annoyed. What had happened to his self-confidence? Meeting Gene seemed to have turned everything upside down, and he was reminded uncomfortably of those first few weeks after he'd left the hospital. He hadn't known until he started getting out again that his wounds were more than physical. To his horror, the crash seemed to have done something to his confidence, too.

He'd never had a problem with women. As egotistical as it sounded, he'd never even thought about it. He'd been married during his racing days, so he had never taken advantage of all the groupies hanging around. But there had always been girls—women—in the pits or the stands, waiting to be noticed, and sure enough, they flocked to him when he showed up—brave, battered, but undaunted—after the crash. They didn't know it, but he couldn't stay away; just being there made him realize how lucky he'd been. Even though his doctor had told him he'd never race again, he could still dream that nothing had changed.

For a while, except for the fact that he wasn't driving, it seemed that nothing *had* changed. He was even treated like a hero, he remembered. Or if not a hero, like a wounded warrior who deserved attention and sympathy. After so many months of pain and difficult therapy, he'd basked in all the attention, but of course, it hadn't lasted. Because he was consigned to the sidelines, he wasn't generating all those heartstopping thrills that the fans—male *and* female—craved. All too soon, the groupies abandoned him for drivers who could fulfill both the expectations and the fantasy. Not long after that happened, he'd stopped going to the track.

He had to admit that the experience had soured him on relationships. Ever since, he couldn't tell if a woman was really interested or just felt sorry for him and would leave when her sympathy ran out. Not wanting to take the chance, he'd settled for superficial dating since his divorce.

And now that he'd met Gene Logan ... what? Was he still sour, disinterested, afraid to let a woman get close?

He didn't know what he felt. Impatient with himself, he wondered what he was worried about. Gene had made it clear during their one dinner date that she was too committed to her work to think about anything else. He had to accept that, forget it and go on to something else.

But damn it, he thought, he couldn't forget. He could try to delude himself, but he knew Gene was in his mind to stay. He couldn't stop thinking about how her eyes sparkled when she was amused, and how that dimple in her cheek flashed when she laughed. She was intelligent and witty and creative, and she could ride a horse like no one he'd ever seen before. It seemed as though there was nothing she couldn't do. Was he falling in love with her?

The sudden thought startled him so much that he jerked the steering wheel and the car swerved. The motion broke his reverie, and he realized that James was looking at him.

"Are you having second thoughts?" James asked.

He didn't want to get into it. "About what?"

James looked at him a moment more. "Never mind. Tell me what's wrong. You looked so serious all of a sudden. First you were smiling, then you turned grim." He shook his head. "I don't like it when you look grim, Ross. It's not good. Something's wrong, isn't it?"

"Nothing's wrong."

James wouldn't listen. "I know what it is. You don't think this is a good idea, either, do you? Come on, admit it."

"I'm not going to admit anything," Ross said flatly. "As usual, you're letting your imagination run wild. Besides, it doesn't matter what either of us thinks right now. We're almost there, so we'll just have to make the best of it."

The gates to Rancho Caballero were ahead, and as they got into line with all the other cars and trucks towing horse trailers that were turning in, James sighed. "This is a mistake," he mumbled. "I just know it."

"Calm down and look for the van, will you?"

Kenny had kindly volunteered to take Achilles to the meet, and as James resignedly leaned forward to scan the colorful, confusing crowd of horses, riders, spectators, veterinarians and other officials who were milling around inside the park, he said, "I don't see it. No, wait! There it is, under those trees!" He gasped. "I think something's gone wrong!"

Ross was too busy trying to maneuver the car through the throng to look. Animals and people and vehicles seemed to be everywhere, and he said tensely, "What is it? What do you see?"

"It's...oh, no!"

"Damn it, James! If you don't tell me—"

He didn't get a chance to finish. Just then, a riderless black horse appeared out of nowhere right in front of him, and as he slammed on the brakes, he and James were thrown forward. Coffee flew everywhere, and James cursed as he banged his hand against the dashboard. The horse didn't even break stride. It galloped on with people in hot pursuit. The car was still rocking when Ross looked at his partner. With coffee dripping off him, James said plaintively, "What are we doing here?"

At the moment, Ross had no answer. The near accident with the horse was still on his mind. Thank heavens it wasn't Achilles, he thought. He saw Kenny's trailer parked just ahead, and drove toward it. Quickly, he scanned the scene, but he couldn't see what James had been worried about until he parked right beside Kenny's rig. That's when he realized that the trailer was empty, and the big white horse was nowhere in sight.

"Oh, what now?" he muttered. He got out and saw with relief that Gene and Shelley seemed to be all right—well enough to be having an argument, anyway. They were so involved in discussion, they didn't even look up.

"What happened?" James called to them.

"Nothing. Everything's fine," Gene said as Ross reached behind the seat for his cane.

James looked around nervously. "But when we were pulling in, I was sure I saw Achilles rearing up and fighting, and . . . what was he trying to do, anyway?"

"He was—" Shelley broke off when Gene gave her a look.

"He lost his balance, that's all," Gene said. "He'll be fine. Kenny just took him for a walk so he could get the kinks out."

"Yeah, right," Shelley mumbled, to another stern glance from Gene.

Ross walked over to where they were standing. Despite the obvious tension between the sisters, he couldn't help thinking how beautiful Gene looked. She was dressed in formfitting white breeches, tall black boots, a short-sleeved green polo shirt, and seemed as comfortable in this chaotic setting as he imagined she appeared in a business meeting at work. She was holding a sturdy regulation helmet with a safety harness and a new protective Kevlar vest.

By this time, Ross had learned enough about eventing to know that riders couldn't compete without protective gear. The helmet and vest had seemed substantial enough back at the store when they came in on special order, but right now, he would have preferred to have Gene suited up from head to toe in cotton batting. Or better yet, he thought, not riding at all. The riderless horse careening around like a loose cannon a few moments ago had rattled him more than he wanted to admit.

And speaking of horses, he thought, when would Kenny be back with Achilles? Just as he was about to ask, he saw the stable owner leading the horse toward them. When Ross saw the obviously agitated Achilles, he tensed even more. Somehow the horse looked bigger than ever.

Pumped up with excitement, Achilles was practically cantering in place beside Kenny, who had to tug sharply on the lead rope every few feet to keep the horse's attention. A sheen of nervous sweat glistened along Achilles's bulging neck, his ears flicked back and forth as though to catch every sound and his eyes looked as though they were going to pop out of his head. As Ross watched, transfixed, Achilles suddenly let fly with both hind feet. Fortunately, no one was behind the horse. Unfortunately, James happened to look over just at that moment.

"Ross, did you see that?" he gasped. Without waiting for a reply, he turned to Gene. "You're not going to ride that horse, are you? Oh, please, tell me you aren't!"

Gene laughed and patted his arm. "He's just feeling good, James. Don't worry. It doesn't mean a thing."

"But—"

"I think James is right," Shelley declared. While Gene looked at her warningly, and Ross turned to her in surprise, she glared at the approaching Achilles. "Maybe this isn't a good idea, after all."

"What are you talking about?" Gene demanded. "We've been over this before. Of course I'm going to ride him. How else are we going to find out how he works under pressure?"

"That's just the point," Shelley said stubbornly. "I think it's too soon to ask him to do something like this."

Gene put her hands on her hips in exasperation. "Something like what? This is just a schooling event, remember? It's not a real competition."

"Still—"

"Still, nothing!" Gene's expression darkened. "What's the matter with you? You're the one who wanted to do this!"

"Well, I was wrong, okay? I think we should just load up and go home."

"Well, I don't."

"And I do!"

"Look, Shelley," Gene said, obviously trying to control her temper. "We agreed. We're here, and I want to see what he can do."

As the two sisters faced each other, Ross wished he could disappear. He didn't know which one of them was right, but as he looked from the sturdy, bigger Shelley, to the smaller, more delicate Gene, he had the sinking feeling that before the decision was made, he was going to have to take sides. It wasn't a pleasant prospect, because he knew he couldn't win no matter what he said. If he agreed with Shelley—and he had to admit that, deep in his heart, he did—Gene was going to be angry. If he agreed with Gene, Shelley would feel betrayed.

On the theory that if he didn't look at either of them, they wouldn't remember he was here, he turned and watched as Kenny approached with the horse. His theory didn't work.

"Ross, what do you think?" Shelley demanded just then.

Impaled by two pairs of eyes, one a challenging green, the other an angry blue, he turned resignedly to the angry sisters. He took a deep breath before saying, "I think it's up to Gene. She's the one who has to ride."

Predictably, Shelley's blue eyes flashed. "But he's my horse!"

Ross decided now was not the time to point out the inaccuracy in that statement. He was trying to think of something tactful to say when Gene jumped in. Tossing him a smile of satisfaction which, mercifully, Shelley didn't seem to see, she said to her sister, "He's not your horse. And furthermore, Ross is right. I have to ride him, and I'm going to do it."

And with that, she turned to another hapless male. "Kenny, will you help me tack him up?"

It was Kenny's turn on the hot seat. He didn't even make a pretense of trying to assuage the increasingly angry Shelley. Dropping his gaze, he mumbled, "Yeah, sure."

"Well, thanks a *lot!*" Shelley cried.

Her mouth in a mutinous line, Shelley glared at them all, then clumped some distance away on the crutches. Ross saw Gene and Kenny exchange a quick glance before Kenny shrugged and went to fetch the tack. It took only moments for them to saddle the horse, and as Gene gathered the reins and bent her leg so that Kenny could help her up, she looked at Ross and smiled tightly.

"Don't worry," she said. "Shelley is being a pill. Achilles is going to be just fine."

Her words did nothing to reassure Ross. Quickly he looked around to see where everyone had gone. He had something private to say to Gene and he didn't want to be overheard. It turned out he didn't have to be concerned. Looking a little sick, James had retreated to the car, and Kenny had hurried after Shelley. They were already deep in a conversation that was punctuated with a lot of gestures—at least on Shelley's part.

Keeping a cautious eye out, Ross edged closer to Gene and the horse. "You don't have to do this," he said, looking up. "Nothing is as important as your safety. I don't care if the horse never competes. I don't want you to get hurt."

"I won't get hurt," she said.

The shine in her eyes and the eager tilt to her chin worried Ross. She seemed to vibrate with excitement, and he realized suddenly that in spite of all her statements about just exercising the horse until Shelley could ride him again, she was starting to enjoy this. That made him feel even more uneasy. Was she going to like it too much?

"Gene—" The sharp report of a whistle interrupted what he was about to say.

"That's for us," she said. Her face practically glowed as she looked down at him. "Aren't you going to wish us luck?"

He would rather pull her off the horse and wrap her in his protective arms. But he could just imagine what her reaction would be to that, so he said, "Good luck. And remember, if you don't think things are going well out there, don't hesitate. Just pull out. I promise you, none of us will think anything of it."

Her eyes were very green and there was a pink tint to her cheeks. "You might not, but I will," she said. She patted the tense Achilles on his arched neck. "And so will your horse. He deserves this chance, Ross. You'll see. It'll be all right." With a smile, she reached down and touched his face. "I appreciate the concern, I really do. But you worry too much. I've done this before, remember?"

Ross wanted to point out that it had been years ago, and in a different time and place, but he just nodded. "We'll be here when you get back."

Gene backed Achilles away from Ross and whirled the horse around. Her eyes sparkling in that way he was beginning to mistrust, she saluted and said, "We'll see you later."

"I hope so," he muttered as he watched the pair head toward the starting point. Clusters of riders and horses were already there, grouped according to experience and ability. Gene joined the "baby novice" group for beginning horses.

"We might as well go now," Kenny said, coming up behind him.

"Go?" Ross asked. He was still preoccupied with Gene and how vulnerable she'd looked on that big horse.

"You want to watch, don't you? There's a vantage point up that hill. You can see almost the entire course."

Ross wasn't sure he wanted to do that. In a sea of bays and chestnuts, their white horse stood out like a ghost. The image unsettled him, and he was so tense now, he couldn't decide if Achilles's conspicuousness was good or not. What was he going to do if, somewhere along the course, he saw that unmistakable coat disappear in a cloud of dust?

But he couldn't just stand here; he had to know what was going on. If Gene was risking herself for their company, the least he and James could do was cheer her on.

"Yeah, sure, let's go," he said. "Do we drive, or walk?"

It was the barest flicker. Kenny caught himself immediately, but Ross saw the other man's eyes drop momentarily to his cane and in spite of himself, he stiffened. "It's not a problem," he said flatly. "I can make it."

Kenny brought his eyes up to Ross's face again. "I never doubted it for a minute. I was thinking about Shelley and her crutches—"

Shelley heard them. "Don't worry about me!" she cried. "Since we're going to do this thing, let's get going and do it!"

She started off before anyone could stop her, heading toward a high hill that made Ross wish he hadn't been so defensive and cavalier. He thought about suggesting they drive, but the set of her shoulders told him it wouldn't be a good idea. Already, other spectators were heading up the hill, and down at the starting point, the riders were being given their last set of instructions. Ross knew that if they didn't move soon, there wouldn't be room for them.

"Come on, James," he called as Kenny ran after Shelley. "Let's go."

Bleakly, James emerged from the car, his handkerchief out. As he mopped his forehead, he said, "Do I have to? I'm not sure I'm ready for this, Ross. I don't think I want to watch."

Ross was too nervous to feel pity. "If I'm going to watch, so are you. Let's get moving."

"Can't we take the car?"

"No, we're going to hoof it like everyone else," Ross retorted. "Come on. They're already getting started."

The climb up the hill was even more difficult than he had anticipated. He had such a hard time with his cane that he didn't know how Shelley managed with the more awkward crutches. He looked her way when he and James finally reached the top and decided from her expression that she'd probably made it on temper alone. The first riders were coming through, and suddenly Shelley pointed. "Look, there she is!"

Ross turned in the direction she indicated. The cross-country course meandered through stands of trees, over creek beds, across roads and ditches, up hill and down, until finally, after a last series of three jumps, it ended in a long, upward pull to the finish line. Some of the jumps were natural: trees fallen over streambeds, branches at the top of a slope. But the man-made jumps looked even more horrifying to Ross. Wagons were piled with hay, fence posts stacked atop one another, high banks fortified with logs and who knew what else.

James stood beside Ross, his hands over his face. "I can't look," he moaned. "How is she doing?"

Ross forced himself to follow the white coat flashing through the trees below them. As he watched, Gene headed Achilles toward a steep slope with a series of steps cut into it. As the horse scrambled up from one to the other, Gene bending close to his neck, Ross wanted to close his eyes and couldn't. He'd never seen anything like it. With Gene urging Achilles on, they crested the top of the hill and started down the other side at what seemed to Ross a suicidal, breakneck speed. Beside him, Shelley was muttering to himself.

"That's it, take him straight down...collect him up a little...don't let him get ahead of himself...."

At last, Ross tore his eyes away from Gene—but only because he had to see what was coming next. He blanched. Horse and rider were heading down the hill. At the bottom was a deep ditch flanked by two fences, the second perched some distance up the opposite slope.

"Good Lord!" he exclaimed. "What's *that?*"

"It's called a coffin," Shelley said.

Ross thought he hadn't heard her right. "A...
coffin?"

"Like a ditch," she said hurriedly. "With big jumps
before and after it. One problem is—"

She stopped. Ross wanted to shake her. "Is what?"
he almost shouted.

Shelley drew in a breath. Ross hardly dared to look,
but when he turned his head on what seemed like a
rusty neck, he saw that Gene and Achilles had reached
the complicated, dangerous jump at the bottom of the
hill. They sailed over the first fence, took a stride,
leapt right into, and then out of the coffin, and before he knew it, were on top of the other fence, and
then scrambling up the hill again. As they headed over
the top and disappeared, Shelley cheered.

"Right *on!*" she shouted. Beside her, Kenny
grinned, while next to Ross, James finally took his
hands from his eyes.

"Is it over yet?" James asked pathetically.

Before Ross could answer, Shelley turned excitedly
their way. "Did you... did you see that?" She was so
excited, she was babbling. "He was great! A lot of
horses are afraid of the coffin, you know. They shy
like mad, and often fall. But not Achilles. He took it
like a champ!"

Ross wanted to be excited—as least as thrilled as
Shelley was. Kenny looked delighted, and although he
wasn't quite sure what was going on, even James
looked pleased. But Ross's heart was still pounding.
It was fear, he felt, not exhilaration, he realized. All
he could think was how scared he'd been when Gene

galloped down that hill, heading toward a suicidal-looking jump with that ominous-sounding name.

I can't do this, he was thinking shakily, when he heard Shelley gasp, "Oh, no!"

His heart dropping like a stone, Ross followed her glance, and froze. The last jump before the final long pull to the finish line was a steep decline to...water. Ross never did know what happened. Just as he turned to look, he saw a fountain of water spraying up and a thrashing commotion in the center of the pool where Gene and Achilles had...disappeared.

"No!" he shouted. He started mindlessly down the hill, but James grabbed him. Just as Ross turned to shake him furiously off, he saw his friend gesture.

"Look!"

Not sure he wanted to, Ross turned back to the course. In the center of the pond, a riderless horse was emerging through the spray that was still raining down. Gone was the white coat; Achilles was dripping with water and colored a muddy brown. Ross was so transfixed by the sight that he couldn't move. Where was Gene? he asked himself in panic. *Where was Gene?*

He was about to start toward the pond again when suddenly Gene appeared. She was soaked and muddy, too, but at least she was on her feet. Ross felt dizzy with relief.

"Oh, damn!" Shelley cried. "If this had been a competition, that fall could eliminate them!"

Ross turned to look at her. *Eliminate* them? he thought incredulously. They were lucky they hadn't been *killed!*

Ross didn't know how they all got down to the place where Gene had led the horse out of the water and stopped on shore. Somehow, even in the confusion of falling and getting drenched and thrashing around, she'd managed to hang on to the reins. She was checking Achilles for any injuries when they arrived, and when she straightened, a relieved look on her face, Ross couldn't help himself. Oblivious to anything but how grateful he was that she was safe, he threw down his cane and hugged her fiercely. She was so surprised that for a few blissful seconds she actually yielded. Then excitement seemed to sweep over her again and she pulled away.

"Did you see that?" she demanded, her muddy face glowing. "Oh, I can't believe it! I know he fell, but at least he tried it. Isn't it wonderful?"

James didn't know what was going on, but Shelley and Kenny seemed to. As they crowded around Gene and the blowing, stamping Achilles, Ross stepped back. He couldn't take his eyes off Gene, for without warning, he had just realized what had been bothering him. He'd seen the look in Gene's eyes, and he knew what it meant. How many times had Marilyn said she'd seen it in him when he'd been racing? It was the look of the competitor, the ace, the champion— the one who didn't care about the odds...the one who would rise to every challenge...the one who wouldn't be defeated.

Even after her fall, Gene still had that look of ea- gles, and as Ross watched her mount up again after she'd sought permission to finish the course, he knew that, without a doubt, they were all in big trouble.

CHAPTER SEVEN

GENE WAS SO ELATED when she crossed the finish line that she invited everyone to an impromptu barbecue at her house. All she needed, she said giddily, was time to take this wonderful horse back to the barn and go home to clean up.

"I'd like to, but I can't," James said, still looking a little dazed. "I promised my wife we'd visit her parents today, so I'll have to bow out."

"Another time, then," Gene said with a grin. She was still muddy from head to boot, but she had managed to wash most of the dirt off her face at one of the water spouts scattered throughout the park. She'd put her head under the faucet, as well, and tendrils of wet hair clung to her forehead and cheeks. She saw Ross staring at her and she knew that she looked a mess. Too bad, she thought. How could her appearance matter when Achilles had done so well? It had been a glorious day.

She turned to her sister. "What about you, Shelley? And Kenny, you, too, of course. You have to come. It's an occasion to celebrate!"

Shelley and Kenny glanced at each other, then Shelley said, "Yeah, sure, Gene. We'll come. It will give us a chance to talk."

"About how well Achilles did today?"

"Yes, that—and other things."

Kenny gave her a warning look. "Now, Shelley—"

She turned to him with a fierce, "Well, I'm sorry, but she has to know!"

"Know what?" Gene asked.

"Never mind," Kenny said, with another look at Shelley. "We can talk about it later."

Gene refused to allow Shelley to dampen her mood. She knew her sister. Shelley probably wanted to review in excruciating detail every jump they'd taken today so she could advise Gene exactly where she'd gone wrong and why. Deciding she'd handle the inevitable critical analysis later, Gene turned to Ross.

"What about you?" she asked. "I know it's short notice, but can you come?"

Ross hadn't said much since she'd finished the trial and rejoined them at Kenny's horse trailer. But then, he'd hardly had a chance. She'd been busy with Achilles, hosing him down and wrapping his legs for the trip back to the stables, and hadn't been able to stop herself from pausing in what she was doing every few minutes to give the horse a pat. She didn't care that his performance had been a little rough. She was proud of him and she wanted to express her feelings. That's when she'd thought of the barbecue idea. They should all celebrate such a red-letter day, and she wanted everyone to come.

Especially Ross?

Just then, Ross asked, "After all you've done, are you sure you want to do this? Won't it be too much trouble?"

Gene knew she'd probably regret it tomorrow, but right now she felt fine. More than fine. If she'd felt any better, she could have run a marathon.

"It's no trouble," she said. "I'll just make a salad and put some chicken on the grill. It'll be a cinch."

"In that case . . . at least let me bring dessert."

She hadn't thought as far as dessert. "Oh . . . you don't have to—"

He smiled. Her enthusiasm and excitement were contagious. "It's no trouble."

She grinned at him. "In that case, be my guest."

They all agreed to meet at her house at six o'clock. Gene gave directions to Ross before he and James left. Then she helped Kenny secure the van with Shelley standing to one side, leaning on her crutches and giving unnecessary directions. Shelley was still behind the trailer when Gene came around to put the ramp up. While Kenny went to start the truck, Gene asked, "What did you want to talk to me about?"

"It can wait."

Gene turned to look at her. "Correct me if I'm wrong, Shelley, but you don't seem to be very happy. When Achilles did so well today, I thought you'd be over the moon, just like I am. Yet you've hardly cracked a smile, let alone offered any congratulations. What gives?"

"I told you we'd talk about it later," Shelley muttered. "Let's let it go at that."

"I'd rather not. I know you, Shelley. Something's wrong, and I'd appreciate knowing what it is."

Her mouth a tight line, Shelley used the tip of one crutch to draw a square in the dirt. Gene knew that Kenny was wondering what the hold up was, but he'd just have to wait. Something was bothering Shelley, and Gene wanted to know what it was.

"Well?" she said.

Shelley wouldn't look up from her doodling in the dirt. "You did good today," she said unwillingly. "But I guess you know that."

"Thanks... I think," Gene said. "But if you feel that way, what's the problem?"

Shelley's mouth tightened even more. "The problem is, I don't think you should ride Achilles anymore." She looked up defiantly while Gene just stared at her uncomprehendingly. "There, I've said it. I knew you wouldn't like it, but that's the way it is."

Gene was too shocked to say anything for a few seconds. Finally, she managed to say, "Look, Shelley, I know how difficult it must have been for you to stand around on the sidelines when everyone else seemed to be riding. I've been there myself, and I hated it. But it won't last forever. Your leg will heal and soon you'll be back in the saddle, too."

Shelley's hands tightened around the crutches. "I knew you wouldn't understand!"

"You're right about that, I don't. What's going on here? You're the one who asked me to ride the horse. I can't believe you've changed your mind now, especially after the way things went today."

"But that's the point, don't you see?" Shelley said angrily. "Oh, I should have known this would happen! It's always been this way. No one can compete with you. It's stupid even to try!"

"What are you talking about? I'm not going to compete the horse. This was just a simple trial today, to see how he'd do under a little pressure. Instead of criticizing me, you should be happy that he did so well."

"I am happy!" Shelley snapped. "But don't you see? I wanted that to be me!"

Gene took a grip on her temper. "And it will be. As soon as you can ride again, it will be you in the saddle, not me. I'll get out of your way, and everything will go back to what it was."

"Yeah, sure."

"What do you mean by that? That's the way it's going to be. We made a deal, remember?"

"Oh, I remember. What I'm wondering now is if you do."

"And just what does *that* mean?"

"You know what it means. I saw your face when you were out on that course. You enjoyed it!"

"I don't believe this! You're accusing me of—" Gene stopped and took a deep breath, trying to calm herself. "Of *course* I enjoyed it. And why not? As green as he is, Achilles is a good horse. Was I supposed to hate every minute?"

"No, but you... but you—"

"What?" Gene demanded. She was out of patience.

"Oh, never mind! I said you wouldn't understand, and I was right. You don't!"

And with that, Shelley whirled so quickly that she almost lost her balance. Gene reached out automatically to steady her, but Shelley glared at her with such fury in her eyes that she dropped her hand. Helplessly, she watched as Shelley headed toward the front of the truck, where Kenny was waiting.

"And you can forget about the barbecue!" Shelley said over her shoulder. "I'm not coming, and neither is Kenny!"

"Hey, wait a minute," Kenny protested. "I didn't say—"

Her face red, Shelley looked at him. "If you go, I'm never speaking to you again."

He looked shocked. "Shelley!"

"I don't care. Her or me, make your choice. But just remember, Kenny Fielding, if I'm not speaking to you, I'm not doing your account books, either!" She must have sensed Gene's astonishment, for she turned irritably back to her. "If you must know, I'm doing Kenny's books. You told me to find something to keep myself occupied and I did." Her lip curled. "Little did I know that while I was trying to get that so-called office organized, you'd be trying to steal my horse away from me!"

"What a rotten thing to say!" Gene exclaimed.

"It's true, and you know it. Come on, Kenny. Let's go."

Shelley didn't wait for Kenny's help. Hobbling furiously around to the side of the truck, she jerked the passenger door open and threw her crutches inside. As she climbed in after them, Kenny looked helplessly at Gene, who—fortunately, she thought now—had come in her own car. He was clearly as unhappy about this new development as she was, and when she saw his face, she said, "It's okay. You go ahead. I'll see you later, when this all blows over."

"I'm sorry about the barbecue—"

"Don't worry about it. It was probably a bad idea, anyway."

"She'll get over it." He looked quickly at Shelley, who was now sitting stiffly in the front seat, her arms crossed and her lips clamped together. He turned to Gene again. "It's just hard for her to be on the sidelines."

"I know." Gene could feel her euphoria fading. It had been such a wonderful day, she thought—and now this. She forced a smile. "I'll call her tomorrow and we'll patch things up. We always do."

Still, he hesitated. "You did real good today."

"Thanks."

"I mean it."

"I know you do."

"Are you going to quit riding the horse?"

Quit? Gene was surprised at how strongly she felt. "No, I won't do that. Shelley's just upset now. She'll come around. And, a deal's a deal."

"Good."

Gene waited until Kenny's rig pulled out and was gone before she went to her own car. But after she'd climbed in behind the wheel, she sighed. Now that all the excitement was over, she was so tired that she wondered if she'd be able to drive home. The argument with Shelley had been even more enervating, and she was glad that the barbecue was off. Now that she thought about it, she couldn't imagine why she'd impulsively invited everyone for dinner. The way she felt now, she'd be lucky to get in and out of the shower before she keeled over. All she wanted to do was fall into bed and go to sleep.

It wasn't until she was pulling out of the parking lot that she remembered one person she had invited who was still planning on coming tonight.

"Oh, my God—Ross!" she exclaimed in dismay.

Well, she'd just have to call him when she got home and say—what? That she'd changed her mind about dinner with him because no one else was coming? She blushed. She might just as well admit that she was afraid to be alone with him. That would be more honest, at least.

No, it wouldn't, she told herself firmly. She was being ridiculous. What did she expect would happen, after all? It was a celebration, not a . . . tryst. It would have been an impromptu party, if everyone else hadn't canceled, so it was no big deal. *Chicken and a salad,* she thought. *A little wine, and he'd go home again.*

Where was the danger in that? Was she so insecure that she couldn't handle a simple dinner . . . between friends?

GENE GOT HOME a few minutes before five. After throwing some chicken in the microwave to defrost, she hurried upstairs. There was enough time to take a shower and wash her hair, but as always, especially when she was in a hurry, her knee-length riding boots refused to come off. She had a bootjack, but long before she finally battled her way free, she'd nearly fallen off the chair twice and was so annoyed that she'd even considered slitting the sides. She might have done just that, if one foot hadn't been caught halfway inside. Stuck as she was, she couldn't even hobble down to the kitchen to get a knife.

Sweat was running down her face by the time she finally freed herself, and as she kicked the boots across the room, she looked at the clock and groaned. She only had minutes to make herself presentable.

Sure enough, she had just finished blow-drying her hair when she heard the doorbell. She should have known Ross would be on time, she thought, as she whipped on some lipstick and headed for the stairs. After such a rush, she felt decidedly off balance.

"Hi," she said, trying not to pant as she opened the door. "You're right on time."

As always, Ross looked as though he'd just stepped out of a bandbox. Wearing a fresh pair of slacks and a light blue sports shirt, he grinned. "It comes from years of having to be on the starting line when the clocker calls."

Instead of flowers this time, he was carrying a big pink bakery box in one hand, and a bottle of wine in the other. Gesturing with both, he added, "I brought the important things."

"I'm glad you did," she said, standing aside so that he could come in. She took the box from him, but let him carry the wine. "Because right now, that's all we're having. I got stuck in traffic on the way home, and I haven't even had time to start the barbecue, much less get the salad together."

"Well, I can take care of the barbecue," he said easily. "And the salad, too, if you like."

"I should have known you were a man of many talents," she said as they went to the kitchen. "And don't think I won't take you up on it. I'm still trying to catch my breath."

"I'll tell you what—why don't you sit down and have a glass of wine while I start the barbecue?" He looked out the kitchen window. The grill was in plain sight on the patio, and he asked, "Are the briquettes out there, too?"

"They're in the garage, by the washer. But Ross, you don't have to—"

"I want to."

She was too glad of the help to argue. "Then have at it," she said. "But I'm not quite helpless. I'll make the salad, and then we'll both have wine while the chicken's cooking."

"Sounds good to me."

She hesitated. "There's just one thing. Shelley and Kenny decided they...had other plans. I hope you don't mind, but it's just you and me tonight."

The smile he gave her did strange things to her insides. "I don't mind at all. But I guess that means—"

She felt a stab of—what? Alarm? Anticipation?

"What?" she asked quickly.

His eyes shone. "That we'll have to eat all the dessert by ourselves."

THEY NEVER got to dessert.

By the time dinner was over, Gene was so giddy from weariness, food and wine that she forgot all about an after-dinner treat. It was a beautiful night, and as they sat outside on the patio, the candle on the table made intriguing shadows across Ross's face. His eyes looked almost black as he smiled at her, and, feeling in a daze, she smiled back.

"You're staring at me again. Why do you do that?" she asked.

"I don't mean to stare. I guess it's because you look so lovely in this light."

She flushed at the compliment. "Everybody looks good in candlelight."

"I don't know about that," he said softly. He moved closer.

Even though he was still sitting across the table from her, his very presence was almost a physical contact. Something warm began to glow inside her. She tried to look away from him, and found that she couldn't. A little breathlessly, she said, "I guess that anything is an improvement on the way I looked earlier today."

"Oh, I don't know. I thought you looked pretty good then, too."

"Soaking wet, with my hair plastered to my face? If I'm not careful, that's the image you're going to get whenever you think of me. Wasn't that the way we met?"

"So it was. I'll never forget that day. You looked so angry."

"I was furious. But I think you'll have to agree that, as a way to impress someone, it doesn't rank right up there at the top."

"I'm not so sure," he said, reaching for her hand. "You inspired me and, believe me, I didn't want to be impressed."

His hand was warm over hers. Or maybe, she thought dizzily, it was her entire body that was feeling warm. It was difficult to focus on the conversation when she was fighting an urge to lean across the table and kiss him.

She pulled herself together. "I could see that. I knew from the beginning that you didn't think I could ride your horse."

"It wasn't that I didn't want you to. I knew right away that you were the kind of woman who could do anything you put your mind to. I just thought—"

"What?"

He held her glance. Quietly, he said, "That if I were responsible in any way for your getting hurt, I'd never forgive myself."

The night seemed to have taken on an electric quality, like the air does before a thunderstorm. Gene could almost feel the ends of her hair crackle, and it seemed more difficult to breathe. *What is he doing to me?* she wondered. It was as though he'd cast some kind of spell. Confused by the feeling, not sure she liked it, she stood abruptly and began to clear the table. As she stacked dishes willy-nilly, she said, "You didn't feel that way about Shelley?"

He stood with her and pushed the tray they'd used to bring everything out toward her. "Of course I didn't want Shelley to get hurt. But that was different."

"Different?" Trying to disguise what she knew had to be the sudden loud pounding of her heart, she threw a pile of silverware on the tray with a clatter. "How?"

"Shelley wasn't you. Gene," he said, taking her hands and forcing her to face him. "What's wrong?"

She wanted to withdraw her hands. Suddenly, even this simple contact was too much. Her heart leapt, and for a moment she felt dizzy again. She had to make herself look up at him. "Wrong?" she said too brightly. "Nothing's wrong, Ross. Would you like some dessert now?"

"No," he said, holding her eyes. "You know what I want. I think you want it, too." He paused, waiting for her reply.

"I don't know, Ross. I do feel something going on here, but I—"

He touched her face. "We'll take it slow."

"Oh, Ross—"

She didn't have time to say more. His other hand was at the small of her back, and as he drew her toward him, she couldn't resist. She lifted her face to his and put her arms around his neck. His body felt lean and hard against hers when they met, and the first touch of his lips was something she realized she'd always been looking for... and had always missed. The warmth that had been glowing inside her burst into heat, and she pressed against him, suddenly weak with desire. Their kiss deepened, and when she felt him tremble, she drew back and said huskily, "Let's go inside."

Without a word, he reached for his cane.

THE BEDROOM WAS upstairs. Ross stopped on the landing—not to catch his breath, but to kiss her again. As their tongues met and heat flooded her body again, Gene wanted to make love to him right there. But the bedroom door was only a few feet away, and when they were inside, Ross tossed down his cane.

"Are you going to be—" she started to say.

He stopped her with another kiss. "I need it to walk," he said hoarsely. "I don't need it for this." He paused, then added painfully, "There's just one thing...."

The streetlight outside cast silvery shadows on his face. She couldn't see his expression and with one tender hand, she touched his cheek. "What?"

He closed his eyes. "My leg ... With all the surgeries and everything, it's... not a pretty sight."

She didn't miss a beat. "I broke my collarbone once," she said. "Now my right side is higher than the left. Is that going to make a difference?"

With a sound like a moan, he pulled her to him again and buried his face in her hair and held her tight. "I want this to be right."

"It will be," she whispered. But her voice was shaking with her need for him, and so was her hand when she reached for his belt.

With a shushing sound, the slacks he was wearing fell to the floor. He tensed again as his mangled leg was exposed to her, and Gene knew that everything depended on her reaction to the sight. Tears filled her eyes as she touched the deeply scarred flesh, and when she bent forward and gently pressed her lips against his thigh, he shuddered and put his head back.

"Oh, my poor Ross," she said, holding him close.

He reached down and gently lifted her to her feet. "My turn," he said softly.

She was wearing jeans and a silk blouse. As though her blouse was made of gossamer, Ross carefully unfastened each of the buttons down the front until he could push the two halves away. His handsome face expressing his wonder, he looked at her. As her bosom rose and fell with her quickening breath, he closed his eyes.

"You're so beautiful," he said almost reverently. He opened his eyes again. "I'm almost afraid to touch you."

"Let me help you, then," she said.

When she took one of his hands and placed it over her breast, he drew a quick breath. Gently, he caressed, then he ran a thumb over her hardening nipple. The touch sent a flood of sensation racing through her. It seemed to take forever but finally their clothing was discarded and they were together on the bed.

He pulled her toward him as they lay, side by side, and when she felt his erection against her legs, she raised her knee and put it over his hip.

The new intimacy aroused them even more. Groaning, he pulled her with him as he rolled over. Now she was on top, his entire length beneath her, and as she straddled him, she looked down into his eyes. It had never happened to her this quickly, but she was ready for him, and, lowering her head to kiss him, she guided him inside.

Nothing prepared her for the feeling that surged through her at this most intimate union. Eyes closed, she balanced on her arms and threw her head back so that she could feel every sensation. Lost in growing passion, she began to move her hips, drawing him in deeper and deeper until she couldn't take any more.

Under her, Ross put his hands on her breasts, squeezing them, kneading the flesh until she didn't think she could bear the wild throbbing that coursed through her. Then he lifted his head to kiss her nipples, sucking them, teasing them with his tongue until her entire being seemed to distill down to these three points of contact. She felt as though she were about to explode.

"Oh, Ross," she gasped, "I don't think I can—"

"It's all right," he said, pulling her down so that he could kiss her. "I'm right behind—"

Whatever else he said was lost, gone in a thundering explosion of pleasure that surged through her. It started at some point deep within and fanned out quickly, keenly, sharply, until every nerve felt on fire. She tried to make sure that he was there with her, but there wasn't time. Her body was no longer her own, but an entity swept into a tide that tumbled her over and over. Just when she thought she couldn't bear it any longer and would have to scream to let go, the intensity of feeling began to abate. Seconds later, she was gently tossed ashore. When she was finally able to look over, Ross was there with her.

"Lord," he said, looking dazed.

Ross LEFT before it was fully light. Gene wasn't sure when. The exciting, exhausting events of the day—not to mention the evening—finally caught up with her, and she wasn't aware of anything until she felt someone kiss her. Drowsily at first, she opened her eyes; when she saw that Ross was perched on the edge of the bed, fully dressed, she tried to sit up. Smiling tenderly, he gave her a gentle push back into the pillows.

"No, you stay here," he said. "I know the way out. I'll lock the door behind me."

She touched his arm. "You don't have to leave."

"Believe me, I don't want to. But I think it's best this time, don't you? You need your rest. If I stay, I won't be able to keep my hands off you."

She didn't want to admit it, but in spite of his delightful implication, she could hardly keep her eyes open. "All right," she said. "As long as you promise there *will* be a next time."

"Just try to keep me away," he said. Brushing back a lock of hair from her face, he bent down and kissed her. "You were wonderful."

She had enough energy to tease him. "You weren't so bad yourself. How do you think I got into this shape? You wore me out completely."

"Oh, I think your wild ride cross-country might have had something to do with that."

"That, or the wild ride I had here."

He chuckled and got up. "I'll call you later."

Gene was asleep before he reached the door.

CHAPTER EIGHT

ROSS WAS SO PREOCCUPIED with thoughts of Gene when he got to work that it took him a moment to realize he wasn't the only one who looked like the cat that had swallowed the cream. James was wearing a big grin as he waited outside Ross's office. He was holding a copy of this morning's newspaper as though it were the Rosetta stone.

"What's with you?" Ross asked.

If possible, James's smile widened even more. "I take it you haven't seen the paper."

Ross hadn't even looked at the headlines. After such a glorious evening with Gene, he hadn't wanted any bad news to mar the day.

"No, I didn't," he said. "Why? What happened?"

James unfolded the sports section and handed it over. "Read it and celebrate!"

Ross looked down at a picture of Gene and Achilles. The photographer had caught horse and rider just as they were coming up out of the coffin jump. In perfect alignment, they were sailing over the incline fence as though it were a matchstick on the ground.

"Isn't it great? Read what it says!" James sounded as if he were ready to pop.

Ross forced his eyes from the picture to the caption below: "Gene Logan and Achilles, the eventing horse sponsored by Outdoor Outfitters, at the horse trials in Rancho Caballero yesterday. Achilles, an eight-year-old pure white Thoroughbred, and Ms. Logan, formerly an international junior champion equestrienne..."

"How did this happen?" Ross asked. "I don't remember any photographers there yesterday."

James looked ready to dance down the hall. "I didn't want to tell you ahead of time in case nothing came of it, but I called the paper."

"You did?" Ross asked, surprised. "And because of that, they sent someone out to cover the event?"

"Well, it wasn't as simple as that," James said modestly. "In fact, I had to do some fast talking when I spoke to Jerry Fazey. You remember Jerry, don't you?"

"The sports editor?"

"Yes. When I told him we were sponsoring a horse, I convinced him it might make an interesting angle. He said he'd try to send a photographer out to the trials yesterday, and do you believe it, he actually did." James grabbed the paper and grinned again with satisfaction. "I hoped something would happen, but I have to tell you, I never expected this. What publicity. Isn't it great?"

"Great," Ross said. He still couldn't believe it.

James looked at him. "You don't sound very happy about it."

Ross tried to think of something tactful to say. James was so pleased with himself that Ross didn't want to confess how uneasy he felt. He knew it made no sense. After all, wasn't this just what they'd been after when they decided to sponsor the horse? He couldn't have asked for better advertising for the company. Still . . .

An image of sparkling green eyes came to him, a look of eagerness, of daring . . . With an effort, he shook it off. James was staring at him with a hurt expression, and Ross forced a grin. "Forget it," he said. "I *am* happy about this, you know I am. Publicity like this is invaluable, just what we intended."

"Damn right!"

James looked pleased again, and for good measure, Ross slapped his partner's shoulder. "I'm proud of you. I hope it works."

"Oh, it's going to work," James said confidently. He touched the paper as though it were a talisman. "Who can resist a beautiful woman on a gorgeous horse? It's got built-in appeal, exactly what we were aiming for. I'm going to have the article enlarged and put in all our stores." His eyes gleamed. "Now maybe I can follow up with something else Jerry and I talked about."

Ross's unease was back full force. Alarms ringing inside his head, he asked cautiously, "What's that?"

"Oh, you're going to love it. When I was telling Jerry about the horse trials, I also suggested he might send a reporter to interview Gene. He said we'd take it one step at a time, but now that the picture has turned out so well, I'm going to call him and twist his arm a little. We could start with an interview and—"

"What do you mean, *start* with an interview?"

James gave him a what-kind-of-simpleton-are-you look. "Oh, come on, Ross! Gene's story is tailor-made for a series of articles!"

"What are you talking about? Gene doesn't *have* a story."

"But of course she does. It's got human interest written all over it. You know, former junior champion rider forced into early retirement, now returning to competition after all these years. It's perfect!"

"Now, wait a minute—"

But James didn't want to listen. A faraway expression coming over his face, he said, "We'll get someone to follow Gene and Achilles as they compete this season. It'll be—"

Ross couldn't let this continue. Forcefully, he said, "Haven't you forgotten something?"

James blinked and looked at him. "Forgotten something? No, I don't think so. What do you mean?"

"Think a minute, will you? Gene isn't going to be the one riding the horse this season. She's just exercising Achilles until Shelley gets back on her feet."

James started to say something, then his mouth snapped shut. From his expression, it was clear that he had forgotten this detail. "Oh...yeah, right," he said slowly. "Well, I guess that takes care of that."

He looked so deflated that Ross said, "Let's not go to extremes now, any more than you can help it, that is. The paper was interested this time. Who's to say they won't be when the season begins and Shelley starts riding?"

His feet dragging, James turned toward his office. "You don't understand."

"Wait a minute. What's to understand?"

James turned back. "Don't you see? The only reason the paper ran the picture this time was because

Jerry liked the 'returning champion' angle. He wasn't interested until I told him that Gene used to ride when she was young, but that she hadn't ridden competitively in years. Now, all this time later, she's back in the ring, so to speak, to take up where she left off. He said it had built-in appeal, and I agree.''

"Yes, but—''

James was never down for long. Beginning to get excited again, he went on. ''In fact, I don't know why we didn't see it sooner. Think about it. How many of us dream about the same thing—having a second chance to try again?''

Without warning, an image of a powerful Formula One car flashed into Ross's mind. Just for an instant, he was behind the wheel and the only thing he could see ahead of him was all that beautiful length of empty track. For a few seconds, he could hear the roar of the engine and feel the throbbing of all that power around him. James was right, he thought before he could help himself. He'd give anything for another chance!

Then common sense returned, and he shoved the fantasy away. It wasn't the same thing, he told himself. He and James had to get a grip here and face reality. They hadn't hired Gene to compete the horse; they'd contracted Shelley. Even if Gene wanted to do it—

And did she? he suddenly wondered. When he recalled the light in her eyes yesterday, and the excitement she couldn't hide, his uneasy feeling returned again. How would he handle it if she did want to do it? What would he say?

That was a good question, he thought. He knew he'd better not admit it to independent Gene, but now that they'd made love, he felt even more protective of her than ever. The idea of her being injured because he and James wanted to boost business was unacceptable to him now. When he recalled the chances she'd taken yesterday, not to mention how dangerous even a simple cross-country training course was, he shuddered. If he felt this way now, it would be even worse if she entered an actual competition. There, the speed would be even greater and the jumps that much more dangerous.

And then there was Shelley to consider, he thought belatedly. Shelley, who'd had the misfortune to break her leg just when she thought her big chance had come. They had approached her first, after all. How could they say they'd changed their minds now that they'd realized her sister could get them more publicity? She'd have every right to be angry. In fact, he wouldn't blame her if she sued for breach of contract. He winced at the thought. They'd get publicity over that, all right. He could see it now: "Big outdoor equipment company ruins rider's dream." Sales wouldn't just go down; they'd drop like a ton of bricks.

"James," he said carefully, "I think we should consider all the ramifications before we jump in and change everything at the last minute. We promised Shelley—"

To Ross's dismay, James said eagerly, "We'll talk to Shelley. I'm sure she'll understand."

Ross couldn't believe his partner was serious. "Is that so? Well, I can't imagine anything she'd understand less. Don't you remember when we first got the horse? Shelley has told us again and again that she's waited for an opportunity like this all her life."

"There will be other opportunities," James said. He sounded callous, but Ross knew he was just trying to find a way out of this difficulty, as was Ross himself. "In fact," James went on enthusiastically, "if Gene and Achilles do well enough, maybe we can buy Shelley a second horse!"

This was too much. "You didn't want to sponsor one horse, remember? Now you want to buy two? Are you out of your mind, or what?"

"Well, it's just one solution," James said defensively. "It doesn't matter what we think, anyway, does it? I just remembered that Gene has said repeatedly that she's only going to exercise the horse until her sister can ride again. Even if we could get Shelley to agree, how do we know Gene would consider a new arrangement?"

Ross didn't say it, but he was sure it would take only the merest nudge for Gene to agree to ride Achilles in competition. The only thing that might stop her, in fact, was Shelley's prior claim to the horse. Gene could protest all she liked about being too involved in her career to do anything else, but would she refuse if they offered her a competition? He doubted it.

James interrupted this depressing train of thought by saying, "Well, we can at least ask them, can't we?"

He sounded as forlorn as Ross felt. "Sure, we can ask. But don't be disappointed if—"

"No, I won't," James promised, too eagerly. "You're right, I know that. For a while, I admit I was getting a little ahead of myself, but I see it now. We did agree to do this with Shelley. It wouldn't be fair to change things at this stage." He paused hopefully. "Would it?"

"No, it wouldn't."

"Well, you can't blame a person for trying, can you? Let me just ask you something, though. When are you going to see Gene again?"

Ross looked at him suspiciously. "Why?"

"Well, I thought... Never mind," James said hastily. "It was a bad idea, anyway. Let's talk about something else. I know. How was the barbecue? Did you enjoy it? You never go anywhere, you know. It's about time you started going out again."

And with that, James was off on another tangent. Ross didn't want to talk about Gene anymore—especially about what had happened last night. So he said neutrally, "The barbecue was nice. I enjoyed myself."

James looked at him curiously. "Well, that's interesting. From the way Shelley was acting yesterday, I thought for sure there would be fireworks."

James was going to find out, anyway, Ross reasoned, so it might as well be now. "Shelley and Kenny weren't there. It was just Gene and me." He saw the light in James's eyes, and added firmly, "Now don't get any ideas. Gene did invite everybody, remember? It just happened to work out this way."

"Oh, I see." James looked sly. "No wonder you look so... different today."

"What do you mean? I don't look any different, I'm just the same."

"Then why do you have that... satisfied look?"

Ross scowled. "I don't know what you're talking about."

"Okay, have it your way," James said with a grin. "It's just nice to know that you're human like the rest of us."

BACK AT HIS OWN DESK, Ross realized it was too late to call Gene at home. She'd already have left for her office, so he'd just have to wait. He was trying to decide what task to begin with when Cindy, the secretary he and James shared, buzzed him. She sounded excited, and when he heard who was calling, he understood why.

"Ross, Mr. Malcolm Quincy is calling for you on line one. He's with—"

"I know who he's with, Cindy," Ross said. Quincy was the West Coast representative for an Australian company called Roo'sters, which produced an array of all-weather gear comprised of hats, boots, cowboy "dusters," jackets, coats and even horse blankets. All were made of the finest materials, long-lasting and virtually indestructible. He and James had been angling for months to get Roo'sters into their stores, but the company was extremely selective about whom they allowed to sell their goods. Ross took a deep breath. He asked Cindy to tell James to come in so they could both listen over the speaker, then he reached for the phone.

"Good morning, Malcolm," he said. "Or should I say, good evening?"

Quincy chuckled. They'd met before, and Ross remembered him as a big man with blue eyes and the tanned face of an outdoorsman. "G'day will do," he said with more than a trace of a down-under accent. "But if that's your polite way of asking whether I'm enjoying myself in God's country, or working for a living here in the land of smog and honey, let me put your mind at ease. I'm sitting on the balcony of a posh hotel not ten minutes from your office, and I just finished reading the sports section of one of your fine newspapers."

James burst into his office, wide-eyed and making all sorts of "what's happening" gestures. Pointing firmly to the chair opposite the desk, Ross said, "Say, Malcolm, James just came in. Would you mind if I put you on the speaker?"

"Not at all, mate. In fact, I guess both of you ought to hear this. Hello, James. I see by this picture in the paper that you blokes have finally done the smart thing and associated yourself with a bit of class." He chuckled again. "And the horse isn't bad, either."

Ross smiled and sat back. Still wearing a do-you-know-what-he-wants expression, James perched on the edge of the other chair. Ross shook his head at his partner, and said to Malcolm, "I'm glad you think so. In fact, we'll take that as a real compliment, coming from a horseman like you."

"Well, I've ridden a few in my time," Quincy agreed. "But I have to say, as a public relations ploy, sponsoring a horse like this is a good move. It got my attention, I'll tell you that."

"It's nice to know we're on the right track," Ross said. "But that photo was taken at a horse trial this weekend. Wait until the competitive season starts."

"It looks like this horse can go the distance. And if that's so, you'll get a lot of publicity out of it. I have to say, the story itself is sheer brilliance."

James shot a triumphant I-told-you-so glance at Ross. "Do you really think so?" he asked.

"I do," Quincy said. "This comeback attempt is a true magnet. I've got to congratulate you on coming up with that angle. It's a winner, for sure. Did you advertise for a rider like that, or what?"

Ross sat forward. "Well, actually—"

James guessed what Ross was about to say, and he practically dived toward the speaker. "Actually, it was a fluke, Malcolm," he said quickly. "But a lucky one, I agree."

"Actually, it's more of a fluke than James is telling you," Ross said, with a glare in his partner's direction. "Originally, we asked Gene Logan's sister, Shelley, to ride the horse, but—"

"And Shelley is a good rider, Malcolm—excellent, in fact," James interrupted. "But then Gene took over, and—"

"Gene didn't actually *take over*, Malcolm," Ross said firmly, with another meaningful look in James's direction. "In fact, she's just exercising the horse until Shelley—"

Waving his hands wildly in the air at Ross in an attempt to silence him, James grabbed the speaker. "But enough about *that*, Malcolm," he said. "We know you're a busy man—"

"That's true," Quincy said ruefully. "In fact, I've got to fly out tomorrow. I know it's short notice, but before I go, I'd like to meet—"

Since this was the opening they'd been seeking for months, James nearly fell off his chair in sheer excitement. Before Ross could say anything, he blurted out,

"Where and when? Just say the word, and we'll be there."

Malcolm chuckled. "Don't get excited, James. I haven't promised anything yet."

"No, no, of course not. I didn't mean—"

Quincy chuckled again. "Never mind. I might change my mind, at that. I like the idea of the horse. It shows you two have some sense of what's really important in this world. But I'd also like to meet your Gene Logan. Anyone—man or woman—who can ride a horse like that deserves a handshake. I realize it's asking a lot, but do you think we all might get together for dinner tonight? I wouldn't be in such a rush, but I can't cancel my flight."

Ross knew James would have cleared his calendar if he'd been having dinner with both the Pope and the president tonight. But they couldn't speak for Gene, and so, before James could plunge in again, he said, "I'll have to ask Gene if she can make it."

"I'll understand if she has other plans, but I'd sure like to meet her before I leave," Quincy said. He paused. "I don't know when I'll be back."

The implication was obvious, and with a quick look at Ross, James said, "I'm sure it won't be a problem."

"Well, if it is, let me know. And like I said, James, this is only a friendly little dinner, all right? If we decide to, we can always do business later."

They hung up, and as Ross switched the phone off speaker, he looked at James. "Well, that was quite the performance," he said mildly. "Do you mind telling me what you were thinking of?"

Nervously, James stood up. "I'm sorry. I know I got a little carried away—"

"A little?"

James reddened. "All right, more than I meant to. But we couldn't let this opportunity slip through our fingers, could we? If we can persuade Malcolm to give us Roo'sters, a lot of our troubles will be over."

Ross looked steadily at him. "Don't you mean, if Gene can charm him into changing his mind, things will be easier for us?"

James's flush deepened. "You make it sound—"

"No, *you* made it sound like something it wasn't. Didn't we agree this morning that Shelley got first choice? You deliberately let Malcolm—and everyone else, apparently—think that Gene is our rider."

James turned away. "Well, maybe she will be," he said stubbornly. "Who knows how long it's going to take Shelley's leg to heal? I think we should just wait and see how things go before we come to blows about it. A lot is at stake here, Ross, in case you've forgotten."

Ross hadn't forgotten. "I just don't like the idea of using Gene to cinch a business deal."

"Why not?" James demanded. "You wouldn't have hesitated asking Shelley to come, if that's who Malcolm wanted to meet."

"Shelley was the one we signed the contract with," Ross said sharply. "Gene is doing us a favor by exercising the horse."

For once, James didn't back down. As he went to the door, he said, "I think you'd better reexamine that premise, Ross. We both saw Gene on that cross-country course. Now, I don't know much about it, but

I do know this—she was enjoying herself." He paused deliberately. "Maybe a little too much."

Ross couldn't deny that he'd thought the same thing, so he said, "I've never seen you this way, James."

His partner stared at him for a long moment. "We've never had this much at stake. Now, do you want to call Gene and ask her to dinner, or shall I?"

Since James had accepted the date for her, Ross was tempted to let him call and try to explain why. But then he shook his head. "I'll call her."

James nodded. Then his expression softened, and he said, "It'll work out, Ross. It has to. You'll see. We've put too much of ourselves into this company to lose it now. After all, what are we really asking Gene to do? There are worse things than being taken to dinner by three men who think she's not only talented, but beautiful, too."

James went back to his own office, but for a few minutes, Ross just sat there. His partner made it sound so simple, but he wasn't sure what approach to take. He could hardly tell Gene in one breath what a wonderful time he'd had last night, and in the next ask her to a business dinner because a prospective client had been impressed by her picture in the paper. He grimaced. It sounded sleazy even without his saying it aloud, and he couldn't shake the feeling that they were about to use her for their own interests.

But that wasn't the only reason he had a bad feeling about this. He could have been more forceful if he'd wanted to be. He was just as guilty as James was in allowing Malcolm to believe that Gene was their rider, when Shelley was the one they'd picked. What were they going to do if they got the Roo'sters franchise on that basis? Malcolm wasn't going to be pleased when he found out he'd been misled.

He sat back. How had things gotten so turned around? The plan had seemed so clear-cut and straightforward until Shelley broke her leg. Now it was a mess. He felt boxed in with no answer in sight, and he wished to hell he'd never even heard the word *horse*.

"Well, you look like you've lost your best friend," a voice said from the doorway. "Would you like a shoulder to lean on, or just a handkerchief to cry in?"

Startled, Ross looked up. His ex-wife, Marilyn, newly blond, was standing on the threshold, grinning at him. At any other time he would have been glad to see her, but she was the last person he wanted to talk to right now. Ever since their divorce, it seemed that Marilyn had developed the disconcerting facility to see him too clearly and he was in no mood for one of her lectures.

Marilyn never waited to be invited. Before he could say anything, she came in, closed the door behind her and sat down opposite him.

"Is this a bad time?" she asked.

"Would it matter if it was?" Ross asked.

"Not in the slightest," she said. She took a pack of cigarettes from her voluminous purse, pulled one out and lit it with a silver lighter. As she exhaled, she said, "Don't say it. I know I promised to give up smoking and I will. Besides, I think it's more to the point to tell you that you look like hell."

"Well, thank you. And here I was feeling so well."

"Is that so? Then what was the attitude of despair I saw when I came in?"

"Just a little business problem." He sat back. "You, on the other hand, look wonderful. Selling real estate seems to agree with you."

"Oh, I've found my niche, that's for sure. In fact, I can't stay long. The only reason I'm out your way at all is that I have to meet a client soon." She looked around for an ashtray, but not finding one, shrugged and drew the wastebasket toward her with a high-heeled foot. "So, since I was in the neighborhood, I decided to drop in and see how my favorite man in the world is doing." She took another drag off the cigarette. "Not well, obviously."

"No, I'm fine. Things have just been a little hectic this morning."

"I'm not surprised. When did you and James get into the horse business?"

He couldn't hide his astonishment. "How did you know about that?"

She laughed. "It's not because I read the sports pages, sweetie, I can tell you that. One of the men in the office saw that picture in the paper and remembered that my ex owned Outdoor Outfitters." She paused again to flick ashes into the wastebasket before adding, "I must say, you always had good taste in women, Ross. Although it was a little hard to tell exactly what this Gene Logan looked like in that vest and under that hat." She looked at him from under her lashes. "Are you two an item, or is it strictly business?"

"Why do you want to know?" he parried.

"Oh, so it's like that, is it?" Marilyn said. With a catlike smile, she settled back. "Well, I don't blame you, darling. In fact, I'm delighted. It's about time you started getting out. You've been a hermit for too long, don't you think?"

Ross was getting tired of everyone he knew feeling free to pass judgment on his love life—or lack of it. "No, I don't," he said. "My life suits me just fine like it is, thank you."

She regarded him calmly. "I can see that you want me to stay out of it."

"I do."

"I know that we're divorced, but that doesn't mean I don't care about you."

"I know you do," he said. "I'm sorry. It's just been a long few weeks."

"I understand. I know you've been under quite a bit of pressure over the company." She took another drag. "It hasn't been easy for any of us, has it? This damned recession just won't go away."

"It hasn't affected you."

"Don't kid yourself. I'm barely hanging on."

He had to laugh at that. "This, from the woman who was top real estate salesperson of the year?"

"That was last year," she said primly. "And it was only for San Diego, not the whole state."

"Give the woman time."

"Flattery will get you nowhere," she said, but he could tell she was pleased that he knew. Finished with her cigarette, she stubbed it out carefully at the side of the wastebasket. When she straightened, she said, "Maybe things will turn around for you and James now that you've got this horse angle to play. I have to admit, it's certainly inventive. If it caught Alex's attention, he who never reads anything but the game scores, it definitely has possibilities."

"I hope so. We've already got a lot of time and money invested in sponsoring this horse."

"I can imagine. But I'm more interested in this Gene person. I can't believe it's just business, as you tried so manfully to imply. There must be more to it than that."

He scowled. "I told you, Marilyn—"

She laughed at his fierce expression. "And I've told you for months now that you should stop living like a monk. Now, get down off your—pardon the expression—high horse and tell me about Gene Logan."

"Didn't you say you were supposed to be meeting someone?" he asked.

"You're not going to tell me, are you?"

"I will when there's something to tell."

"Promise?"

"Cross my heart."

"I guess that will have to do."

"I guess it will," he replied. They both stood up. "Let me walk you to your car."

"That's nice, Ross, but it isn't necessary." Rising on tiptoe, she gave him a quick, affectionate kiss as he walked her to the door. "How's the leg these days?" she asked lightly. "Still keeping you up at night?"

"Not so much," he said.

He appreciated it when she left it at that. Wagging her fingers at him, she started to leave, only to turn back with a twinkle in her eye. "I'd still like to meet Ms. Logan," she said mischievously. "It's been a long time since I've seen that look on your face, Ross. Whoever this woman is, she's been good for you."

"I thought you said I looked like hell."

"I changed my mind. In fact, now that I think about it, I'm sure I mistook that look of despair for one of being in love." She looked at him seriously for a moment. "But then, maybe those two conditions are interchangeable sometimes, don't you think?"

They looked at each other for a moment. Then Marilyn smiled again and said, "Goodbye, love. It was nice seeing you."

"Likewise."

After she had gone, Ross returned to his desk to make the call to Gene. He wished he could just ignore this looming dinner meeting with Malcolm and concentrate on last night's wonderful interlude, but he'd told James he'd do this, and he would. The phone rang twice at the other end before it was answered by a male voice.

"Greetings, this is Gene Logan's office, Wally speaking."

"Hello, this is Ross Malone. Is Gene ... um ... Ms. Logan able to take a call?"

"I'm sorry, but she's out of the office.... No, wait a minute. She just came in. Would you hold, please?"

It seemed an eternity before Gene came on the line. Ross had already thought of a half-dozen ways to phrase the invitation, but the instant he heard her voice, he forgot every one.

"Hi," she said. "I'm sorry you had to wait."

"It wasn't long," he said. How could just the sound of her voice could make him feel like humming? It was an effort not to picture them in bed together, even more difficult to resist thinking about how she'd felt in his arms. And when he remembered the sweet taste of her mouth, and how soft her skin was, he closed his eyes. *Not now!* he told himself, and asked, "Is this a bad time?"

Her laughter made him feel weak. "No worse than any other. It seems that every time I turn around, there's another problem to solve."

He suddenly wondered if the air-conditioning had gone haywire. Without warning, he felt hot. Working at the knot in his tie with his free hand, he said, "I know what you mean."

"I stopped in to check on Achilles on the way to work this morning. He's just fine, all four of his legs look good, and he's eating like there's no tomorrow."

He'd forgotten all about the horse. "Oh, that's good."

She chuckled. "You don't sound very impressed."

"Oh, I am. I...um...was just thinking about something else."

"You mean the fact that I fell asleep last night?" She sounded embarrassed. "I'm sorry, Ross. I was going to call you and apologize as soon as I came in. There was no excuse. I...that is...I didn't—"

Even her voice sounded pink, and he laughed. "Don't worry about it. I knew you were tired."

"Yes, but that's no reason. Oh, and thank you for fixing the coffee and tidying up. It was so thoughtful of you."

"Well, I didn't want you to have to do it when you got up."

"Thank you. You don't know how much I appreciated it," she said. Then she added a soft, "But...you didn't have to leave, you know."

She sounded so warm that he took a chance. Lightly, he said, "I won't, the next time."

"I'll hold you to that."

"When can I see you again?"

"I don't know," she said with what he hoped was genuine regret. "Things aren't going well with the new line of greeting cards, and I'm going to have to work late every night this week, I think. But don't worry," she added quickly, "I'll get out to the stable early in the mornings to ride Achilles before I come to work."

The last thing he wanted to be concerned about now was that horse. Wishing they could just forget Achilles and concentrate on how much time they could spend together, he forced himself to think of his duty to the company.

"I'm not worried about the horse. I know you'll take good care of him." He took a deep breath. "But I need to ask you something important, Gene. I'll understand if you say no."

"What is it?"

"I hate to ask you this, especially since you've just told me how busy you are, but would it be possible for you to come to dinner...tonight?"

"Oh, Ross, I'd love to, but—"

"I wouldn't ask if it were just me," he said, and then added quickly, "Well, maybe I would, since I want to see you again. But this isn't what you think. We got a call this morning from a man named Malcolm Quincy, who represents Roo'sters—"

"The company that makes those wonderful horse blankets?"

"Those, and all sorts of additional outdoor equipment. Well, anyway, he saw the picture in the paper—"

"Picture?"

"You haven't seen the paper this morning?"

"No, I didn't have time."

He wanted to groan. This made things more difficult. "It was a picture of you and Achilles taken at the horse trials. Malcolm happened to see it, and he called and asked when we'd decided to sponsor a horse."

"But that's wonderful! The season hasn't started yet, and already you're getting some press. Oh, wait until Shelley hears."

"I hope she'll be as pleased as we are," he said, not wanting to think about Shelley for the moment. "You wouldn't know this, but James and I have been angling for months to get the Roo'sters franchise, so when Malcolm called and asked us to meet with him for dinner, naturally we jumped at the chance. Having his products in our stores will almost certainly boost sales."

"Especially if you get those horse blankets."

"We'll take everything we can put our hands on," he promised. "But the point is, Malcolm is a horseman, and he was really interested in Achilles. So James and I were wondering—" he crossed his fingers "—if you wouldn't mind coming to dinner with us when we meet with him. After all," he added hurriedly in case she brought up Shelley again, "you've been riding the horse, and you can tell him more than we can."

"But—"

He wondered what he was going to say if she refused. Or worse, he thought suddenly, if she insisted that Shelley go in her place. Before she could do either, he added a persuasive, "Besides, it would be a good excuse for us to see each other again, wouldn't it?" Feeling like a heel, he threw himself on her mercy. "Please, Gene, I'd really appreciate it."

"Well, in that case, how can I say anything but yes? Sure, I'll come. What time?"

"About eight? I know that's rushing you, but Malcolm has to fly out tomorrow morning."

"Eight is fine. I'll look forward to it."

"So will I," he said fervently. "Thanks, Gene."

He was so relieved, he sagged in the chair when they hung up. Sweat was running down his face, and he took out his handkerchief. Well, it didn't matter. The thing was done, she was coming, and somehow, some way, he'd make it up to her, he thought. But in the meantime, what in the *hell* had happened to the air-conditioning? It was hotter than Hades in here, and the day hadn't even started yet.

CHAPTER NINE

GENE KNEW she shouldn't have agreed to go to dinner with Ross; already, this week was shaping up to be a nightmare of one crisis after another. But she hadn't been able to deny herself. As much as she wanted to do him the favor he'd asked, she wanted even more to see him. So she'd said yes, thinking that she'd justify the stolen time by working the rest of the night, if necessary, to pay for it. It would be worth it for a few hours of being with him.

She was just thinking that she was acting like a lovesick teenager when Wally appeared in the doorway.

"Yes?" he said.

She looked at him blankly. "What?"

"Earth to Gene," he retorted, grinning. "You called me in, remember?"

For a few seconds, she couldn't remember what she'd wanted him for. In fact, she couldn't remember buzzing him in the first place. Then it came to her, and she said hastily, "Yes, right ... Would you see if you can find a copy of this morning's paper at that stand down by the corner?"

"Yeah, sure," he said easily. "Which one?"

She'd forgotten to ask Ross what paper had published the picture. "Oh...all of them. I mean, just those for California."

"Okay." He studied her a moment, then he asked, "Gene, are you all right?"

"Yes, I'm fine. Why?"

"You seem a little distracted this morning."

A little distracted? With so much on her mind, it was a miracle that she could remember her own name. She tried to smile, then was mortified when it turned into a yawn, instead. Sheepishly, she said, "I guess I'm a little tired."

"And no wonder, with all you're trying to do. By the way, how did the horse trials go? Did you manage to stay on the horse the entire way around this time?"

She gave him a mock glare. "Thanks for the vote of confidence. And for your information, I did manage to stay on him—until we came to the pond. We fell there, but—"

"You fell?" he echoed. "Why didn't you say anything?"

"Because it was just one of those things."

"Just one..." He looked shocked. "You weren't hurt?"

"Only my pride," she said cheerfully. Then, seeing his face, she added, "It wasn't a big deal, really. These things happen all the time in eventing."

"You're crazy, you know that?"

She grinned. "You know, the thought had occurred to me, but it's too late now. I'm committed."

"You should be committed, all right," he said. "Honestly, Gene, do you really think you should be taking such chances?"

"People do it all the time."

"Not ordinary people. Not people with any common sense. Not people with a healthy regard for life and limb!"

"Why, Wally," she said, "I didn't know you cared."

"Of course I care!" Apparently realizing she was teasing, he added, "Just think of it. If something happens to you, where am I going to be? Looking for another job, that's what."

"Gee, and here I thought your motives were strictly altruistic. I didn't know you were such an opportunist at heart."

"Well, now you know. So, be careful out there, you hear?"

"I *am* careful. It was the horse that fell, not me."

"Like that matters!"

"Well, it does, in fact," she said, thinking of it. "In a way, that was almost the best part."

Wally rolled his eyes. "You know, I've anticipated this for a long time, but now I'm sure. You've definitely gone around the bend."

"No, listen to me. I say that because at least the horse *tried* to take the jump. He didn't stop—" she winced with the memory of her first wild ride on Achilles "—on the other side and let me sail over by myself."

"Oh, I see. He gets credit because this time he went with you, so you both ended up taking a bath."

"Sarcasm will get you nowhere," she said loftily. Then she laughed, thinking that she really was proud of Achilles. He might have failed in this bid to have a clean go, but at least he'd given it all he had. There was a lot to be said for that, and she looked mischievously at Wally. "I knew you'd understand."

"The only thing I understand is that you're out of your mind," he said, and glanced at his watch. "By the way, did you forget the meeting with Mason? It was scheduled to start at ten."

Her joking mood vanished. "Oh, Lord, I did forget!" Horrified, she jumped up and looked wildly around. "I know I was supposed to take something, but what was it?"

He pointed. "That folder on your desk."

When she looked at it as though she'd never seen it before, Wally added helpfully, "It's got the résumés of the illustrators you might want for the new line."

Where was her mind? As she snatched up the folder, she forgot all pride. "Was there anything else?"

Grinning, he pointed again. "The figures on the paper bids we've been working on. We talked about them this morning when you came in."

"Oh, yes, right." She grabbed that, too. "Is there anything else I've forgotten?"

"No, that's everything."

Files in hand, she made a beeline for the door. On the way out, she said, "I don't know what I'd do without you, Wally. Thanks!"

"It's my job," he called after her. "I'm used to it."

"I'm so glad," she called over her shoulder. "Because I'll expect a new paper supplier lined up by the time I get back."

On that note, she left him standing in the hallway while she hurried off to her meeting with the boss.

WHEN GENE RETURNED to her office two hours later, Wally had gone to lunch. Before leaving, he'd placed a neat pile of newspapers on her desk. Too tense to do anything at the moment but push them aside, Gene sat down and took a deep breath.

The meeting with Mason hadn't gone well. Her boss normally gave her all the latitude she needed to do her job. But he was getting impatient with the setbacks she was having with the new division, and she couldn't blame him. She felt even more guilty about it because she knew it was her fault that things hadn't moved more quickly. Even so, she just couldn't confess that she hadn't been devoting as much time and energy to her job as she usually did. It made her sound frivolous and incompetent, two things she definitely was not.

Oh, really? Then how did she explain what had happened this morning? She had never forgotten a meeting before; she had never forgotten so much as a memo or a note. Now she couldn't seem to remember anything.

The problem was that she'd been spending too much time at the stables instead of the office. But at this point, she didn't see what she could do about it. She'd made a commitment, to Shelley, and to James and Ross—not to mention, to the horse. She couldn't back out now. She'd known it would take some time and effort on her part; that was why she'd opposed the idea in the first place. There was nothing to do but carry on until Shelley was well again. She had to admit it would be a relief not to have to go to the stable every day. Maybe then everything could get back to normal.

Normal? a little voice whispered at the back of her mind. Suddenly, she wondered what "normal" was. Was it coming in to work early every morning and staying late because there was nothing at home to return to? Was it thinking of nothing but the greeting card business because you didn't have anything else to occupy your time and energy? Was it not having a life outside this office?

"I've got a life away from this place," she muttered. "I do. And I have other interests, too."

Did she?

Yes, she did. She had her caricatures, her drawing. But she'd never done anything with that, so did it count?

Increasingly annoyed with this interior inquisition, she reached for the newspapers Wally had put on her desk. She needed distraction, and she turned to the sports section of the first one. By chance, she'd selected the right paper, and when she saw the photo of herself and Achilles on the lead page, she forgot her problems and sat back with a murmured, "Oh, my..."

Her first thought was a delighted, if guilty, realization that the photographer had done them justice. The camera had caught them at the apex of the second fence of the coffin jump, and miraculously, considering the fact that this was their first test in public, they were both in perfect form.

A lucky coincidence, she thought with an ironic smile. Still, she was pleased to see that her head was up, and Achilles's ears were pricked forward as they both looked eagerly ahead to the next jump. Only she had to know that at that moment, Achilles had been about to pull her arms out of their sockets from sheer strength and momentum. The picture made them actually look like a team, and it made her feel proud... until she remembered Shelley.

"Oh, boy," she said. What was Shelley going to think of this? Things were already tense enough between them. A picture like this could only add to the strain, and she was just reaching for the phone to give her sister a call when it rang.

Wally was back from lunch. Out by his desk, he picked up, saw that she was in and put the caller on hold. "It's for you, Gene," he called. "Some guy named Jerry Fazey. He says he's the sports editor of the *Tribune*."

Since she was looking at the morning edition of that same newspaper, she asked, "What does he want?"

"To talk to you about your comeback attempt."

"My comeback...!" She didn't know what he was talking about until she looked down. She hadn't read the caption underneath the picture yet, but when she did, she gasped. How had the paper come up with the idea that she was going to be competing the horse? Or worse—her heart skipped a beat at the idea—that she was using Achilles to jump-start her career as an equestrienne? Wondering why Ross hadn't mentioned this, she reached quickly for the phone. She had to stop this before it got started or Shelley was going to have a fit.

"Good morning, Mr. Fazey," she said into the receiver. "This is Gene Logan."

"We haven't met—yet, but it's nice of you to make time to talk to me," a male voice said. "I know you must be busy, so I'll get right to the point. Have you seen the picture we ran of you and your horse at the trials yesterday?"

"Achilles isn't *my* horse, Mr. Fazey," said. "You see, I—"

"Oh, I understand. Achilles technically belongs to Outdoor Outfitters, I'm aware of that. They're the company that's sponsoring you."

"No, you don't understand," she persisted. "I'm only riding the horse until—"

"Yes, and that's just the point. You certainly *do* ride that horse. I don't know much about the sport myself, but the phone has been ringing off the hook ever since the morning delivery. We've already had several dozen calls wanting to know more about you."

"I can't help that," she said. "I—" She broke off, realizing what he'd said. "You've had calls?"

"Indeed, we have. You're news, Ms. Logan. The public is always interested in stories like yours."

"But I don't have a story!"

"Oh, but you do. And since you've generated so much attention already, we did a little digging on you and came up with some amazing facts. You had quite a riding career as a youngster, didn't you? All those championships before you were old enough to drive. And then . . . tragedy. One jump away from winning a prestigious international championship, and your horse goes down. What was his name? White Cotton—"

"High Cotton," she said. She sat back, quite overwhelmed.

"Right, *High* Cotton. Sorry. I told you, I wasn't much up on horses. But I am on good stories, and the amazing thing is why yours wasn't made into a movie.

It has all the prime ingredients, you know. A kid, a horse, near victory, then...disaster. Disney would have made a fortune. There wouldn't have been a dry eye in the house."

The thought that she and her special horse could have been exploited repulsed her and she said, "Well, that's very nice, Mr. Fazey, but it was long ago. Years in the past, as you've pointed out yourself."

"Yes, but now you're back in competition once more," he said smoothly. "You'll pardon me if I sound cynical, Ms. Logan, but however you might view it, your story was news then, and it is now."

"I still don't think you understand—"

"Oh, but I do. Picture it—a twist of fate stole your victory and caused the destruction of an animal that obviously meant a great deal to you. Now, after years away from competition, you're going to try again."

"Mr. Fazey," she said firmly. "I'm trying to tell you—"

It was as though she hadn't spoken. "It takes courage to do that, Ms. Logan," he went on. "As you said yourself, a lot of time has passed. But don't you see? You're living the dream. Imagine the number of people who would love to go back and change the course of their lives, but can't. Maybe they're prevented by circumstance, or reluctance, or fear of failure, or just plain cowardice. Who knows? Who cares? The point is, you'll be an inspiration, I guarantee it."

"The *point*," she insisted, "is that I don't want to be an inspiration. You're not listening to me. I'm trying to tell you that I'm only riding the horse until my—"

"But don't you see? You've already captured the imaginations of all sorts of people. The calls we've had this morning prove it. Everyone wants to know about you and that horse. They'll want to follow your progress, see how it all turns out."

"But—"

"I know, I know. You can accuse me of exploiting this for my own gain, and maybe you'd be right. It's a given that the more people who read about this, the more papers we'll sell. But think about this, too. Outdoor Outfitters will also gain because they're sponsoring the horse. They'll be happy, we'll be happy—and you'll be happy, because you'll be doing what you do best. We'll all win. There won't be a loser in the bunch."

Just for a moment, she was tempted. It sounded so enticing that she—

She stopped, appalled by the direction of her thoughts. What was she thinking? She had to remember Shelley. She couldn't do this. She couldn't even *think* about it.

"So," Fazey said, interrupting her frantic reverie. "When can I send a reporter to do an in-depth interview? I'd also like some pictures, maybe at the place where you keep the horse, definitely while you're riding. Oh, and if this takes off like I think it will, we'll need a schedule of upcoming competitions, so we can report on those, too."

Gene put her hand to her head. How had this happened? What was Shelley going to say? She cringed. She knew what Shelley was going to say. Maybe what was more important was how Ross and James were going to feel. When Ross had told her about the picture, she hadn't imagined it might lead to this. What was she going to do? She knew what she had to do. She had to convince Jerry Fazey that the story should be about Shelley and Achilles, that's what. If the *Tribune* was going to write about anyone, it had to be her sister and the horse.

"Mr. Fazey, would you still be interested in following Achilles if someone else was riding him?" she asked.

She could almost see him frown. "Someone else? Who do you mean?"

She took a deep breath. "Well, as I've been trying to tell you, my sister was originally supposed to compete Achilles, but she broke her leg. That's why I took over. I was just going to exercise the horse until she could ride again."

"I see," he said. She thought she'd gotten through to him until he went on enthusiastically. "Now that I think about it, this is even better! Okay, listen. As I understand it, you were doing a favor for your sister, right?"

"Yes, but—"

"But then, when you started riding again, you realized how much you had missed it. You saw it as a chance to go back and redo the past. You decided you wanted to compete again!"

She was aghast. "No, that's not the way it was!"

"But that's the angle we'll play! It'll be wonderful, you'll see. Oh, hey, I just realized that I'm late for a meeting. I'll get back to you about sending a crew out for that interview. We'll do it soon, I promise. I don't want to lose momentum. Thanks, Ms. Logan. It was nice talking to you."

"Wait!" she cried. When all she heard was a dial tone, she slammed the receiver down. "Damn!" she exclaimed. What was she going to do now?

There was only one thing to do—call Ross. He'd know how to handle this, she thought. All she had to do was tell him about Fazey's call just now and he'd—

Her shoulders slumped. She *couldn't* ask Ross to cancel the interview. Publicity like this was the reason he and James had purchased the horse in the first place. If the *Tribune* ran a story, especially a continuing story about Achilles, the name of Outdoor Outfitters would be before the public all the time. Any company would have to pay dearly to get the advertising coverage Fazey was offering for free. As he'd pointed out just now, everybody was going to be happy with this.

Everybody except Shelley, she thought. And herself, she added quickly. But it was Shelley she was most worried about. If their positions had been reversed, she knew how she'd feel. She'd be furious.

At the thought, she sat forward and reached for the phone again. Before things got any worse—although how that could happen, she wasn't certain—she had to call Shelley and find out if she'd seen the picture in the paper.

To her dismay, Shelley wasn't home so Gene left a message asking her sister to call back as soon as she got in. Then she called Kenny.

"Fielding Stables," Kenny said.

"Hi, Kenny, this is Gene."

"Hey, how's it going? After all that action yesterday, are you able to walk today?"

She blushed as she thought of the activity she'd engaged in *after* the cross-country trials. "Just barely," she said. "In fact, I was late for work today. Listen, Kenny, I haven't been able to get hold of Shelley, and I wondered if she was there with you."

"She was, but she had to go to the doctor."

Shelley hadn't mentioned a doctor's appointment, and Gene's heart skipped a beat. "Is something wrong?"

"No, no. It's just routine, she said. But between you and me, I think she's going to try to talk the doc into fitting another cast. She says she's tired of lugging around that big thing. I don't blame her."

"Nor do I," Gene agreed. Cautiously, she asked, "Did either of you see the paper this morning?"

"You mean the sports section of the *Trib?* Yeah, I saw it when I got up. Congratulations, Gene. That was a great picture. Good publicity, too. You and Achilles looked great."

"Thanks. Do you think Shelley saw it?"

"Oh, yeah," he said meaningfully. "But don't blame me, Gene. I didn't show it to her. One of our boarders made sure she saw it." He paused. "You know how people are."

"What was her reaction?"

"Do you really want to know?"

"I'm not sure," she said. "Do I?"

"Let's just say she wasn't too happy. In a way, it's understandable, don't you think? The caption did sort of imply that you were going to be riding the horse."

"I know. That's why I wanted to talk to her. Kenny, I didn't say that—"

"I know you didn't. I tried to tell her that, but...well, you know how she is...." His voice trailed off for a moment, then he added optimistically, "I'm sure she'll get over it."

Gene knew that if Shelley had been angry about the picture, she was going to come unglued at the news that the paper had called for an interview. Still, she'd get it all straightened out—somehow.

"I hope so," she said. "In the meantime, if you see her, will you ask her to call me? I left a message on her machine, but she's with you more than she is at her place."

"Yeah, and she's doing a really good job here, too. You should see the office. You wouldn't recognize it."

"That's great."

"I think so, too. In fact," he went on admiringly, "after she went over all the books and sent out new statements, I've actually got money coming in. From people who haven't paid in months!"

"Imagine!"

He laughed. "I know. I know. I should have hired her on a lot sooner." His voice turned even warmer. "I think I'll keep her around for a while."

Gene couldn't help teasing him. "As exasperating as she is?"

"Aw, that's just an act. You don't know because you're just her sister. But underneath all that bluster, Shelley's really sweet and kind and gentle."

At her end of the phone, Gene raised an eyebrow. "If you say so."

"Oh, I do."

"I'll take your word for it. You obviously see a different side of her than I do."

"Now, Gene—"

"I was just kidding," she assured him. "Now, don't forget. If you see my sweet and gentle sister, please have her call me. Oh, and by the way, I'm coming out tonight to ride for a while. Not a hard workout, believe me. But after yesterday, I think Achilles and I both need to get some of the kinks out."

"I hear you. See you later."

GENE DIDN'T get a chance to talk to Shelley until later that day, after she'd ridden Achilles. It was a perfect Southern California evening, warm and balmy with just a hint of a breeze, and after all her trepidation, an easy canter around Kenny's lower pasture had done wonders for her sore body. By the time they walked back to the barn, she felt almost human again, and she was humming as she put Achilles in the cross-ties. She was just taking off the saddle when Shelley came down the aisle. The instant Gene saw her sister's face, she knew she was in trouble.

"Well, well, and how's the celebrity tonight?" Shelley mocked. "Still untacking your own horse? Carrying your own saddle? I'm surprised you don't have a groom to do such lowly chores for you."

With a sigh, Gene deposited the saddle on a nearby rack. As she grabbed a brush, she said, "I take it you saw the paper."

"How could I miss it? The only thing lacking was that the picture wasn't in color."

"I didn't know about the picture, Shelley. Not until this morning."

"You didn't talk to a reporter?"

Gene knew that now was not the time to mention her conversation with the sports editor. "I told you, I didn't know anything about it. You have to believe me, Shelley. I wouldn't do that to you."

"I don't know what you'd do anymore."

Gene stopped brushing the horse and turned to her. "How can you say that?"

"Well, what do you want me to think?"

"Look, Shelley, it was only a picture—"

"Yeah, sure. But it was *your* picture on *my* horse. Now everybody thinks you're going to be riding Achilles this season instead of me."

"It's a mistake, Shelley. I told you. I'll set it right."

"How?"

"I'll talk to Ross. He'll—" Gene suddenly realized something about Shelley was different. "You're not on crutches!"

"Gee, you noticed."

Gene had noticed something else. Gone was the full-length plaster that had encased Shelley's leg from thigh to foot; in its place was a new cast that started just below her knee and ended at her toes. "And the doctor changed your cast!"

"About time, too. By the way, he said that the way my leg is healing, pretty soon I'll be out of this thing entirely."

"That's great."

"Is it? What will you do then, Gene? Flip a coin to see which one of us is going to ride Achilles? What if you lose? What will happen to your big 'comeback' then?"

"I told you." Gene could feel herself getting angry, and she tried to control herself. "It's all a big mistake. I never said anything about a comeback. It's a fiction the paper dreamed up."

Shelley tightened her lips. She obviously wanted to believe Gene, but she had a lot riding on this, too. "I should have known something like this would happen."

"Don't be ridiculous. No one could have predicted this."

"Maybe *I* should have! You always got all the attention, even when we were little. It was always, 'Gene this' and 'Gene that,' remember? There was nothing you couldn't do, and now it's happening all over again." Shelley's voice rose. "Maybe I should just give it up right now and let you have the damned horse! It's what you want, anyway!"

"That's not true!" Gene denied. But she felt her cheeks flame, and she knew that she looked as guilty as she suddenly felt. Before she could say anything, Shelley saw her expression, and her own face changed. She started off, but Gene quickly grabbed her arm. "Wait. We have to talk about this."

Shelley tried to jerk her arm away. "I saw the look in your eyes just now. I know what you want."

"No, you don't. Look at me. . . . *Look* at me!" she repeated when Shelley tried to pull away again. When her sister angrily met her glance, she said, "I'm going to ask you again, Shelley. Do you want me to exercise this horse for you or not? Because I'll tell you, I'm getting sick and tired of your accusations. You're the one who asked me, remember? Say the word, and I'll walk away right now. You can find someone else to ride Achilles until you can, I don't care. I don't need this. I've got enough problems of my own."

Shelley stared at her for a long moment. Then her face crumpled, and she looked close to tears. "No, we'll leave it the way it is for now," she said, her voice choked. "I told you before, I don't want anyone else riding that horse."

"Oh, well, that's nicely put. You know what? Maybe you'd better find someone else to ride him, after all. I think I just changed my mind about doing you this favor."

Shelley scrubbed at her face with her hands. "Oh, I don't think so. I know you, Gene. You're enjoying this. You can deny it all you like, but I can see it in your eyes, in the way you ride. But just remember. Achilles is *mine*. And when I'm well again, I'm going to ride him, not you!"

And with that, she turned and stalked off. Gene was so angry that she actually started after her. Then she stopped. She despised herself, but Shelley was right. She *was* enjoying this. She could deny it all she liked, but the truth was that until her sister was able to ride again, she couldn't give Achilles up.

But what was going to happen when that cast came off?

CHAPTER TEN

WHEN SHELLEY LEFT Gene standing in the barn aisleway, she was so angry that she needed to talk to Kenny. He lived in a trailer just off the main stable, and when she knocked at his door a few minutes later, he opened it with a surprised look on his face.

"Shelley! What are you doing here? I didn't hear your car."

Suddenly, she didn't want to go into the entire argument with Gene. It seemed so stupid now, and she felt embarrassed about raising such a fuss. So she said, "That's because I parked at the barn and walked down. It's such a relief to get rid of those crutches and use my own two feet."

He grinned and looked down as he opened the door. "Come on in. And congratulations on the cast change."

"Thanks. But are you sure you're not too busy?"

"For you? Never. Would you like a soda or something?"

She didn't know what she wanted. "Okay. Whatever's handy."

As he headed toward the little kitchen to get the drinks, he said, "I thought you'd be with Gene tonight."

She looked at him sharply. "Why?"

Surprised at her tone, he turned. "Well, to celebrate, I guess. It's not every day you browbeat a doctor into giving in to your wishes."

"Oh...right." She managed a weak smile and said, "Gene's busy tonight."

"Oh. Well, that's all right. If you want, maybe we can send out for dinner or something later."

She didn't know that she'd stay that long. Already she felt restless, unsure of herself, wondering just why she had come. Hedging, she said, "Maybe...."

As Kenny started into the kitchen again, she saw a videotape on top of the TV. Still feeling unsettled, she picked it up. "What's this?"

Kenny looked at her, then just as quickly away. "Uh...it's nothing."

"Nothing?" His tone made her suspicious. "Then why do you have it around?"

"I always have tapes around. Video is the new thing, remember? People constantly send me stuff on their horses to evaluate—aw, Shelley, you don't want to watch that," he said, as she put the tape in the machine. "Come on. Let's have—"

He was too late. As soon as she saw the opening scene, Shelley knew it was a recording of yesterday's horse trials. A group of riders and horses were milling around the starting line, and right there in the center, like a giant white bull's-eye, was Achilles. His snowy coat was impossible to miss in that group of bays and chestnuts, and she turned accusingly to Kenny.

"Why didn't you tell me you taped this?"

"I didn't. One of my students bought a new camcorder and wanted to try it out. She gave me the tape this morning. I haven't even watched it yet."

"Good," she said grimly. "Because we're going to watch it right now."

"Oh, now—"

"Why don't you want me to watch it? Are you afraid I'll see that Gene rides better than I do?"

"Is that what you think?"

She didn't know what to think. She knew she was being childish, but she couldn't help it. Watching Gene ride the horse in person was one thing; being able to analyze every movement and observe everything again was something else. She wasn't going to leave until she'd watched it through to the end.

"Come on, Shelley, you don't have to do this," Kenny said as she sat down in front of the television.

"Yes, I do. Are you going to watch with me, or not?"

On the tape, several horses had already gone through the starting point. It was Gene's turn, and Shelley's eyes narrowed as she watched how easily Gene controlled the eager horse. Achilles clearly knew something was about to happen; he was practically dancing in place as he waited for the signal to get started. Gene just sat there as if the horse had turned to stone.

"Kenny," she said, not taking her eyes off the screen, "do I look like that when I ride Achilles?"

With a heavy sigh, he came and sat beside her on the narrow couch. Reluctantly, he said, "You and Gene have different styles of riding. You know that, Shelley."

"You mean that she just rides better than I do."

"I *mean* that you and she have different ways of riding. One isn't better than the other. They're just different. Why can't you leave it at that?"

She didn't know why; she just couldn't. Unhappy with his answer, she turned back to the screen just as Gene was given the signal to start the course. She didn't say another word until the pair, much the worse for wear, crossed the finish line. Then she switched off the VCR and the TV and just sat there.

Kenny couldn't hide his impatience. "Aren't you going to go through the whole tape frame by frame?" he asked. "I thought for sure you'd want to watch all the jumps in slow-motion over and over again. Or, do you only want to be half-miserable?"

She flushed. "I've seen enough."

"Well, good. Maybe we can think about dinner then."

He started to get up, but she didn't move. "Gene *is* better than I am. It's not my imagination, so don't try to deny it. The evidence is right there. She handles the horse better than I do. He responds to her better than he ever did to me."

Kenny sat down again. "That's not true."

"Yes, it is, and you know it. Don't lie to me, Kenny."

He tried to reach for her hand, but she pulled away. Sighing, he said, "You want the truth? All right, I'll give it to you, as I see it, anyway. Gene *does* ride the horse better than you do—no, wait," he said quickly, as her eyes darkened. "Hear me out. The *reason* she rides the horse better than you do is that she's been riding him longer. You broke your leg before he'd been here a week. Gene started riding him right away, and because she was the one who began to discipline him, he's started to respond to her."

"That's a—"

"Wait a minute. That doesn't mean that Achilles won't work for you when you can ride again. Come on, Shelley, you've been around horses too long not to know that."

She knew she was going to cry. Fiercely, she held back the tears. "I know that a horse responds best to the person who trains it. And we're talking about Achilles, and my sister, who is the best rider I've ever known. You saw the way she handled him, right from the first. She was never afraid—"

She stopped, realizing too late that she'd said too much. Quickly, she turned away so he wouldn't see her face.

"Is that what's really wrong?" he asked quietly. "Are you *afraid* of the horse?"

"No!" She didn't want to admit it, even to herself. "No, I'm not afraid. That wasn't what I meant to say at all!"

She had to get away from his obvious sympathy. Wondering what had gone wrong, she tried to get up from the couch. The damned cast still hampered her, and she glared at it angrily, wanting to take a chain saw to the thing to get it off. Flailing at Kenny's offer of help, she made it to a standing position. She looked around for her purse, remembered that she hadn't brought it with her, and said, "I'm going home now."

He got up, too. "Let's talk about it."

"We've said enough."

"At least let me walk you to your car."

"I might not be able to ride worth a damn, but at least I can walk without help again. I can get to my own car by myself, thank you very much!"

"Aw, Shelley—"

She didn't want to listen. Her hand on the door, she flung herself out of the trailer and down the steps with such force that she nearly lost her balance again. Only her pride kept her upright, and without a backward look, she stalked—clumped—off. She could feel Kenny's eyes on her as she went, and for some reason, that made her even angrier. She knew she was acting like a jerk, but she couldn't help herself. *Why did this have to happen just when things were starting to go so well?* she asked herself furiously. *Why now?*

There was no answer, of course; there never was. All she wanted to do, she thought self-pityingly, was to ride. Was that so much to ask? Apparently, it was, for here she was, stamping along on her broken leg, and she hadn't even touched a saddle for weeks.

Her car was just ahead, but as she started for it, a crazy idea took hold of her and she stopped in her tracks. The more she tried to dismiss it as stupid and dangerous, the more alluring it became. Who was going to know? she thought. The barn was empty; everyone had gone home for the night. She knew Kenny kept to a schedule, and he wouldn't come down for a last check of the horses until ten o'clock.

She glanced at her watch. It was barely eight o'clock—plenty of time to settle her doubts right now, if she wished. Why wait until the doctor gave her permission to ride again? She'd known people who rode with broken arms, wrists, ribs. There was no reason she couldn't ride with a broken leg. After all, it was well-protected by this damned cast.

Before she could think about what she was doing, she entered the barn. Achilles's stall was down the aisle, and when she came up to it, she looked through the bars. As big as a mountain, but placid for once and looking a little drowsy after his dinner, the white horse glanced curiously at her. Apparently he wasn't used to visitors at this time of night.

"Well, what do you think, boy?" She took the halter and lead rope that hung on his door and went into the stall. "Are you up to a little night ride?"

The new cast was lighter and shorter, but she was still so awkward that saddling took longer, and more energy than she'd thought. Also, because he didn't appreciate the prospect of another ride after he'd already been put away for the night, Achilles made things difficult. He jerked his head when she put the bridle on, and then puffed up when she tightened the girth. By then she was so aggravated that she forgot her apprehension. The problem, she thought, after he was saddled and ready, was how she was going to get on him.

She noticed a bench nearby that would do as a ladder, but demon that he was, Achilles wouldn't stand still after she'd climbed up on the perch. Every time she tried to put her free foot in the stirrup, he'd move over—just far enough so that she risked falling if she tried to jump up.

"Hold still, or you'll be sorry," she panted, after she'd moved him parallel to the bench for the sixth time. By now, she was sweating. Annoyance acted like a spur, and on this attempt she managed to throw herself ungracefully atop his back before he realized it. She was already acquainted with his habit of hopping around when he was first mounted, so she quickly regained her balance and grabbed the reins.

Nothing happened. When he stood there quietly, just like the gentleman he was supposed to be, she relaxed a little. Thinking this wasn't going to be as bad as she had thought, she signaled him forward. To her amazement, he actually obeyed. As sedately as a Victorian lady out for a ride on her well-trained little pony, she and Achilles left the barn for the outdoor arena. The floodlights were still on, and even though she might not be able to do much, at least she'd be able to see where they were going.

"Now we'll see what we can do together," she said. She still felt clumsy with the cast, and her leg stuck out at an awkward angle, but who cared? All she wanted to do was take Achilles around the arena a few times to prove to them both that she could do it. Finesse, she thought, could come later.

Heartened by the fact that Achilles seemed willing to work a little now that he was outside, she cued him into a slow trot. When he responded without fuss, she had to give Gene a grudging point. She remembered the first time *she* had tried this same simple thing. Achilles had balked, spun around and tried to get her off. Now he was going forward as smooth as silk—

No, wait!

She'd gotten a little off balance as they turned. Her cast bumped against his side, and instantly, Achilles increased his speed. Suddenly, it seemed they were going very fast. The weight of the cast pulled her down and she couldn't get straight in the saddle, no matter

how she tried. Even worse, the more the horse felt her
dragging to the side, the faster he went.

"Whoa!" she cried. Still trying to drag herself upright, she pulled on the reins, making him more resis-
tant. By this time she'd lost her stirrup on the cast side,
and she had to grab onto the front of the saddle to
keep from falling off.

This was a nightmare! she thought, and abandoned
all dignity by trying to scream for help.

"H...*ooof!*" she gasped, as Achilles rounded another turn. More off balance with every stride, she felt
like a rag doll, flopping every which way. Every time
she tried to straighten, the horse would speed up.

"Help!"

Once more she tried to scream, but ended up with a
whisper. Achilles was galloping now, dangerously out
of control. She knew that if she didn't stop him, one
or both of them was going to get seriously hurt. With
a last effort, she jammed her left foot hard into her
remaining stirrup, took a grip on the reins, and hauled
back.

"*Whoa!*" she screamed with all her might.

This time, he stopped. Unfortunately, as had happened before, she didn't.

Before she could react to the sudden cessation of
forward motion, momentum flung her forward, and
it was obvious that she was going to fall again. She
tried to grab onto something, but her clutching fingers missed his mane and she headed toward the
ground. Before she could stop herself, she landed directly on her broken right leg.

There was a sickening crunch. She tried to look
down, but a mind-numbing bolt of pain shot up her

leg, through her body and out the top of her head. The pain was so fierce that she cried out. The next thing she knew, Achilles was taking off across the arena, reins dangling, saddle askew, heading right for one of the jumps.

"Oh, God," she gasped. She tried to yell at him to stop, but the quick movement sent another shot of agony surging through her and everything went black.

CHAPTER ELEVEN

THAT SAME NIGHT, Gene dabbed a last bit of perfume behind her ears, then stopped a moment to stare at her reflection. It had been a rush after leaving the stable, but she was ready for the business dinner with Ross and Malcolm Quincy. She was wearing a teal-colored sueded silk dress with matching low heels. She knew the color was good for her; why, then, did she look so pale?

Slowly, she recapped the perfume bottle and set it aside. She knew what was wrong with her, and it had nothing to do with the color of her dress. She was upset about that scene with Shelley. The fact that she hadn't been able to get in touch with her sister hadn't helped. She had already called Shelley's apartment several times since she'd come home, with no result. Kenny wasn't answering either, so Gene hoped they were together, and that he'd talk some sense into her. Kenny was a good man, she thought. If anyone could straighten Shelley out, it would be him.

The question now, she thought glumly, was: who was going to set *her* straight? Only a few weeks ago, things seemed so clear. She'd been happy with her job, or so she'd thought. She'd been set on her career. She had things in order. She was happy.

But then a white horse—appropriately named Achilles, she thought—had deflected her, and now things weren't so simple and straightforward at all. Tonight was a good example. She should have made an excuse when Ross asked her if she'd meet him and Malcolm Quincy for dinner. Instead, she'd said yes. She hadn't even really wondered what Shelley was going to think—or even more importantly, how Shelley was going to feel about being left out. She hadn't considered her sister at all. It wasn't like her to do that.

Or was it? When she thought about how Shelley had accused her of trying to take over, she cringed. Then she felt defensive. She was doing Shelley a favor. There was no reason for her to feel guilty. It wasn't her fault that her picture had appeared in the paper.

But she'd gotten a kick out of it, hadn't she?

She turned away from the mirror. She couldn't look at herself anymore. The truth was that she had enjoyed the attention and publicity almost as much as she was enjoying riding Achilles.

Abruptly, she got up. She hadn't thought of it until Shelley's accusation, but she had been in the limelight almost constantly in her youth. When she looked back on it now, it seemed that in those days she couldn't turn around without a flashbulb going off in her face. The sports media had been fascinated with her because she'd always been the youngest rider ever to win this competition or that, or the youngest ever to hold one national title or another.

She might as well admit it, she thought with a sigh. She had loved all the applause and the acclaim. High Cotton had loved it, too, she remembered wistfully.

And they usually had won, Gene thought nostalgically. From the first time they competed until that last horrible incident, it seemed that blue was the only color they knew.

The doorbell rang, jolting her out of her reverie. Relieved to return to the present, she grabbed her purse and looked around to make sure she hadn't forgotten anything. Then she hurried downstairs to greet Ross.

"Hi," she said when she opened the door.

Instead of answering, he pulled her into his arms and kissed her. The instant their lips met, she felt herself melting. It was all she could do to pull back after a moment and look dizzily up into his eyes.

"I'm sorry," he said, his eyes on her face. "But I've dreamed about doing that ever since I left last night."

"Don't be sorry," she said, one hand over her heaving chest. "As a greeting, I'd say that ranks right up there at the top."

Reluctantly, he released her. But he sounded a little breathless himself when he said, "I'd like to pursue this, but I don't trust myself. If I touch you again, I'll forget all about dinner."

Her pulse was pounding, but she managed a faint, "It's just as well. One more kiss like that, and I'd probably never let you out of here."

"One more kiss like that, and I wouldn't go."

She took her keys from the hall table, and as they walked to the car, Ross put his hand on her elbow. The gesture made her feel lighter than air, and she flushed when she realized she was wondering how she was going to get through the evening without putting her hands all over him. She felt warm every time she looked at him, and when she thought about how that single kiss had affected her, she wondered how soon dinner would be over so they could be alone again.

"I wish we didn't have to go," Ross said, after they were in the car and on their way. "I'm sorry I dragged you into this, too."

"You didn't drag me into it. I came willingly, remember?"

"Still—"

She reached for his hand. "I don't mind. But it's too bad James couldn't come. You said he was pretty excited about this."

"He was, but who can anticipate a baby-sitter crisis? With his wife out of town, he had to stay home with the kids."

She smiled. "He'll probably want a word-for-word repeat of the conversation. Did you bring your tape recorder?"

He smiled, too. "He'll have to make do with my faulty memory." He squeezed her fingers. "Thanks again, Gene. After a day at the office, this is probably the last thing you wanted to do tonight."

"Oh, no, I'm looking forward to meeting Mr. Quincy. I've seen some of his company's advertising, and it's very effective. Whoever thought of that kangaroo logo with the bush hat was brilliant. It's a wonderful advertising gimmick."

"I think so, too. Even if someone can't remember the name, the symbol is unforgettable."

"How can anyone forget the name?" she said with a laugh. "Roo'sters. It definitely has cachet. And the products aren't bad, either. I had one of their horse 'rugs,' as they call horse blankets, for years and years.

It wore like iron. In fact, I probably still have it around somewhere."

"No doubt it's just as good as the day you bought it," he said, and laughed. "Listen to us. We sound like a commercial."

"Maybe we should work up a little proposal," she teased, "and spring it on your Mr. Quincy at dinner."

"Believe me, if I thought it would work, I'd try to talk you into it."

He sounded so fervent that she said, "This account means a lot to you, doesn't it?"

"James and I have been trying to get Roo'sters in our stores for years. Everything they make is top quality, not only the horse gear. But as I said, they're very particular about who they allow to sell their products. The fact that Quincy called us this time might be just the break we need."

His words reminded her that she hadn't told him yet about the *Tribune*'s request for an interview. "Do you think it's just because my picture was in the paper?"

"Well, Quincy is quite a horseman himself, you know. And he was very complimentary about your riding."

Was it her imagination, or did Ross suddenly seem uncomfortable? She looked at him for a moment, then she glanced away. She was simply transferring her discomfort onto Ross because *she* felt guilty. Why didn't she just tell him about Jerry Fazey and get it over with?

"I'm sure he was just being nice," she said. "It's difficult to tell much from a single picture, you know."

"Well, I'm not a horse person at all, and I could tell how well you ride from that photo. Don't you think that someone who knows horses could see the same thing?"

"I suppose." She knew she had to tell him about the interview request, so she tried to lead into it by saying, "I'm flattered that he approved, but it doesn't really matter. Shelley is going to be competing the horse."

"Yes, we told him that. But he wanted to meet you."

"I see."

He looked at her. "You *are* having second thoughts, aren't you?"

"No, I'm not—not about dinner, anyway. It's just—" She stopped, biting her lip. But she couldn't put off telling him any longer, so she said, "Ross, Shelley and I had words tonight—"

"About this dinner with Malcolm?"

Gene shifted in her seat. This was getting worse and worse, she thought. She was keeping things from everybody, and she wasn't sure why. She should have told Shelley about having dinner tonight with Ross and Malcolm Quincy, but she hadn't. She should have told Ross about Jerry Fazey's request, but she hadn't done that, either. Why was she being so secretive? What was the point?

She knew what the point was. If she told Ross about the interview, or mentioned to Shelley that Malcolm Quincy had asked to meet her because he'd seen her picture in the paper, she'd have to face the fact that this was really Shelley's job, and get out of the way so her sister could take over. But she just wasn't ready to do that, and it wasn't because Shelley was still in a cast.

"She doesn't know about the dinner. I didn't tell her."

"Did you think she'd be upset?" Ross asked.

Upset? Knowing Shelley, she would have been furious at being left out, Gene thought. But she said, "Well, it just didn't seem a good idea at the time, Ross. She was already so annoyed about that newspaper photo. She thinks I did that on purpose."

"But you had no control over that."

"I know, but try convincing her. I told her it was just a coincidence. The photographer could have taken anyone's picture. I just happened to be there when he took the shot."

As though his collar was suddenly too tight, Ross stretched his neck. "Well, not exactly."

It was his expression more than his words that roused her suspicions. Suddenly, she realized that she'd been so preoccupied with the *fact* that Jerry Fazey had called, that she'd forgotten to wonder *why* he had.

"Ross, did you have something to do with that picture?"

He looked even more unhappy. "It wasn't me, it was James. He knows the sports editor at the paper, and they thought it might be a good story."

"Well, that's just great. I wondered how all that business about this supposed 'comeback' of mine got started. I suppose James was responsible for that, too."

"I'm afraid so."

"No wonder Shelley doesn't believe me. If I were in her place, I'd be upset, too."

"I'm sorry, Gene. I didn't mean for this to happen, honest."

"Well, neither did I."

"I guess the question is, what are we going to do about it?"

"After we have dinner with your Mr. Quincy, you mean?"

He winced at her sarcasm. "I never should have asked you."

"No, you should have asked Shelley."

"And you could have suggested that she come instead of you, too."

"That's a nasty thing to say!"

The fact that he'd struck a nerve made her react more strongly than the situation warranted. She flounced around to stare out the window. She could feel his eyes on her, but she wouldn't look at him, and they drove in tense silence the rest of the way to the restaurant. But he turned to her after he'd parked the car and reached for her hand.

"I'm sorry," he said. "I shouldn't have said that."

She still wouldn't look at him. "You're right. You shouldn't have."

"I did try to make it clear to Malcolm that Shelley is the one who's going to be riding the horse, but James—" He stopped. "Never mind, it's my problem. But I promise you, I'll get this straightened out tonight. We can go in there right now and tell Malcolm the dinner's off, if you like. Or, I can go in by myself and tell him. It's up to you. What do you want?"

She didn't know what she wanted. Ross's comment still rankled, all the more because she knew he was right. She *should* have insisted that Shelley take her place. Why hadn't she? Because—she had to admit it—she was enjoying all this sudden attention a little too much. But was she the kind of person who would deny her own sister an opportunity because she wanted the spotlight to herself? Wincing at the thought, she reached for the door handle, her mind suddenly made up.

"We're here, so we might as well go in," she said. "But I'm going to make sure Mr. Quincy knows the exact situation. Is that understood?"

Ross looked relieved and wary at the same time. But he said, "Yes, it is. You tell him whatever you want."

"I'll tell him the truth."

"Yes, of course, that's what I meant." Quickly, he got out of the car and came around to her side. Since he'd gone to so much trouble, she took his hand when he offered to help her out. When she was standing beside him, he said, "I'm sorry this has become so difficult, Gene. I didn't want it to be this way, not after..."

His voice trailed off, making Gene feel even worse. She still hadn't told him about the interview, but she decided to put it off. She didn't want anything more to come between them, and she certainly didn't want to prolong this argument.

"We're both at fault," she said. "So we'll just have to make it right. Mr. Quincy will understand—don't you think?"

Ross looked as though he didn't know what to think. Gene knew he was as ambivalent about the situation as she was.

"Well, we'll just have to see how it goes," he said finally. He gazed into her face. "I don't care what happens, just as long as you and I are all right." He paused. "Are we?"

She didn't have to think about *that*. "Oh, yes, Ross," she said. "I don't want to fight, not about this, not about anything. I'm so sorry about it all."

The corners of his mouth twitched—in amused relief, this time, she thought. "All of it?" he asked.

It was that twitch that did it. "Well, not *all*," she said, her eyes glinting. "There are *some* aspects of this that I'm not sorry about at all."

"Me, neither."

They were standing close together, and when he put his hand on her waist and slowly pulled her into the shelter of his body, she didn't resist. His eyes never leaving her face, he bent his head and kissed her.

Gene couldn't believe the effect he had on her; it was as though with one touch of his lips, her entire body began to weaken. Her legs and arms trembled, her head started to spin. She'd never reacted to a man this way before, and when she leaned against him for a moment and breathed in his scent, she felt lightheaded, giddy—and ready for anything. She wanted that kiss to go on and on, but she knew that if it did, she'd be tempted to pull him back into the car right here in the parking lot.

"I think," she said shakily, when they finally broke apart, "that we'd better go in."

His voice was hoarse. "I think you're right."

They had spent so much time in the parking lot that Malcolm Quincy was already seated at a table. As she approached, Gene could tell, even though he was sitting down, Quincy was a big man. Her first impression was confirmed when he stood as Ross introduced them. Everything about Malcolm Quincy seemed big to her, from the hand that enveloped hers, to his booming voice, to the bush boots he wore. The footwear should have looked incongruous with his sport coat and tie, but the outfit suited him.

"I saw your picture in the paper, Gene," he said as they all sat down. "The way you were riding that horse made me want to saddle up one of mine, myself. I wish I'd seen the trials in person."

She was pleased at the compliment. "I think the photographer caught us at a good time," she said modestly. "Achilles—the horse—is still very green. As for me, I haven't been in a saddle for more years than I care to count."

"You could have fooled me," Quincy said as Ross ordered a bottle of wine from the waiter. "Tell me, what's this about your making a comeback after all this time away?"

Gene shot a quick glance at Ross before she answered. Then she plunged in. "I'm afraid that story has been exaggerated, Malcolm. You see, I'm only riding the horse until my sister is able to do it again. She broke her leg, and—"

Quincy waved his hamlike hand expansively. "I've always said that someone's bad luck can be someone else's good fortune. You're a perfect example of that philosophy, wouldn't you say?"

Gene didn't know what to say. She shot another hasty look at Ross, who was preoccupied with tasting the wine that had just been brought to the table. She could see he wasn't going to be much help, and she was irritated. Then she realized she might be expecting too much from him. If Malcolm Quincy believed this "comeback" fantasy the press had spun, it was her job to burst the bubble, not Ross's.

She turned back to the Australian. "Actually, I wouldn't say that," she said cautiously. She knew how much Ross wanted this man's business, and she didn't want to offend him. But she couldn't allow him, or anyone else, to think that she intended to get back into competitive riding.

"You're just being modest," Quincy insisted genially. "Now, I can understand your not wanting to step on someone's toes—especially if they're in a cast," he added with a wink. "But you have to think of yourself. Why, anyone with half an eye can see from the photo that you were born to ride."

"That's nice of you to say," she said. She understood Ross's reluctance to argue Quincy's point, but this was ridiculous. Why was he sitting there, not saying *anything?* She sent a glare his way, but Quincy went blithely on.

"I'm not just saying it," Quincy said. "I mean it. I've been in this business a long time, and I know how things work. At Roo'sters, we took a little one-room outback store and built it into an international business. You don't do that by accident."

"No, no, you don't," she agreed, trying to signal Ross without Quincy noticing her do it. She gave him a sideways glance and saw that he seemed to be enjoying the exchange between her and his guest.

"A hook, that's what it takes," Quincy said. "You can have the best advertising in the world, pledge yourself to the highest cause, but if you don't have a hook to get people's attention, you're going to remain a little backwoods store. Now, take James and Ross, here. I was beginning to think that concept had eluded them, but they're on the right track now."

Gene saw her opening and took it. "Oh, yes, I agree. Sponsoring a horse was a great idea—"

"Oh, sure, as far as it goes. But finding you, a rider with a story of her own—*that* was a brilliant touch."

"But I'm trying to tell you, Malcolm, I don't *have* a story," she said desperately. "Please, you must understand. It's all been a mistake, an exaggeration by the press. Shelley is—"

"Charisma, that's what it takes," Quincy said as though he hadn't heard a word. "You've got it, Gene. I saw that right away."

"I don't have anything," she protested. "Shelley is the one who's going to be riding, when she's well again."

"I'm sure this Shelley is a good rider, but I doubt she has what you do, my dear," Quincy said. "You've got something special, and I'm not the only one who sees it. That's why the press picked up on it."

"The press picked up on it because James is a friend of the sports editor," Gene said firmly. She'd given up waiting for Ross to help. She turned directly to him and commanded, "Tell him, Ross."

With a smile, Ross obliged. "That's true, Malcolm," he said. "Jerry Fazey is a friend of James's."

Gene turned back to Quincy. "You see?"

The Australian waved his hand again. "Details. If there hadn't been a story there, the trials never would have made the paper. We all know it. No, *you're* news, Gene, whether you want to admit it or not." He paused as the waiter came to take their order. Then he continued, "I saw it right away. And now that I've met you, I see it more clearly than ever. It's hard to explain charisma, you know. Only a few people have it, but when they do... well, there's nothing that can match it."

No matter what she said, Gene couldn't sway Quincy from his opinion. She gave up halfway through dinner, and they talked of other things. She wasn't sure she should bring up the subject again as they stood outside the restaurant saying goodbye, but she didn't have to worry. Malcolm did it for her.

"Well, I'm glad I got a chance to meet you, Ms. Gene Logan," Quincy said, enveloping her hand again in his big one. He looked at Ross, then back at her, turning into a businessman before her eyes. "But if I were you, I'd think about this riding business again—you and Ross and James. It's clear that you're up to the challenge, Gene. And if I may be so bold as to offer an opinion, I think you'd relish the chance to make a comeback after all these years. I can see it in your eyes."

"Now, Malcolm—"

"I didn't say anything before now, but I used to ride competitively myself in my younger days. Before age and girth caught up to me, that is," he added with his booming laugh. Then he turned serious again. "But it wasn't so long ago that I don't recognize a fellow

competitor when I see one. That's why I like Ross
here, so much. Why, if it weren't for that bum leg of
his, I bet he'd still be racing around hell-for-leather in
those high-powered cars. Wouldn't you, Ross?''

Ross shifted uncomfortably. ''Oh, I don't know,
Malcolm,'' he said, with a glance at Gene. ''It's hard
to say.''

''Oh, bull pucky,'' Quincy pronounced. ''You know
it's true, and so do I.'' He turned again to Gene.
''Now, don't take this the wrong way, my dear, but
Roo'sters is a big company, and we would certainly
consider putting some of our products in Outdoor
Outfitters stores if you're riding that horse. No, no,
don't tell me about your sister again,'' he said as she
opened her mouth. ''As I told you before, one person's misfortune is another one's chance. There's opportunity here for all of us. This thing could generate
a lot of interest. It wouldn't hurt Roo'sters to be there
when it does.''

Gene could feel Ross's eyes on her, but she had to
try one last time. ''Malcolm—''

''No, no, don't say anything now. You think about
it. You too, Ross. I'll be in touch.''

A limousine appeared as if by magic. The driver
stepped out and opened the door, and Quincy climbed
in with a wave. The big car sped away. Left alone on
the sidewalk, Gene and Ross looked at each other.

''I don't know about you,'' she said, ''but I feel as
if I've just spent the evening with a whirlwind . . . or a
bulldozer.''

''I felt the same way when I first met Malcolm,''
Ross said. ''He is a little overbearing, isn't he?''

"A *little?*" They began walking back to where he'd left his car, but she turned accusingly to him. "And you weren't much help. Why didn't you say anything when he was going on and on about all that charisma stuff?"

Ross calmly unlocked the passenger door of the car. "Because I agreed with him," he said. "And also," he added before she could protest, "because I thought you could take care of yourself."

That took the wind out of her sails. She couldn't think of an immediate reply, so she got into the car. As they started off, she said quietly, "I can't do it, Ross. I know how much the Roo'sters account means to you, but I can't take the horse away from Shelley. It wouldn't be right."

"I know."

"You do?"

"Yes, of course. Don't worry about it. Things will work out."

She looked at him gloomily. "Are you sure about that?"

He shrugged. "Roo'sters would be nice to have, but we haven't had any of their products in our stores until now and we still got by."

She knew she should just drop it while she was ahead, but she had to say, "Yes, but you said that things were different now. You need—"

"Those are my problems, Gene—mine and James's. Yes, we would like the Roo'sters account, I don't deny it. But there will be other accounts, other products. Now that you and I have...what we have, the last thing I want is to come between you and your sister. Things will work out."

"But how?" she persisted. "I don't like to admit it, but Malcolm was right. To get ahead, especially these days, you need a hook."

"Let me ask you something. Do you want to compete the horse in Shelley's place?"

Gene hesitated just a fraction too long. Even she could hear the uncertainty in her voice when she answered, but she couldn't help it. "No, of course I don't." Then, annoyed with herself, she added, more forcefully, "No, I don't. I told you that. In fact, I—"

"Then, why are we discussing it?" He reached for her hand. "Let's talk about something else."

Gene didn't want to talk about something else. She couldn't seem to stop worrying this subject to death. As they pulled up in front of her house, she asked, "Would you like to come in?"

"Only if you promise we won't talk about my business problems."

Just moments before, Gene couldn't seem to let the topic go. Now, seeing the look in his eyes, business was the last thing she wanted to talk about. Suddenly a little breathless with anticipation, she crossed her heart.

"I promise."

"In that case, I accept."

Arm in arm they walked up to the front porch. When she took her key out, she realized that her fingers were trembling. Ross saw it, too. He put the crook of his cane over one arm and took the key ring from her. Then, with his free hand, he pulled her toward him.

"I can't wait any longer," he said. "You looked so damned beautiful all through dinner that it was all I could do to keep my hands off you. If I don't kiss you now, I'm going to—"

As their lips met, Gene forgot all about going inside. She forgot about Malcolm Quincy, and Ross's business problems, and her own doubts and self-recriminations. There was only the touch of his lips on hers, the glorious feeling of his strong arm pressing her into him, and the feel of his lean body. Wanting to experience even more of him, she wrapped her arms around his neck and wound her fingers through his hair. The scent of him was in her nostrils; even through her silk dress, his touch burned. She knew that if this blissful contact went on, she'd pull him over to the porch swing and make love with him right there.

"Let's go inside," she whispered, her lips against his.

She didn't know how, but he managed to unlock the door without letting go of her. Their arms still around each other, they went inside. Then he reached behind him with one hand and shoved the door closed. He threw down his cane, her keys clanged as he tossed them onto the hall table. Both arms free, he grabbed her to him as though he'd never let her go and buried his face in her hair.

"God, what you do to me," he murmured hoarsely. "If anything ever happened to you, I don't think I could bear it...."

As swept away as she was by sensation, something in his voice alarmed her. She pulled back a little so she could look into his face.

"Nothing's going to happen to me," she said.

His arms tightened around her. "No, I won't let it...."

Another alarm bell sounded in her mind. Remembering his reluctance to let her ride Achilles, she wondered briefly if he planned to stop her now, but then she forgot about it when he put a hand under her chin and tipped her head up to his.

"I love you, Gene," he said. "I love you like I've never loved anyone before."

She was too surprised to reply. "Ross—"

He put a finger over her lips. "No, don't say it. I know it's too soon. I shouldn't have told you, but I wanted you to know. I can't help myself. I think I loved you from the moment I first saw you walk in through those hospital doors. I didn't even know who you were at first, but even so, I knew. You were worried and concerned, but you were still the most compelling woman I'd ever seen."

She didn't know what to say. Uncomfortably, she tried to pull away. "You're embarrassing me, Ross—"

"Why?" He searched her face, his eyes glinting in the dim light. He had never looked more handsome to her, more magnetic...more urgent.

Her lips felt stiff. This wonderful thing was happening, and she didn't want to ruin it by saying or doing something foolish. "I don't know why," she said. "Oh, Ross, I—"

Just then, the phone rang.

She'd been so involved that the noise made her jump. She turned blankly in that direction as it rang again. "Who in the world would be calling me at *this* hour?"

Before she could answer, her machine picked up. It took Gene a moment to realize it was Kenny at the other end. His voice sounded so different.

"Gene, will you call me as soon as you get home? I'm at Shelley's place. We just got home from the hospital again. She tried to ride Achilles tonight and refractured her leg. But don't worry. She's all right—now. She didn't want me to call you, but I thought you should know. She'll be mad when she finds out what I've done, and she already feels foolish enough, so...take it easy on her, will you? I'll talk to you later. Bye."

He hung up before Gene could gather her wits.

The intimate mood that had sprung up between Gene and Ross vanished as they looked at each other in dismay. Then Gene said, "I can't believe it. I'm going over there right now."

"I'll take you."

Feeling close to tears, Gene looked at him and asked, "How could she have done such a stupid thing?"

"I don't know," Ross said, reaching for her hand. He gave her fingers a comforting squeeze. "I guess we're about to find out."

CHAPTER TWELVE

KENNY ANSWERED the door when Gene and Ross arrived. Before Gene could ask what had happened, he put a finger over his lips and jerked his head toward the closed bedroom door.

"Shh," he said. "She's asleep, I think."

Gene was relieved to see that Kenny didn't look as pale and worried this time as he'd been before. Did that mean this wasn't as bad as she had imagined on the way over? "How is she?" she whispered.

"She's doing all right, all things considered."

"And her leg? What did the doctor say?"

"He said she was lucky. X rays show that the bone shifted only marginally, so they were able to recast without surgery. But she'll be in a cast for a while longer."

Gene's expression went from concerned to grim. "Great."

They all went into the living room. When they were seated, Ross asked, "What happened? Do you know?"

"I'm not clear on all the details," Kenny said. "On the way home, she told me she didn't want to talk about it, so I left it alone. All I know is that she tried to ride Achilles tonight—"

"And the horse threw her!" Gene exclaimed. "I can't believe she'd even try such a stupid thing. She knew how dangerous it was. What's the matter with her?"

"One thing at a time," Kenny said. "I know how worried you are, Gene, but one thing Shelley made clear was that the horse didn't throw her. She insisted that she fell."

"And there's a difference?" Ross asked.

"There is to her," Kenny replied.

"Wait until I see her!" Gene was almost shouting. "What difference does it make if she fell or if the horse tossed her off? Isn't the important thing that she tried to ride with her leg in a cast?"

"I agree with you, Gene," Kenny said. "But Shelley was adamant about that point. I guess she's afraid that Ross and James will get rid of the horse if they think Achilles is to blame."

"I see," Ross said. "So if the horse had thrown her, it would mean it was his fault. Since she fell, it was hers."

"Something like that."

"Aren't we splitting hairs here?" Ross asked. "The point is that, no matter how it happened, she hit the ground."

Gene looked at Kenny again. "What else did the doctor say?"

"Not much," Kenny said unhappily. "I guess we're just going to have to wait and see how it goes."

"Oh, swell," Gene said. "I can just imagine Shelley's reaction when she heard that!"

"If it had been ordinary circumstances, she probably would have been mad. But as it was, she was almost meek."

"Shelley's never been *meek* in her entire life!"

"Well, she feels awfully foolish right now. She knows what a stupid thing it was to do," Kenny said. "Actually, I think she's madder at me than she is at herself."

"At you?" Ross said. "Why?"

Kenny glanced quickly at the irate Gene. "Well, like I said, she wanted me to promise not to call you."

"That figures," Gene said. "I'm glad you did. In fact," she added, "*I* would have been even madder at you than at Shelley if you hadn't."

Kenny smiled wanly. "I figured that, so I didn't think I had much to lose. Still, maybe what happened was my fault."

"Don't be ridiculous! Shelley is a grown woman. She knew what she was doing. Or she should have."

"Why do you think it was your fault?" Ross asked curiously.

"Well, if she hadn't found that damn videotape of the trials and insisted on playing it, I don't think this would have happened," Kenny said.

"What videotape?" Gene asked.

"Oh, one of my students got a new camcorder and tried it out Sunday at the cross-country. I got a copy, and like a fool, I left it sitting on top of the TV."

"But what does that have to do with Shelley trying to ride again?" Ross asked.

"That's a good question," Gene said. "What *was* she thinking of? Did she have an attack of nostalgia, or what? She hasn't been off a horse that long. Did she think she was going to forget how to ride, or something?"

"It wasn't either of those things," Kenny said quietly. He glanced toward the closed bedroom door, and then hunched closer to them before continuing. Even then, he dropped his voice. "I think she was jealous."

"Jealous?" Ross repeated. Gene sat, suddenly silent. "Of what?"

"Not of what. Of whom," Kenny said. He glanced at Gene again. "Achilles's white coat is pretty hard to miss, you know. It wasn't difficult to see you and Achilles all over that tape. When Shelley saw how you rode that course..."

"But she was right there!" Gene exclaimed.

"I know. But it was different seeing it on tape. You'll see, when you watch it."

"Oh, for heaven's sake!" she said impatiently. But she knew her face was turning red. She glanced away from the truth she could see in Kenny's eyes, muttering, "I thought we had this all settled."

"Well, you know how she is," Kenny said. "I tried to tell her that she was just as good a rider in her own way as you are in yours, but she wouldn't listen. I've never seen her this way, Gene. She's seen so many other people ride—some better than she, many worse. But when it comes to you—"

Gene couldn't sit there any longer. She jumped up. "But why does she have to compare herself to me? I've never said anything—"

"You don't have to." Kenny met her eyes. "The way you ride speaks for itself, don't you think?"

"I don't know what to think! I wish I had never agreed to this. If I hadn't said I'd ride the horse, none of this would have happened!"

"She still would have broken her leg," Kenny said.

"And we still would have had to find someone to ride the horse until she was well," Ross added.

She looked angrily at them both. "But it wouldn't have been me, don't you see?" She threw herself down on the couch again. "I should have known this would happen. Shelley always has been jealous of me. I should have agreed to ride and then made a mess of it. Maybe *that* would have made her happy!"

"You don't mean that," Kenny said. "You're just upset."

"Damned right, I'm upset!"

"It's not your fault, Gene," Ross said. He reached for her hand. "You couldn't do anything differently, and you certainly can't be responsible for what Shelley tried to do tonight."

"I'm not sure of that," she said.

"I am," Ross said firmly. "Now, the thing to do is to decide where we're going from here."

"I know where I'm going," she said. She jumped up again. "I don't care if Shelley's asleep or not, I'm going in to talk to her right now."

Kenny looked alarmed. "What are you going to say?"

"I don't know. I'll think of something. But I'm sure of one thing...."

"What's that?" Ross asked anxiously.

"I'm not going to ride anymore if it's going to upset her this much, that's what!"

"Now, Gene—" Ross started to say.

"I don't think that's—" Kenny began to say at the same time.

She didn't want to listen to their opinions. If she did, she might change her mind, and she couldn't do that. "No," she said firmly. "If Shelley is so unhappy with the situation that she risks breaking her neck to prove God knows what, then I'm just going to have to bow out. You can get someone else to exercise Achilles until Shelley's well again, Ross. Kenny can find another rider, I'm sure. Can't you, Kenny?"

"Well, I don't know, Gene," Kenny said, with a quick glance at Ross. "Achilles is a lot of horse."

"I know that!" she said, clenching her fists. "But you have people hanging around the stable all the time, just begging for a chance like this. I know that *one* of them can handle Achilles! As I've proved, he's not impossible to ride!"

"Gene, don't you think you should consider this?" Ross asked.

She turned to him. "I have considered it! Don't you see? This was supposed to be so simple when we talked about it, but now it's more complicated than ever. And guess who's the biggest complication? Me! So I think I'll just solve everyone's problem and go back to what I was doing before Shelley ever got this stupid idea. And when that reporter from the *Trib* calls, I'll just tell him—"

She stopped abruptly. "What reporter?" Ross asked.

She could have bitten her tongue. Why had she mentioned that reporter? Weren't things bad enough?

"Yeah, what reporter?" Kenny asked.

She glared at them both. She felt defensive, and with good reason, she thought. She *knew* she should have told Ross before this. Now it was going to sound as though she'd been hiding something—which she *had* been, she reminded herself scathingly.

"I was going to tell you, Ross," she said. "But, what with one thing and another..." When she saw the look in his eyes, she felt even more foolish. Deciding it would be best to come clean, she started over again. "Jerry Fazey called me today, and—"

"Jerry Fazey, the sports editor of the *Tribune?*" Kenny asked, sounding impressed.

"Yes, that's the one." She knew her face was bright red; she could feel the heat. She made herself look at Ross. "He wanted to know if I'd do an interview for the paper. About this supposed comeback of mine."

"And what did you tell him?" Ross asked quietly.

"Well, I made it clear that Shelley was riding Achilles, of course!" she exclaimed. "Or, at least that she *will* be when her leg heals. Needless to say, that was before I knew about this latest stunt of hers."

"I see," he said.

"That's all you have to contribute?"

"What do you want me to say?" he asked. "I knew the paper was interested, but—"

"But what? And what do you mean, you knew the paper was interested? That's not what you told me before. Why didn't you say anything? At the least, you could have told me how to handle it when Fazey called!"

"In the first place," Ross said, "I didn't know Fazey was going to call you. And in the second, I figured you could take care of yourself. After all, what is there to say? You've told us all again and again that you're only going to ride the horse until Shelley is fit. So it doesn't make much difference if they want to interview you or not, does it?"

"No, it doesn't. And I told him that, too!"

"And?"

"And what?"

"What did he say?" Ross asked.

If she'd wanted him to know what Fazey had said, she thought unfairly, she would have told him. She cringed when she remembered that conversation. At this point, she had to question if she had really tried to convince Fazey of the situation regarding Achilles. Had she been as forceful as she should have been in driving home her point?

Ross repeated his question. "What did he say, Gene?"

She didn't want to get into all that now. "Oh, Ross, you know how reporters are," she said impatiently. "He had his own agenda, and he wasn't going to listen to anything I said. He's insisting that I give him his damned interview!"

"It seems we have a problem, then."

"A *problem?*" She looked at him incredulously. "That's all you can say?"

"What do you want me to say?"

She knew she was overreacting, but his reasonable tone aggravated her. What she *wanted* him to say was that he understood her dilemma, they were all caught in a situation not of their own making and that soon it would be all over and everything would get back to normal again because he had a solution to the problem.

Was that really what she wished? Or was she fooling herself again?

Had she been lying to herself all these years? she thought suddenly. She'd told herself that she was no longer interested in horses, that she'd outgrown her childish hobby, that she'd moved on to other things. Now she realized it wasn't true. Maybe she'd thought that if she said it enough times, it would be, but she knew now that even if she said it a thousand times a day for the rest of her life, she'd still want to ride competitively. She'd never lost her taste for it, she thought. She had just postponed it for a while.

And now that she'd been given a glimpse of what it could be like again, she couldn't give it up, especially when she had the opportunity to ride a horse like Achilles. She knew how Shelley felt. Achilles *was* a dream horse. She'd tried to hide the knowledge from herself, but she had known the instant she first laid eyes on him that he was destined for greatness. Even standing in his stall, Achilles had something that made him stand out even more than that pale coat of his. What that magnificent creature had was star quality.

Talk about charisma, she thought, recalling the conversation with Malcolm at dinner. She wasn't the one who had it: Achilles did. Even though he was still green and untrained, he could be one of the best, as good as, if not better than—she had to admit it—High Cotton. Achilles had the same courage and heart, and just that hint of recklessness that High Cotton had possessed. Together, those qualities made the great competitive horses.

That thought brought her up short, and she bit her lip. If she felt this way, Shelley must feel it even more keenly. After all, Shelley was the one who loved horses and riding so much that she'd made a career out of it. She was the sister who had not forsaken the sport. Given that, how could Gene take back her decision now, just because she'd found a horse she couldn't give up?

"Gene," Ross said, interrupting her thoughts. "Don't make us choose between you and Shelley. Not now, at any rate."

She looked at him blankly. She knew she couldn't tell him what had been going through her mind. The idea was too new, and she needed time to think about it. Going back to a career in riding would be a big step. She had to make sure she knew what she was doing.

"I'm not making you choose," she said unsteadily. "Haven't I told you all along that I wouldn't?"

As though he sensed something going on, he replied quietly, "I know what you've told me, but I think things might have changed."

"Changed?" She couldn't meet his eyes.

"Yes, changed. After what happened tonight, we still don't know the situation. Until we do, there's no point in causing hurt feelings. I think we can all agree that Shelley won't be riding for a while, so I think we should just table this discussion for now. Then we can be fair to everyone—especially Achilles."

Gene had been feeling increasingly impatient with him during this speech. The more he said, the more convinced she became that he was looking for an easy way to postpone the inevitable. Now she wasn't so sure. It was his mention of Achilles that caused her doubt. Even Shelley would have to agree that the horse was a prime consideration. After all, in competition,

Achilles was the one who had to do most of the work. He deserved the best rider they could put on him. The only question, she thought uneasily, was which of the Logan sisters was that rider?

"I agree," she said. Suddenly, she felt very tired. All she wanted to do was go home.

Kenny had been silent until now, but he glanced at Ross. "Are you thinking of backing out?" he asked.

"I don't know," Ross said. "I have to admit that when James and I first thought about this, we didn't realize the difficulties involved."

"No one could predict that Shelley would break her leg," Kenny said. It was clear to Gene that he was on her sister's side. "If that hadn't happened, everything would have worked out just fine."

Ross glanced her way, then at Kenny. "Unfortunately, it didn't turn out that way, did it? I don't know what James is going to say, but I admit I'm wondering if we shouldn't rethink this whole thing."

"But you're getting great publicity out of this, Ross," Kenny said. "I thought that's what you wanted."

He didn't see Gene glare at him, which was just as well, she thought. She'd hoped she'd safely negotiated the conversation away from the problem of the newspaper, but now that Kenny had brought it up again, they might as well deal with it.

"Kenny brought up a point that got lost somewhere along the way," she said. "I know Jerry Fazey is going to call back about that interview." She looked evenly at Ross. "What do you want me to say when he does?"

"Tell him the truth," Ross said. "That you're just riding the horse until Shelley can do it."

"I *did* tell him that," she said. "Or, at least, I tried. But he said that was an even better angle because it inspired me to compete again. He sounds just like Malcolm."

"Who's Malcolm?" Kenny asked.

"He represents Roo'sters," Gene said.

"Oh, yeah," Kenny said with an understanding nod. "That company that makes the great horse blankets."

"Among other things," Ross said. "James and I have been trying to get their products in our stores for years." He paused, then added, "He wasn't interested until he saw that picture of Gene and Achilles in the paper."

Kenny looked from one to the other. "Oh...I see," he said. He sat back. "That's kind of good and bad, isn't it?"

"Yes, at the moment, it certainly is," Gene said grimly. Then her frustration erupted again. "What I'd like to know is why everyone is so interested in this fantastic comeback story of mine. *I* never said anything about it. In fact, I never even *thought* of it until—"

She stopped—too late. She hadn't meant to betray herself like that, and she looked quickly at Ross, hoping he hadn't heard. But of course he had, and now he was staring at her as though she'd just confirmed something he'd already known. And in a way, she thought desperately, she had.

"You were saying?" Ross said calmly.

"Never mind," she said. "It wasn't important—"

"What wasn't important?" a new voice asked.

Startled, Gene turned toward that direction. She'd been so preoccupied that she hadn't heard Shelley come in, but there she was, standing on her crutches on the living-room threshold. When Kenny saw her, he jumped up to help, and to Gene's amazement, Shelley actually let him assist her to one of the chairs by the couch.

"I thought you were asleep," Gene said.

"How can anyone sleep with all the noise in here?" Shelley said. "I've been listening to you argue for what seems like hours, and I decided it was time I joined in."

"I'm sorry if we disturbed you," Ross said. "How do you feel?"

"Like a jerk, if you want to know the truth," Shelley said. She glanced up at Kenny, who was still hovering over her. "You don't have to stand there like that. I've done enough stupid things for a lifetime. I certainly won't do any more tonight."

Again, to Gene's surprise, Shelley softened her words by reaching for Kenny's hand. Briefly, she brought his fingers to her cheek, then she smiled up at him and added softly, "But thanks."

Kenny's hand lingered on Shelley's neck. "Can I get you anything?" he asked.

She shook her head. "No, right now, I just want to talk."

Gene looked at her warily. She couldn't help wondering how much Shelley had overheard, and she asked, "About what?"

"Well, it's obvious, don't you think? About the competition that's coming up, of course," Shelley said. She looked around at their blank faces. "That *is* what you were talking about, isn't it?"

Gene had regained enough of her composure to remember how upset she still was at Shelley for pulling such a stunt. "As a matter of fact, we weren't," she said. "We were talking about you."

Shelley reddened. "I already admitted I acted foolishly."

"Yes, you did. Now I want to know why you did it."

"Do you want us to leave you two alone?" Ross asked.

"Yeah, that's a good idea," Kenny said. "Come on, Ross. We'll wait in the kitchen."

"You two stay right where you are," the sisters commanded in unison. They looked at each other, then Shelley added, "This concerns you, too."

With identical expressions of caution, both men settled back into their places.

"Now," Shelley said. She looked at Ross. "The first thing I want to say is that I'm really sorry, Ross. I know I screwed up, and I have no excuse. I guess I...I just wasn't thinking. But I promise you, it won't happen again."

"You don't have to apologize, Shelley," he said kindly. "We're all just glad it wasn't worse."

Shelley's lower lip trembled, but she quickly composed herself. "Thanks, I appreciate that." She took a deep breath. "I guess the next thing we need to decide is what we're going to do from here, right?"

"What do you mean, where we're going to go from here?" Gene asked. Suddenly, the decision seemed crystal clear. No matter how much it hurt, she wasn't going to ride Achilles anymore. She couldn't take the horse from Shelley; it would cause too great a schism in their relationship. And she knew if she kept working the horse until Shelley recovered, she wouldn't be able to give him back. So she said steadily, "I know you're not going to like this, Shelley, but since you won't be able to ride for some time yet, I think the logical thing for Ross and James to do is to find another rider—"

As she'd expected, Shelley instantly objected. "Oh, no, it's not! Now, listen to me, everyone. I've thought about this a lot. The season is coming up too fast to find another rider who can ride Achilles as well as Gene can—"

Gene saw where this was going. "That's not true. There are dozens of good riders around who would give their eye teeth for a chance to ride a horse like that. All you have to do is look."

"But we don't have to look, don't you see?" Shelley said. "We've got our rider right here in this room. Come on, Gene, you know you—"

Gene jumped up again. "Oh, no, you don't! I agreed to exercise the horse until you could ride again. I never agreed to compete him!"

Shelley looked at her. "But you want to, you know you do. And it won't be for the entire season, because I'll be able to ride long before it ends. Oh, please, Gene! There's a perfect opportunity coming up. It's only a small local competition, but it will give you a chance to see—"

Gene couldn't listen to this; it was too tempting. Resisting the impulse to put her hands over her ears, she said, "No, I told you. I mean it, Shelley. Don't ask me. I won't do it."

"Why are you acting like this?" Shelley demanded. "I know it's not because you're afraid!"

Yes, I am, Gene thought suddenly. *I'm afraid that if I actually compete Achilles once, I'll never be able to give him up.* Already, she could feel the pull of competition, the urge to see how well she and Achilles could do in an actual contest. She wanted to do it so badly she could practically taste it. That's why she couldn't.

"Please, Gene," Shelley said. For help, she turned to the silent Ross. "You agree, don't you, Ross? You want Gene to ride, I know you do. Look at the publicity you're already getting—and that was just from the horse trials. Yes, I saw the picture in the paper, and yes, I admit I was jealous—but that's past now. I only want what's best for the horse, I swear. And it won't be forever, you know. I'll coddle this leg so much it will heal in half the time, and then I'll take over from there. Please say yes, Ross! It's the perfect solution, and we all know it."

Ross looked quickly at Gene, who just as quickly looked away again. She was torn by so many conflicting emotions that she didn't know what she wanted him to say.

"I don't know, Shelley," he said, stalling for time. He glanced at Gene again. "If Gene doesn't want to ride, I don't see how—"

Shelley turned frantically to Gene again. "You know what a great horse Achilles can be, given the chance," she pleaded. "If he misses out of the start of the season, he might never catch up, and it will be so unfair! You know what he's capable of as much as I do. Maybe even more than I do. How can you step aside and watch another rider compete him? What if he's ruined? Gene, you know how I feel about Achilles! I don't want anyone else to have him!"

What about me? Gene wondered, as she stared at her sister. *Would you want me to have him?*

But she didn't say it. She couldn't. And since she couldn't think of a way to deny what Shelley had just said, she looked dully at Ross. "What do you say?"

Ross didn't answer for a moment. He seemed to be struggling with his own inner demons. Finally, he shook his head and said, "It's up to you."

Shelley seized the moment. "Oh, thank you, Ross. I knew you'd agree!" She turned to Gene again. "Come on, sis. What do you say? Please . . . for me?"

Gene looked at Shelley, who was gazing at her so expectantly, and then at Ross, who had so much riding on this, and felt trapped. *They didn't know what they were asking,* she thought, agonized. They were depending on her to pull them through. . . .

And then?

"What do you say, Gene?" Shelley breathed.

Gene couldn't refuse her any longer. She would just have to deal with the situation when it came around, she thought, and took a deep breath. "All right, I'll do it—for now. But—"

Shelley was up and out of the chair before Gene had a chance to finish. Hobbling forward a step without her crutches, she threw her arms around Gene's neck. "Oh, thank you, thank you, you won't regret it!" she said. "You're the best sister in the world. I'll never forget it!"

Kenny was standing right behind Shelley, waiting to catch her if she fell. Ross was still sitting on the couch. Gene scanned both their faces to see whether they had somehow seen through her. If they had, she couldn't tell. Quickly, she looked away and gave Shelley a hug in return.

It will work out, she told herself shakily. *It has to . . . for all our sakes.*

CHAPTER THIRTEEN

IF GENE COULD HAVE, she would have seen Ross every day over the following weeks. Unfortunately, they were both so busy during the days leading up to Achilles's first competition that she had to settle for the times their schedules meshed. Ironically, her newspaper interview caused such a sensation that Outdoor Outfitters was working overtime to fill orders, while she was spending so many extra hours riding, she often had to go back to the office at night. But she and Ross did meet for dinner regularly, and better yet, they even managed to sneak some blissful evenings at her place, where they forgot about eating in favor of other pleasures.

One evening in particular stood out in her memory. It was the night the *Tribune* article appeared about her and Achilles. Ross brought champagne, flowers and about a dozen copies of the newspaper to her house. They sat together on the living-room couch to read the interview, which took up nearly two pages in the sports section.

Gene had insisted that Shelley be included in the article. So, in addition to pictures of Gene holding the horse, Gene on the horse and Gene and the horse taking a jump, there was a comical photo of both her and Shelley giving the long-suffering Achilles a bath. She laughed when she saw that, but then her smile faltered when she saw the article's headline, which read: Former Champion Rider Denies Comeback Attempt.

"Well, Jerry Fazey kept his promise...I guess," she said. "I told him we had to be clear about the fact that my riding Achilles was only temporary. I wanted it in writing that this comeback idea was just that—an idea."

Ross reread the headline. "I'm not sure he's done that, but I guess we could say that he kept to the literal truth. Still, with these pictures... What did Shelley say?"

Gene had spoken to her sister before Ross arrived and had been relieved that Shelley didn't seem angry about the ambiguity of the article. In fact, she thought, Shelley had been more accommodating than she might have been if the circumstances were reversed.

"Shelley knows that things get exaggerated in the paper," she said. "But she couldn't argue that at least I had tried to make the situation clear."

"And you tried to include her. That picture of you and Shelley giving the horse a bath proves it."

"I know. But still..."

"The article did mention that until she broke her leg, she was Achilles's rider."

"That's true. But she feels left out, and I can't blame her." Gene took a sip of the excellent champagne. "She was happy about a couple of things, though. One is the publicity that Outdoor Outfitters is getting because of the article."

"We're happy about that, too. It's amazing. We've had several dozen calls inquiring about the company and the products we sell. What Malcolm will do remains to be seen, but the publicity campaign is obviously working." He touched his glass to hers in salute. "Thanks to you."

"All I did was talk to the reporter."

"You did more than that. If you weren't so—"

"If you say 'charismatic,' I'm going to pour this champagne over your head." She hadn't cared for the slant the article had taken; it made her sound like Elizabeth Taylor in *National Velvet*. But older, she thought, in sudden amusement, and had to smile.

"What's funny?"

"Oh, nothing. I'm just glad that Shelley wasn't upset."

Ross put his arm around her and drew her close. His lips in her hair, he murmured, "What else did she say?"

Gene had trouble concentrating when they were this close. As she nestled by his side, she closed her eyes, enjoying the feel of his body next to hers. He always shaved before he came over, and a faint aroma of his after-shave still clung to him, fresh and spicy, making her want to breathe in deeper. She loved the way he smelled.

"What's that?" she murmured. "Oh, Shelley... right. Well, she was also pleased about the publicity push this gives eventing." Gene sat up a little so she could keep her mind on the conversation. "We all know that the big stars of the horse world are the racing Thoroughbreds, of course. And then, maybe the show jumpers. It's difficult for eventing horses and riders to get much notice. I don't know why. What they do is just as spectacular as racing and jumping, don't you think?''

Ross had made it clear that he didn't want to think about that. Since they'd become involved, he didn't like to discuss the spectacular part of eventing at all. In fact, recently he'd made several comments about how dangerous cross-country was. Gene was touched by his concern, so she hadn't told him the eventing rider's motto: No guts, no glory. She doubted that would offer any comfort.

They hadn't discussed eventing that particular night, either, she remembered. In fact, they hadn't talked much more about the article at all. They sat close together, arms around each other, finishing their champagne. Then, the newspaper scattering to the floor, they went upstairs, where they began another discussion, one infinitely more satisfying.

Gene couldn't remember ever being so happy. Ross was perfect as a companion, he was intelligent, amusing and generous with his emotions as well as his time. As a lover, he was that rare kind of man who was just as interested in her pleasure as he was in his own. Maybe more interested, she thought luxuriously, as she fell asleep much later that night, his arms around her.

ON THE MORNING of her first competition with Achilles, Gene's perfect lover was silent as they drove together to Bellweather Farm, just outside San Diego, where the meet was being held. Gene was nervous about the upcoming contest; even though she had put as much spare time into riding as she possibly could, she was having last-minute doubts. Maybe she wasn't ready for competition.... Maybe Achilles wasn't...

Maybe it was too soon for both of them. Ross's pensive mood didn't improve matters. She had counted on him to help her quell all the butterflies vaulting around her stomach. But he just sat there, stolidly keeping his eyes on the road.

"What's the matter?" she finally asked. "You haven't said a thing since we got into the car. Is something wrong?"

He shook his head. "It's just early, I guess."

"It's not that early. Come on, Ross. I know you better than that. Has something happened that you don't want to tell me?" She had a sudden thought. "Are you having problems at the office? Isn't the publicity working?"

"Oh, the publicity is working just great. We've seen another upsurge in sales since that second article appeared."

True to his word, Jerry Fazey had assigned a sportswriter to do a follow-up article on Gene and Achilles. It had been published yesterday, along with another flattering photo. Gene had been satisfied to see that the two dreaded "C" words—comeback and charisma—had been omitted from the brief article. Instead, the caption had simply read: Gene Logan and Achilles, the duo sponsored by Outdoor Outfitters, prepare for weekend event.

"Then, what?" she asked Ross, reaching for his hand. She noticed that his fingers, usually so warm and comforting, felt cold this morning, and she looked at him again. "Something *is* wrong," she said. "Are you sick?"

"No, I'm fine. It's nothing. I mean...it's stupid. Forget it."

"How can I forget it? If something's wrong, you have to tell me. How am I supposed to concentrate if I'm worried about you?"

He sighed. "All right, then, if you must know—I'm the one who's worried, all right? That's all it is. I'm just concerned about you."

She was touched by his concern, but she said, "Ross, we've talked about this before. I've told you, everything is going to be fine."

He erupted so suddenly that she jumped. "How can you be so sure? Here you are, about to risk life and limb on a horse that *I* bought—and for what? So that we can sell a few more sleeping bags? So that Roo'sters will allow us to stock their all-weather gear?" He shook his head. "I don't know, Gene. The more I think about it, the more I'm sure this is the craziest idea we ever had. What do James and I know about sponsoring horses, anyway?"

Gene started smiling halfway through his diatribe. Long before he reached the end, she was trying not to laugh. She knew he was worried about her, but if that's all it was, she could deal with it. For a while, she'd thought it was something *serious*.

"I appreciate your concern, Ross, but don't you think you're overreacting...just a little?" she asked. "After all, Achilles and I have been working very hard these past few weeks to be a team. And it's not as if we'll be competing over our heads. We're still in the baby-novice class. It'll be a piece of cake."

"Yeah, right," he muttered, clearly unconvinced. "You can say what you want, but I can't help how I feel. What if something happens?"

"What if something does? We can't take all risk out of life. It would be so boring that way, don't you think?"

"No, I don't. And at this point, I'll take boring over sheer terror any day."

She laughed. "You don't mean that."

"Oh, yes, I do."

"I know you don't. Come on, let's change the subject. If you're not careful, you'll make me too scared to ride, and I'm nervous enough already."

He gave her a wildly skeptical look. "You, nervous? Don't make me laugh. You haven't got an anxious bone in your body."

If you only knew! she thought. But she couldn't say just how apprehensive she felt about the upcoming competition, or he'd be even more disturbed. So she said lightly, "Then I'm a good cover-up artist, I guess."

Obviously eager to change the subject himself, Ross said, "Speaking of artists, how's work going? You haven't mentioned the new line in a while."

Work wasn't the topic she would have chosen to discuss, but she was glad to have something else to talk about, so she said, "At this point, I'm not sure there's going to be a new line. I'm still having trouble finding the right illustrator. No one seems to have the same concept I do."

"Then why don't you do it yourself?"

"Me? I'm no artist!"

"Oh, yes, you are. And you have a wall full of pictures to prove it."

"Those aren't pictures, they're caricatures."

"It's the same idea."

"It's not the same thing at all!"

"Tell me what makes it different?"

"Well, for one thing, I don't have any training—"

"So, you're a natural talent. What's wrong with that?"

She started to laugh, until she saw his face. "You're serious!"

"Hell, yes, I'm serious. I've seen your work. It's good, Gene. Better than you obviously believe. I think that if you wanted to, you could do a line of cards yourself."

"That's absurd!"

"Why? I've seen some of those card lines at the store. A five-year-old could draw better. Very few are as clever as the ones you've done. Just think of it."

She didn't want to think of it. The whole idea was too silly. "Ross—"

He didn't listen. His enthusiasm growing, he said, "You could start an entire new career with horse-based caricatures. You could call it, 'From the horse's mouth,' something like that. What do you think?"

"I'm flattered, Ross," she said. "But I couldn't draw for a living. The caricatures relax me. I'm just playing around when I do them."

"Like you're playing around with this?"

They were almost at Bellweather Farm. Signs lining the road directed them where to go, and when he gestured toward the activity, she immediately felt defensive.

"I don't know what you mean."

"I think you do."

"No, I don't," she insisted.

"Let me make it clear, then," he said. "Are you just playing around with this riding business, or are you starting to take it seriously?"

"Why are you asking me this now?" she parried. "What difference does it make? It won't be that much longer before Shelley is able to ride. Then the question will be academic."

"I wonder."

Her voice rose. "What does *that* mean?"

He glanced at her. "Hey, I didn't mean to make you angry."

She was angry. "Then don't talk about things that don't make any sense!"

Surprised by her tone, he said, "Gene—"

"Never mind," she said childishly. "I don't want to talk about it anymore."

His jaw tightened. "Okay, fine. We won't."

She didn't reply. She didn't want to admit that his questions had been much too close to the mark, but in any case, she didn't want to think about it right now. She needed all her concentration for the three phases of the upcoming competition or she'd make a fool of herself.

And then what would the paper say? she asked herself angrily. They'd get publicity all right, just the kind Ross didn't need. How would he feel about *that?*

They reached the parking lot, and as Ross stopped the car, he turned to her. "I'm sorry, Gene. I really didn't mean to upset you. I know you're doing this for James and me, and I appreciate it."

He sounded so contrite that she couldn't be angry. Besides, she thought, she didn't want to fight with him anyway—not now, or ever.

"I'm sorry, too," she said. "I guess I'm on edge. Maybe I'm a little more nervous about this than I thought."

"I understand." He hesitated. "I'm just as nervous. In fact, I'm downright terrified." He leaned awkwardly across the console and kissed her cheek. "Now let's go find the others."

He started to get out of the car, but she held him back. It cost her, but she had to say it. "Ross, are you really worried? Because if you are, I...I won't do this."

When he didn't answer right away, she was afraid that he'd take her up on it. She was wondering what she'd say if he did, when he said lightly, "I *am* worried, but that's my right, isn't it? After all, you mean a lot to me. Still, as much as I'd like to at times, I know I can't wrap you in cotton. I do want you to do this. I know it means a lot to you, too, so go out and give it your best. Now, come on, your horse is waiting."

Gene wanted to believe he meant what he said, but she was troubled when they went to find the others. She noticed that Ross's limp suddenly seemed more pronounced, and the thought that she was the cause made her feel even worse. She slipped her hand in his. He looked at her and asked, "Still got those butterflies?"

She tried to smile. "No, those flew away long ago. They were replaced by vultures that are milling around, bumping into one another."

"You'll do just fine. In fact," he said, unable to suppress a sigh, "knowing you, you'll be the best." He smiled. "Where's your competitive spirit?"

She was about to tell him that she'd left it behind
when she saw Kenny's rig. It was too late to change her
mind, so she pasted another sickly smile on her face
and went to change. She'd already stashed her clothes
in the trailer's dressing room, and when she emerged
a few minutes later in the formal riding attire required for the dressage phase, the first event of the
competition, Ross whistled.

"Wow," he said. "You look great."

"I hate men whistling at me," she said as she
rubbed her cold hands together. "But thanks."

Shelley and Kenny were getting Achilles ready, and
Gene was pleased to see that the horse, at least, looked
relatively calm—or as calm as he ever looked. Even so,
Gene could feel him practically vibrating from excitement underneath her as she mounted, and she knew
that the hard part was just ahead. The dressage phase
was especially difficult for horses as physically fit as
eventers. When they wanted to run full-out, they were
required to be controlled and precise. A lot of competitions had been lost in the dressage arena because
the horses couldn't settle down enough to finish the
test, and Gene was determined that wasn't going to
happen to her and Achilles. She was adjusting the
reins when Ross approached.

He put a hand on her thigh. "I just wanted to wish
you good luck."

When she saw how anxious he looked, she leaned
down and gave him a quick kiss. "Don't worry," she
whispered. "There's not much that can happen in a
dressage arena."

His blue eyes turned dark. "It's not the dressage
part I'm worried about."

She straightened again. "Let's take it one phase at a time, all right?"

Before he could reply, Shelley came up with last-minute instructions. "Now remember what I said about..."

Gene had heard it all several times before, but she listened patiently, anyway. Despite her own conflicts about this, she sympathized with Shelley's frustration. The cast was scheduled to be removed—finally!—in just a short while, and Gene knew that to be so close and yet so far away for Achilles's first meet was difficult for Shelley. She couldn't think ahead to the day her sister got the go-ahead to ride from her doctor. She'd decided she would just have to deal with it somehow. So she just nodded until Shelley had finished recounting all the possible pitfalls she was likely to encounter, then she looked over at Kenny. Shelley might have appointed herself official instructor, but he was still the trainer.

"Any last-minute advice?" she asked.

Kenny obviously had more confidence in her ability than Shelley did. "If you don't know it now, it's too late to go over it," he said. "Just watch the shoulder-out. He likes to cheat on it."

"Got it," she said. "Well, I guess we're ready. Here goes."

DESPITE HER TREPIDATIONS, Gene and Achilles got through the dressage test in fairly good order. They even managed to get a decent score. Shelley was thrilled that they performed so well, and Gene was delighted that what she considered the hardest part was over. With his explosive energy, Achilles was better suited for the next two events, the cross-country in the afternoon, and the stadium jumping the following day.

As Gene changed out of her formal attire into the more casual breeches and polo shirt she'd wear for the next phase, she was humming. All her hard work with Achilles these past few weeks was paying off, she thought. She was so proud of her horse, and she couldn't wait to see how well he performed next. Like the other riders, she had walked the cross-country course before the competition started to memorize the problem areas and the best approaches to the jumps. Her nervousness had been replaced by excitement, and she was looking forward to meeting the challenge head-on.

Ross seemed more at ease, too. He laughed and joked with everyone over the picnic lunch they'd brought, and only started to look anxious again when he realized Gene had only picked at her food.

"Aren't you hungry?" he asked, when Shelley and Kenny went over to the trailer to check on Achilles. He gestured at her almost-full paper plate. "You only had half a sandwich, if that."

"I don't like to ride on a full stomach," she said. "But don't worry, tonight I'll make up for it. I'll eat enough to feed an army."

He gave her delicate frame a skeptical look. "Somehow, I doubt that."

"Oh, really?" she said archly. "Well, you're taking us all out to dinner tonight, aren't you? All I can say is, you'd better have your wallet handy."

"That's James's department. Since he couldn't be here this morning, he agreed to spring for dinner."

"You'd better give him advance warning, then," she said, her eyes twinkling. She pushed her plate toward him. "In the meantime, help yourself. I don't want it to go to waste."

"Don't mind if I do," he said, picking up the other half of her sandwich. "I've got to store up extra energy for all the work I have to do this afternoon."

"What work are *you* going to do?"

He winked at her. "Cheering, of course."

She laughed, pleased that the tension that had sprung up between them this morning was gone. She was even happier to see how relaxed he was, now that the competition had started. A few minutes later, they walked arm in arm over to Achilles, and then, soon after that, it was time to saddle up again. She was giving the girth a last tug to make sure it was tight enough when she sensed someone behind her. Before she could turn around, Ross had put his arms around her and kissed her.

"What was that for?" she gasped when they finally broke apart.

"What do you think? Good luck, of course."

She put a hand to her chest. "Many more like that, and I won't have strength enough to get on the horse."

"In that case—"

He reached for her again, but she slipped away from him. "Don't you dare!"

"I was only trying to help."

"If you want to help, you can give me a leg up—but that's all," she warned. "No hanky-panky. At least," she added slyly, "until tonight."

He reached for her bent leg and tossed her lightly into the saddle. "I'll hold you to that."

She grinned down at him. "I'll look forward to it."

A few minutes later, to a host of well-wishes that followed her, she headed toward the starting line. She was the third to go in her group, and as she waited for the signal, she could feel Achilles's eagerness to get going. He tossed his head and danced under her, and she put a calming hand on his neck.

"Don't worry, you'll get your turn," she promised. He snorted in answer, and then it was time to go. She'd barely put her heel into him before he leapt ahead, and they were off.

The first part of the course wound through some trees. The wavering shadows cast by the afternoon sun were disorienting and Gene was alert in case Achilles tried to run out on her. But, more like a seasoned trouper than a novice, the horse took it in stride, tearing through the wooded area until they reached the first jump. When Achilles took it with almost contemptuous ease, Gene was sure she could hear Shelley screaming with excitement in the background. She might have shouted with joy herself, except that she knew she had a drop jump coming up over the next hill.

After all Kenny's training, Gene knew the drill. So did Achilles, by this time. They took the drop in perfect form, Achilles jumping forward and downward, Gene leaning back and balancing his head on a long rein. They seemed to be in the air forever, but then she felt the thud of his two front feet, and knew they were safely down. She was just looking ahead to the next jump, when it happened.

Achilles stumbled. The next thing she knew, the world had turned upside down. As if in slow motion, they turned a somersault, and when momentum separated them, her only thought was that Achilles was going to break his neck. She was just opening her mouth to cry out when everything went black.

"GENE, Gene! Can you hear me? Can you hear me? Oh, please God, say something!"

Gene heard Ross's voice from far away. Confused for a moment, she wondered what he was doing at the end of a tunnel. She tried to open her eyes, but the glare was too bright. Where was she? What had happened? Why was everyone shouting—and what was all that shaking? Were they having an earthquake?

Then, she realized someone was shaking her shoulder, and everything came back to her in a rush. This time when she opened her eyes, she saw Kenny and Shelley and Ross staring down at her. She grabbed Ross's hand. Her mouth was full of something—it tasted like dirt. She spat it out and said hoarsely, "The horse. Is Achilles all right?"

"He's fine," Ross said, his face drawn and white. "How do you feel?"

She tried to sit up again, but he held her back. "Don't move," he ordered. "The paramedics are coming."

She looked up at him. "Did I break something?"

"I don't think so, but we want to make sure. Does it hurt anywhere?"

Experimentally, she tried to move her arms and legs. They seemed to work. At least she could feel fingers and toes and everything in between. "I'm okay," she said. "I want to sit up."

"I think you should wait," Shelley said anxiously.

"I don't." She was feeling a little sick, and she thought sitting up would make her feel better. She held out a hand. "Here, help me, will you?"

Ross reluctantly helped her to a sitting position. The world tilted a little, but when it settled back again, she announced, "I'm going to stand up."

"Oh, Gene, I don't think you should," Kenny said.

"I'm okay—honest."

"But you blacked out," Ross said worriedly. "You could have a concussion."

"I don't have a concussion," she said. "I don't even have a headache. I'm *fine*." She looked at Shelley. "Find out if I can have permission to finish the course."

"Finish the course!" Ross exclaimed. "Are you out of your mind?"

She scrambled to her feet. "I'm not going to let a little fall stop me," she said. This time when the world stayed where it was supposed to, she knew she was definitely all right. "Don't *worry* so much. I'll be all right."

His expression fierce, Ross got to his feet, too. "I'll say you will. You're going to go to the hospital right now and be thoroughly checked out."

"Oh, no, I'm not!"

"Oh, yes, you are!"

She wasn't going to stand here arguing about it. While she'd been lying on the ground, the competition had gone on, and she wanted at least to finish the course before it was too late. She also wanted to check Achilles herself to make sure he was all right. *Brave horse!* she thought. It hadn't been his fault that they'd gone down. It was just a misstep that could have happened to anyone.

"Where's Achilles?" she asked.

"He's over there," Shelley said, pointing to a clump of trees. Gene looked that way, too, and was relieved when she saw that distinctive white coat. "The vet's already checked him," Shelley added. "Aside from a little cut on his nose, he's okay."

"Thank the Lord." She started toward him and, over her shoulder, she said, "I'm going to check him out myself, and if he's okay to go on, we're going to complete the course. I'll meet you all at the finish line."

"Gene, you can't do this," Ross said sharply. "I won't let you."

She stopped. Slowly, she turned. Her eyes were very green. "I beg your pardon?" she said.

He flushed, but held his ground. "I'm sorry, I didn't mean to put it so baldly. But I'm responsible for you and the horse, and I can't let you continue until you've been examined by a doctor."

She couldn't believe he was doing this. With a mighty effort, she held on to her temper. She didn't want to waste any more time.

"Fine," she said between her teeth. "If it's so important to you, I'll do it later. Right now, I'm going to finish what I started."

And, after quickly conferring with the vet to make sure that Achilles was fit, that's exactly what she did.

ROSS WAS WAITING for her at the finish line. Shelley and Kenny were there, too. So was James, who had arrived in the interim and had obviously been filled in on the situation. Gene saw James's anxious expression and smiled to reassure him, but it was Ross she was most concerned about. When she saw him pacing, his limp even more conspicuous than his thunderous expression, she knew she had a lot of explaining to do. Quickly, she checked out with the officials and handed Achilles's reins to Kenny, who had volunteered in a low voice to cool the horse down. Then she went to face Ross. He was so angry, he immediately grabbed her arm and pulled her to one side.

"Are you satisfied now?" he demanded, his voice shaking with fury.

Gene hadn't expected congratulations for finishing, but she hadn't anticipated Ross's towering rage, either. His eyes looked almost black as he glared at her. She didn't like his expression, and she could feel herself getting angry in self-defense.

"Yes, as a matter of fact, I am," she said. "I see that you could care less right now, but just in case you're interested at a later date, Achilles was wonderful on the rest of the course. He's going to make a great eventing horse."

Ross could hardly get the words out. "Right now, I don't give a damn if he could be champion of the world. What in the bloody *hell* were you thinking about?"

"Well, I wasn't thinking about winning—not this time, at least. But next time—"

"There isn't going to be a next time!"

She thought she hadn't heard right. "What?"

"You heard me!"

"No, I didn't. I can't believe you said that. What do you mean? Are you telling me I can't ride the horse?"

"Not if you're going to risk your life to do it!"

This was ridiculous. Beginning to get really angry, she said, "I told you, I felt fine!"

"For God's sake, *you blacked out!*"

"So what? Aren't I the best judge of whether I'm all right, or not?"

"No, you aren't. And I think you proved that."

She suddenly realized they were shouting. After a quick glance around, she lowered her voice and said icily, "I don't know what's gotten into you, Ross, but if you can't conduct a reasonable conversation, then we're not going to discuss this at all."

"Oh, yes, we are!" he declared as she started off. He reached out and grabbed her arm. "You're not going to run off this time. We're going to settle it once and for all."

She wasn't going to engage in a stupid struggle to free herself. Coldly, she said, "It *is* settled. We agreed that I was going to ride the horse, and I'm going to hold you to that agreement."

He looked at her as though he'd never seen her before. And maybe he hadn't, she thought defiantly. That spill out on the course had jolted a lot of things into place for her. She'd tried to hide the knowledge from herself, but there was no denying it now. She wanted to see this through. She wanted to win with Achilles . . . in fact, she wanted to take him as far as they could go.

She knew how Shelley felt about the horse, but there would be other horses for her sister. Achilles was hers now, and no one was going to take him from her.

She looked at Ross. "This conversation is over," she said. "I've got a horse to see to."

"Oh, no, you don't." If possible, he looked even more furious with her. "I don't care what kind of agreement you think we had. You're not going to ride Achilles anymore. I forbid it."

"You *forbid* it?"

"Yes, I do. *I* decide who rides that horse, and since you're not going to listen to reason, it's not going to be you."

She stared at him incredulously, only vaguely aware that James and Shelley had joined them. She didn't even glance their way. Her voice shaking with rage and disbelief, she said to Ross, "You don't mean that!"

"Indeed, I do." His eyes were like ice, as cold and implacable as his voice. "If you won't agree to quit, then Outdoor Outfitters is no longer going to support the horse."

James heard that last, and he gasped. "Ross, what are you saying?"

Ross barely glanced at him. "Stay out of this, James. This is between Gene and me."

"Oh, no, it's not!" Shelley cried. "What about me?"

"Shut up, Shelley," Gene said tightly. She stared at Ross as she said, "You wouldn't do that. What about all this great publicity?"

"I don't give a damn about the publicity. I'm trying to protect you."

"Protect me!" Her face turned crimson. "What kind of paternalistic garbage is that? I don't want your protection! What gives you the right?"

"I love you, Gene. That's what gives me the right."

She looked at him in sheer disbelief. "You know, I think you really believe that. Well, here's a news flash for you, Mr. Ross Malone! Just because you think you love me doesn't mean you can dictate how I live my life. You don't own me! You can't tell me what I can or can't do!"

"Oh, yes, I can. I can tell you that you're not going to ride my horse!"

She was too angry to think it through.

"Fine. Then sell Achilles to me."

"Wait a minute!" Shelley cried. She looked in horror at Gene. "Gene, what are you saying? You can't do this!"

"Shelley's right," James chimed in. He looked pleadingly at Ross. "Ross, wait a minute. Think of all our plans. Think of the publicity we've gotten. Think of—"

"Be quiet!" Ross said tersely. He didn't take his eyes off Gene as he said, "The horse is not for sale."

Gene held his glance. "Everything is for sale. Go ahead. Name your price."

"Ross!" James shouted.

"Gene!" Shelley cried.

They didn't hear. Locked in a contest of wills, they were oblivious to anything else.

"Either you sell me that horse," Gene said tightly, "or we never see each other again."

Ross didn't hesitate. "I won't be threatened, Gene."

She looked straight at him. "Neither will I."

"Oh, Lord," James moaned.

"Gene, I can't believe you're doing this!" Shelley cried.

Gene couldn't believe it, either. But it was too late now. She and Ross had both said too much. Just as bad, she had betrayed her sister—and James, and even

Kenny. What was she doing? she asked herself. Was it worth it?

Yes, it was, she thought. It was time to stop worrying about everyone else and think what *she* wanted. They were all staring at her with surprise and disbelief and—in Ross's case, helpless rage—but she didn't care. She'd work it out somehow, she vowed. She'd find another horse; she'd do what she should have done long ago. *Because one thing was for sure,* she thought fiercely. *No one was going to stop her now.*

Her head high, she left without another word. A few minutes later, she called a cab and went home... alone.

CHAPTER FOURTEEN

"IT'S YOUR FAULT, you know," Marilyn said to Ross one night at a restaurant where they'd met for dinner.

When his ex-wife had called him that afternoon, apparently out of the blue, to ask if he was free for dinner, Ross had been so surprised that he had agreed to go. At the time, he'd thought that anything was better than going home to an empty apartment, as he had been doing for the past two weeks. Now he wasn't so sure.

Marilyn had let it slip over cocktails that James had called and asked for her help. It seemed that his partner had also told her all about the fiasco at the three-day event—was it only two weeks ago? he wondered, distracted. It seemed a lifetime since he and Gene had quarreled. It was bad enough that they had done it in public, but a few days later they'd had another sharp exchange when, fool that he was, he'd called to apologize. Her voice cold, she had asked him if he had changed his mind either about her riding, or about selling her the horse. When he had replied negatively to both, she had said goodbye and hung up.

"Did you hear what I said, Ross?" Marilyn asked, breaking into his dire thoughts. "Or are you just choosing to ignore it?"

Deciding that he'd speak to James in the morning, he glared at her over the steak he'd ordered. "I heard you. You said this whole thing was my fault. I don't agree, but just how do you figure that?"

Calmly, she speared a little piece of her salmon with her fork. "As I understand it, you're the one who had a fight with this Gene person. James said that everything was fine until—"

"James talks too much," he said flatly. He reached for his wine. "The proof is that he brought you into this."

"Now, Ross. James is just concerned."

"And I'm not? As the saying goes, 'We're rapidly going to hell in a hand basket.'"

"But you could stop that slide, couldn't you, darling?" Marilyn said sweetly. "According to James, all you have to do is apologize."

Ross glowered again. His busybody partner and interfering ex-wife apparently didn't know everything. He'd already tried that. "James doesn't know what he's talking about. And, if you'll excuse my being blunt, neither do you." She was right, and he knew it. But he still didn't like her meddling, and he told her so. "If you don't mind, I'll handle this my own way, thank you."

"Fine." She took another bite of salmon. "I just hope you handle it better than I did."

Her oblique remarks had always annoyed him when they were married. He realized that they still irritated the hell out of him. "And just what does that mean?"

"Well, darling, you have to admit, I didn't handle things well at all where you were concerned. That's why we're divorced."

"That's not the only reason." He knew he was going to regret it, but he added, "Go on."

"There's nothing to go on with. You realize, of course, that I don't know the whole story—"

"Neither does James, no matter what he thinks."

"You're right. Only the people involved know what really happens in a relationship, and sometimes even then one of them is in the dark." She sighed. "When I look back on our situation, I wonder at times if we'd still be married if I'd done things differently."

"You keep saying that," he said impatiently. "Why don't you explain what you mean?"

"All right, I will. You know, it sounds like you and this Gene person are a lot alike."

"Stop calling her 'this Gene person,'" he said irritably. "Her name is Gene, and we're nothing alike."

"All right...*Gene*. And of course, you're alike. You don't want her to ride that horse because you think it's too dangerous. But you wanted to race those cars when they scared me to death."

"It's not the same thing."

"Oh, but it is. The difference is that I learned the hard way that you can't protect someone by forbidding them to do what they love. Don't you remember how I begged you, how I *pleaded* with you not to race because it was so dangerous?" She paused. "Don't you remember what you used to say to me?"

He looked away. "No, I don't."

"I do. You said that you cared about my feelings, but you couldn't give up racing, even for me. You asked me to understand. And when I couldn't—"

He said dully, "You divorced me."

She put a hand on his arm. "Not because I wanted to, darling. Because I *had* to. I knew you loved me, but you loved what you were doing even more."

"That's not true." He put his hand over hers. "I did love it, but in a different way."

"I know that now. I didn't know it then, so I did the only thing I could to protect myself. I got out." She smiled sadly. "I've since learned that some people are different, Ross."

"Different? What do you mean?"

"I mean that people like you and Gene have talents and abilities that the rest of us lack. Don't you see? You're the stars in our lives, the people who dare, who inspire. The ones who do the things we can only dream about."

"I was only a race car driver," he said. "Anyone can do that."

"Not true. And you were more than that, anyway." She looked into his eyes. "And so, I think, is Gene Logan."

Ross thought of Gene and Achilles and the picture they made. The image he had in his mind was one of them soaring over some impossible jump, both in perfect form, already looking ahead to the next challenge. He knew that Marilyn was right. Gene *was* a star, one who inspired, one who gave everyone in her sport—and those who could only watch from the sidelines—something to aim for. He'd always known that. He just hadn't wanted to accept it. Because he knew that if he admitted it, he also had to acknowledge that there was nothing he could do to protect her. When she was out there on that cross-country course, danger was all around.

"You feel about Gene the way I used to feel about you," Marilyn said softly. "I can see it in your face."

He turned helplessly to her. It was useless to deny it; she knew him too well. "What should I do?"

All her hard-won wisdom was in her wistful smile. "I can't speak for you," she said. "But think of this. I know you're worried about Gene getting hurt. I was worried about you, too. But I was also terrified that you'd leave me one day."

"Leave you?"

"Oh, not in the way you think, not by walking out or getting involved with someone else. I mean, in your mind. People like you and Gene go where the rest of us can't follow. But even though...even though *you* can no longer do what you used to do, Gene will never leave you behind. Don't you see, Ross? You're one of the special people, just like she is. She can't leave you, because you've been there. Like her, you *know* what it's like."

The words were out before he could stop them. "Maybe that's why I'm so scared for her, and for me, too."

Her fingers tightened sympathetically on his arm. "I know," she said. "But don't you see, darling? You, of all people, understand what drives her to be the best. And if taking chances, or putting herself in danger, is part of that drive, she accepts it—just like you did when you were racing. Just like you'll have to, if you want to be with her." She shook her head in regret. "I couldn't do it for you, Ross. I've always been sorry for that. But if you want to, you can do it for her."

"I don't know, Marilyn—"

"I do. Because you and she *are* alike. You understand each other." She paused one last time. "All you have to do is let yourself see that, too."

GENE WAITED two weeks before she called Shelley. She'd planned to do it sooner but then she'd had another bitter exchange with Ross and she'd needed time to cool down. He said he'd called to apologize, but when she asked him if he'd changed his mind about her riding Achilles, or buying the horse outright, and he said no, she knew there was nothing more to say.

He just doesn't understand, she thought angrily. And if he didn't realize how much this meant to her, it was obvious that he didn't know her at all. So there was no point in trying to mend a relationship that seemed to have been doomed from the beginning. Somehow, she'd just have to forget him and go on.

But she couldn't forget her sister. They hadn't spoken since that awful day at Bellweather Farm, and she hated the angry silence between them. Also, she had to admit she wanted to know how Achilles was. After these past few months of intense training, she missed riding. But she missed that big white horse even more.

"Well, well," Shelley said. "It's been a while since I've heard from *you.*"

"Yes, well, we didn't exactly leave on the best of terms, did we?"

"And whose fault was that?"

Gene knew she deserved this, but it was still a little hard to take. "Mine. I admit it. I guess I got a little carried away."

"A little?"

"Look, I'm sorry."

"You should be. You know, Gene, the only reason I asked you to ride in the first place was because we were family. I didn't dream that my own sister would betray me."

"I didn't *betray* you, Shelley."

"What do you call it, then? It looked to me like you couldn't wait to get your hands on my horse so you could steal him right out from under me."

"That's not how it happened. I know I handled things badly, and I'm sorry. That's why I called, to apologize."

Shelley was silent. Finally, she said, "Was that really the reason?"

"Yes. Don't you believe me?"

"Well, I thought you might be calling to gloat about what happened at the Pacific Three-Day Event this past weekend."

"I read about that in the paper. Did you ride?"

Shelley was silent again. "You really don't know?"

Something in Shelley's voice alarmed Gene. When she thought of all the horrible things that might have occurred, she said, "Don't tell me he fell again!"

"No, it wasn't that."

"What, then? Don't keep me in suspense, Shelley! Did something happen? Were either of you hurt?"

Again, Shelley hesitated. Finally she said, "All right, you might as well know. You'll probably find out, anyway. The truth is, he refused a jump three times." Her voice rose. "*Three* times! It was a simple brush wall, too, something you've taken him over a hundred—"

Shelley stopped, but not quickly enough. What she hadn't said vibrated between them. After another short silence, which Gene didn't know how to fill, Shelley said sullenly, "I bet it does your heart good to have me admit that the horse works better for you than he does for me."

"How can you say that, Shelley? I know I acted like a jerk, but I don't deserve that."

When Shelley answered, Gene could hear the tears in her voice. "I'm sorry, Gene. This is hard for me to say. I know you don't wish me ill, but do me a favor, will you? I really think it would be better if you didn't come to the stables for a bit."

Gene was silent for a while. When she finally spoke, her voice was strained as she tried to cover her feelings. "I think you're right, Shelley. Don't worry, I won't bother you. I guess after all that's happened, we both need time to get over it."

Carefully, she replaced the phone. She was sitting with her head in her hands when Wally came in.

"Trouble?" he asked sympathetically.

She didn't want to go into it now, so she shook her head and said, "No more than usual. I can handle it." She saw that Wally was carrying a sheaf of messages. "Are all those for me?"

"Every last one." He looked at her face. "Maybe you'd like to go over them later?"

"No, I might as well tackle them now."

He gave her the stack, but on his way out again, he paused. "Gene, are you all right?"

She'd started sorting through the memos. At his question, she began to say something flip to cut off any discussion. But then she saw the concern in his eyes, and said, instead, "Right now? As a matter of fact, I'm not. But I'll get over it."

Still, he hesitated. "Do you miss riding?"

Gene had briefly told him what had happened at the disastrous three-day event. "Sometimes I miss it," she said. "But then, I really don't have time to dwell on it. We've been so busy—"

To her horror, she suddenly felt close to tears. Quickly, she looked down so that Wally couldn't see her face. After a brief struggle, she was able to control her voice sufficiently to say, "Enough with the personal problems. We've got too much to do to get bogged down with all that."

Wally looked at her indecisively for a moment. "Okay, whatever you say. But remember, if you want to talk, I'm here."

"Thanks. Now, we'd better get back to work."

Gene intended to heed her own advice as Wally returned to his desk, but the memos he'd given her kept blurring before her eyes. Finally, she got up and closed her door. Then she sat down again, her hands over her face. She'd gone over it a million times in her mind, but she still couldn't get it right. Whenever she thought of Ross, she felt . . .

Well, what had she expected? she asked herself scathingly. Had she really thought he'd beg her forgiveness? That when he called, it would be to say he'd been wrong? Maybe she'd believed that he'd show up one day and ask ... no, *plead* for her to reconsider?

Oh, who was she kidding? She'd known he'd never do any of those things. She'd wanted him to say that he couldn't live without her, that he'd do anything, say anything, agree to anything she wanted, just as long as they continued to see each other, but what had he done?

He'd told her he hadn't changed his mind, that's what.

Her lips tight so she wouldn't break into sobs, she turned away from her desk and stared at the wall. *I hate Ross Malone,* she told herself. And on the heels of that thought, *No, I don't.*

How could she, when she hadn't done anything to patch things up between them, either? She hadn't called him. She hadn't asked to be forgiven for that scene at the three-day event. They were both at fault.

The situation should have been so simple, she thought mournfully. Instead it had become this Gordian knot. And now Shelley was competing Achilles. Until today, she had believed that somehow, she and Ross would work this out. She knew that he was trying to protect her, but damn it, she didn't need his protection. What she *needed,* since he was the owner of the horse, was his permission to ride Achilles.

It was too late. She had to forget all this and get on with her life. Resolutely, she turned around again. The untended memos on her desk met her eye and she had to fight an irrational impulse to sweep them all into the wastebasket and just walk out.

To what?

Now, *that* was a good question. After making her losing stand with Ross, she had vowed that, since he wouldn't sell Achilles to her, she'd go out and buy her own horse. But she hadn't even started to look at prospects. The truth was, she wasn't interested in another mount. Achilles was the only horse she wanted. She might as well admit it.

As soon as you saw Achilles, you thought High Cotton had come back to life....

Without warning, something her sister had said flashed into her mind, and she wondered if she really had subconsciously been trying to substitute one white horse for another. She'd been so devastated when High Cotton had died. When she'd first seen Achilles in his stall, looking so much like another white horse she'd lost too soon...

She closed her eyes. Maybe Shelley was right, she thought. Maybe she had been trying to revive a dream that had been destroyed the night her horse had died. She had denied it until now, but it could explain why she'd become so... obsessed. That was the only word for it, she knew, and she felt like a fool.

High Cotton is *gone,* she told herself. She couldn't recapture the past. It was an impossible, childish fantasy. And now, after everything that had happened, she couldn't even look to a future with Achilles. In her compulsion to fulfill a dream that had ended too soon, she had alienated almost everyone she knew—including Ross Malone. She couldn't blame him for standing firm. In his view, she had chosen Achilles over him. If he hadn't walked away, she wouldn't have respected him. But how could she ever make it up to him?

A tear slid down her cheek, and then another. She grabbed a tissue to stem the tide, but it was too late. The horse of her dreams, the man of her dreams—both had become so much a part of her. And both, she thought as the tears flowed freely, lost to her forever.

WITH HIS OFFICE DOOR closed, Ross sat behind his desk, staring at the printout of the latest sales figures he'd received moments ago. Try as he might, there was no other way to interpret them. Sales were down, and that's all there was to it. Disgusted, he shoved the offending pages away and reached for his coffee cup. Just then, someone knocked.

He didn't want to talk to anyone now, but since he couldn't pretend he wasn't here, he said tersely, "Come in."

James poked his head in. "Got a minute?"

"Yeah, sure," Ross said. He reflected sourly that if this downward trend continued, he'd soon have all the time in the world.

James entered and shut the door behind him. He was carrying a copy of the same sales printout Ross had been reviewing. "Have you seen these?"

Ross took a sip of his coffee. It was cold, and he set the cup down with a grimace. "I saw it."

"You know why these figures are down, don't you?"

Ross knew. Sales had dropped off as soon as the publicity surrounding Gene and Achilles had stopped. James had tried, but when Jerry Fazey found out that Gene was no longer riding the horse, he hadn't been interested in doing a story on Shelley. The paper hadn't even sent a photographer to cover the Pacific Three-Day-Event this past weekend.

Not that it would have mattered, Ross thought moodily. Shelley had ridden Achilles for the first time in public and had promptly been eliminated from the cross-country course after the horse had refused a jump three times. He was trying to be fair and not blame Shelley for something that probably wasn't her fault, but he couldn't help wondering how Gene would have handled it. A fall was one thing. A three-time stubborn refusal was something else.

And Ross knew what the problem was although he didn't want to admit it to James—and he certainly would never say anything to Shelley. The truth was that, try as she might, Shelley just didn't have the rapport with Achilles that Gene did. At first, Ross had thought it was because Gene had ridden the horse so much. He'd hoped that once Shelley had a chance to spend some time working him, things would even out. So far, it hadn't come about. Shelley was competent, no doubt about it. But even to Ross's untrained eye, Achilles seemed to be going through the motions with Shelley. The horse just didn't have the bond he'd had with Gene.

He tried to tell himself he was being ridiculous. After all, he scoffed, what difference did it make *who* rode the horse? But still, when Gene had been riding

Achilles, they'd had an aura that captured attention. Jerry Fazey had seen it; so had he, and anyone else who had watched rider and horse in action. And what about the customers who asked why Gene was no longer riding the horse? The phones had been ringing all week, people calling to find out what had happened to Gene.

"Well?" James said.

Ross focused on his partner again. "Don't start with me, James," he warned. "I'm not in the mood for it."

James took a seat opposite him, the printout on his lap. "We have to talk about it, Ross."

"We already have talked about it. I'm not going to change my mind."

"But if you just called Gene and apologized—"

"I told you before, I tried that, and it didn't work!" He slammed his fist down on the desk for emphasis. "And even if I tried again, what then? Are we going to pull Shelley off the horse and give him to Gene? Is that what you want?"

"I don't know what I want," James muttered. "God, what a mess!"

"Yes, well, we're just going to have to wait it out."

Apparently, that was too much for James. "We might not be *able* to wait it out." He waved the printout wildly. "You've seen this. You know what it means just as much as I do. When Gene was riding the horse, when the *Tribune* was writing about her, sales were climbing. Now we're right back where we started!"

"And that's my fault?"

James looked at him a moment, then obviously decided to lay all his cards on the table. "Isn't it?" he demanded as Ross stared at him in surprise. His face turned red, but he persisted. "You're the one who quarreled with her! You're the one who let this interfere with good business! If you're not the one to blame, I don't know who is!"

Ross turned a little red-faced, too. "And just what do you suggest?"

"I *told* you. You have influence with Gene—"

"Ha! She won't even speak to me now."

"You don't know that! You haven't really tried!"

"No, and I'm not going to! I told you, James, it's over between us—"

"This has nothing to do with *you!*" James shouted. "This is business! My God, I don't believe your ego!" He waved the printout again. "We're going down the tubes, and all you can think of is your hurt pride!"

Ross started to reply, then took hold of himself. With great effort, he said, "Look, we've been over and over this. Even if by some *miracle* I managed to patch things up with Gene, what would it change? Shelley would still have the horse."

James stood up. "You know what, Ross? This doesn't have anything to do with Shelley. We all know how it works. If we really wanted to, we could switch riders. Shelley would be upset, but she'd get over it. We'd smooth the way somehow. After all, *we* own the horse, so we can decide who rides it. No, the problem isn't Shelley. In fact, I don't even think the problem is Gene. You know what I think?" Breathing heavily, James bent closer. "I think the problem is *you.*"

"What? Me?" Ross was outraged. "You don't know what you're talking about!"

"Yes, I do. You think about it."

"No, *you* think about it! Now, do you mind? I've got work to do."

Slowly, James straightened. "You're right," he said. "And so do I."

"Where are you going?"

"Never mind. You've got your plans, I've got mine. I'll see you later."

"James!"

He was shouting at a closed door.

"Damn it to *hell!*" he cursed. He started to reach for the printout, but it slipped from his fingers. Even from the floor, the falling sales figures seemed to stare accusingly at him. He reached down and stuffed the pages in the wastebasket.

"It's not my fault," he muttered. But he couldn't help wondering if that were true, why did he feel so empty?

ROSS WAS THOUGHTFUL on the way home. Now that his anger had cooled, he was able to consider the situation with a clearer head, and he squirmed. First Marilyn, he thought. Now James. Was Shelley going to be the next one to tell him what a pigheaded, stubborn fool he was?

But as he unlocked the door to his empty, lonely apartment, he knew no one else needed to tell him where he'd gone wrong. He might as well admit it. He loved Gene. These past weeks without her had been sheer hell. After that last argument, he'd dialed her number a dozen times, only to hang up again before she answered.

Marilyn was right, he thought. He had been afraid, but not for the reasons he'd given himself. He had tried to convince himself that his overprotectiveness sprang from fear of seeing Gene hurt, but now he knew that what had scared him even more was the idea she would hurt him, too. He knew he'd never be able to keep up with her, not the way he was now. So he'd tried to eliminate the possibility of her leaving him behind by forbidding her to ride.

But his partner and his wise ex-wife had made him see that he wasn't protecting Gene as much as trying to stifle her, which was even worse. He could buy every horse in existence, he thought, and he still wouldn't be able to shield either of them from reality. Risk was a part of life. Once, he'd understood that, and accepted it. In fact, he'd relished the challenge. Could he learn to accept it where the woman he loved was concerned?

He glanced at the clock. It was almost eleven, he saw, and was relieved that it was too late to phone Gene. Even if he found the courage to call her, what would he say? It wasn't enough to tell her he'd been wrong. Was he ready to give her what she wanted? He was still debating when he realized the answering machine light was blinking. Without thinking, he pressed the play button and listened, stunned.

"Ross, are you there?" Shelley's voice cried on the tape. She sounded almost hysterical. "Oh, I hate to tell you like this, but Achilles is sick. Really sick. We've had the vet out and it doesn't look good. I'll be at the stables all night, so please call as soon as you come in, no matter what time it is. We need to know what to do in case—'' her voice broke ''—in case he doesn't make it.''

CHAPTER FIFTEEN

A WEEK AFTER ACHILLES had emergency colic surgery at the new equine hospital in San Diego, Ross and James met with Kenny and Shelley at the clinic. It was early evening, and the horse was still in intensive care. The veterinarian in charge, a capable blond woman named Dr. Katrina Vale, had called them in for a consultation.

Ross knew the news was bad when he saw the doctor's face. He tried to brace himself. In his mind's eye, he could still see the horse when they'd taken him out of the trailer the awful night they'd brought him in. As the attendants had carefully led Achilles to the operating room, his head had hung down, his feet had dragged and patches of sweat had darkened his coat.

Tonight, the doctor came right to the point. Her voice low, she said, "I'm afraid the time has come to make a difficult decision. As you're aware, some colic cases are extremely hard to treat. And even though things looked positive for a while, we're still not getting the response we'd like. Achilles isn't eating and his intestinal tract still seems to be shut down. Unless the situation changes almost immediately, I think you should consider...alternatives."

Shelley looked stricken. "We *can't* put him down," she said in a choked voice. "He's such a good horse. There must be something else you can do."

The doctor looked sympathetic, but she shook her head. "We've done everything we can. In fact, because Achilles seemed to have such a strong will to live, we've gone further than we usually do. But it's been a week, and we still can't hear any gut noises to indicate that the G.I. tract is operative. Without that—"

"But how can it be operative, when he hasn't eaten anything?" Shelley cried.

"That's exactly the point," the doctor replied quietly. "Sometimes the animal knows better than we do—"

Shelley shook her head violently. "No, I won't believe that! You said yourself that he wanted to live!"

"Yes, I did. But even the strongest horse can only fight so long before the forces of nature take over." Dr. Vale glanced at the silent Kenny, then at James, and finally at Ross. "I know how difficult this is for everyone, so you'll want to discuss it. You can let me know tomorrow, if you like."

Ross made himself ask. "How...long before we have to make a final decision?"

"I promised myself I'd give the horse eight days," the doctor said. "If there was no response by that time..."

Tomorrow was day eight. "I understand," Ross said.

She held his eyes for a few seconds, then she nodded and left. The instant she was gone, Shelley whirled around to Ross. "He can pull through, I know it!" she said fiercely. "All we have to do is give him a chance."

Kenny took her hand. "We gave him a chance. Come on, now, you don't want him to suffer, do you?"

"No, of course not. But I just know there's something else we can do!"

"You heard the doctor. She said they've done everything they can," Kenny said gently.

"There's one thing we haven't tried," Shelley said.

"What's that?" Ross asked kindly. He knew how much Shelley wanted to save the horse. They all did. He wanted to give Achilles every chance, so if there was some possibility they had overlooked, he would pursue it.

"We can call Gene," Shelley said.

James had been standing to one side, quiet for once. He blinked and said, "I beg your pardon?"

"We can call Gene." Shelley's face began to glow. "She and Achilles have a special bond, you know they do. Dr. Vale said that everything would be okay if Achilles started to eat. Well, Gene can do anything with that horse. If anyone can make him do that, she can. What do you think?"

"You know, it just might work," Kenny said.

"I think so, too," James agreed, sounding enthusiastic for the first time since he'd found out Achilles was sick. He turned to Ross. "What about you?"

Ross didn't know what to think. He was too busy trying to reel in his emotions. He still hadn't called Gene. The moment when he'd felt capable of baring his soul had been interrupted by Achilles's surgery.

The longer he waited, the more impossible it seemed. Then, when the horse got so sick, he felt he couldn't call just to tell her about that. He had suggested to Shelley that she let Gene know about Achilles, but Shelley had muttered something about waiting to see what happened. He hadn't pressed her, but it wasn't hard to put two and two together. Gene had been conspicuously absent from the stable, so he guessed that she was deliberately avoiding the place. Whether Shelley had asked her to stay away or not, Ross didn't know. He was just glad they hadn't run into each other.

Now it seemed they were about to do just that, he thought with a grimace. Kenny and Shelley and James were waiting for his answer. He knew that he couldn't deny Achilles a last chance because he hadn't been man enough to tell the woman he loved what a fool he'd been.

"All right," he said reluctantly. "Go ahead and call—"

Before he could finish the sentence, Shelley dashed off to find a phone.

GENE WAS AT HOME trying to get some work done when the phone rang. *Damn,* she thought. *I'm never going to get this project off the ground.* She tossed aside the résumé of yet another illustrator, and answered the phone with an impatient, "Hello?"

"Gene?" It was Shelley, her voice high-pitched and anxious. "Listen, promise not to say anything until you hear me out, okay? I know what I said, but this is more important than hurt feelings. I know we should

have told you before, but... Oh, Gene, Achilles is sick!
He's had surgery, and he's going to die if you don't get
down here!''

For a shocked moment or two, Gene wondered if
Shelley was playing some kind of awful joke on her.
Achilles was sick? He'd had surgery? He was going
to... *die*....

Without warning, Gene's mind flashed back to the
night High Cotton had been put down. She could see
her horse lying in the arena, his white coat spattered
with blood—

She closed her eyes against the awful image. The
couch was nearby, and she grabbed the back of it,
taking a deep breath, and then another. By sheer force
of will, she made her nausea pass.

"Gene, are you there?'' Shelley shrilled.

"I'm here.'' She tried to keep her mind on bare details. "What happened?''

"It's too long and involved to go into now.
Just... please, could you come down here? It's been
a week, and the vet said that if things don't change by
tomorrow, she's going to have to... to...''

She didn't have to finish the sentence. Gene understood even if she couldn't believe what she was hear-
ing. The last time she'd seen Achilles, he'd been so
healthy and so full of life. To think now that he could
die made her feel faint again. How could this have
happened? she wondered in sudden, futile anger—and
then knew it didn't matter. The point was that it *had*
happened, and she had to see him. Even if she couldn't
do anything, she had to be there... to say goodbye.

My beautiful Achilles! she thought, and said to Shelley, "Where are you?"

"At the San Diego Equine Hospital. It's on—"

"I know where it is. I'll be there as soon as I can."

She hung up the phone and grabbed her purse. It wasn't until she was in the car that she wondered if Ross would be there. Not that it mattered. Achilles was the only consideration right now, and at the thought that the horse might die, she began to sob.

For weeks, she had tried not to think of Achilles. But as she zoomed onto the freeway, she knew she could never forget how beautiful he was, or how glorious it felt to ride such a powerful creature. Against her will, images kept coming, and when she remembered the first time she saw him, with his white coat gleaming under the stall lights, she put a hand to her mouth, trying to hold back another flood of tears. How angry she'd been when he had tossed her into the water that day—and how satisfied she'd felt when they had, a long time later, completed a flawless round of jumps in the indoor arena. After all the hours and hours of practice, they had finally become a team. And what had happened? Because of a stupid quarrel, she had abandoned him. Did he wonder what had happened to her? Did he care? At the thought, she sobbed again and drove faster.

It seemed to take forever, but she finally pulled into the parking lot in front of the animal hospital. It was dark by this time and the clinic was closed. There was no sign of Ross's car. Thankful that she wouldn't have to face him, she parked and hurried inside. She couldn't rid herself of the feeling that she was too late until the blond woman sitting at the desk looked up and smiled wanly.

"I'm Dr. Vale," the woman said. "And you must be Gene Logan. Shelley told me you were on your way."

Gene acknowledged that she was Shelley's sister. Then she asked tersely, "What's the situation?"

Her heart plummeted when Dr. Vale told her.

"I don't know what you can do," the doctor finished kindly. "But of course you're welcome to see Achilles. Shelley and the others went out to a coffee shop for a few minutes to... talk about the situation, but I'll show you where—"

She was interrupted by the ringing of the phone. "I'm on call," she explained, reaching for it. "But you go ahead, he's easy to find. Just go through those doors there into the hospital wing. He's in the third stall on the right."

The interior of the clinic was dim and quiet. As Gene entered and looked around, she saw only one stall lighted from the inside. Quietly, she made her way toward it. But when she came closer and saw what was inside, her breath caught.

She hardly recognized her big, bold horse. His head hung low, and he'd lost so much weight that his hipbones and his ribs stood out. The white coat that had gleamed with good health looked dull—as dull as his once-bright eyes. Intravenous lines ran into both sides of his neck from two containers suspended above him on racks, and there was a huge bandage wound around his belly where the surgery had been done. As she stood there, frozen by the sight, Achilles took a shallow breath. His whole body shook, and for a horrible moment, she thought he might fall over from the effort.

The sight was so pitiful that she wanted to turn around and run out the way she'd come. But she couldn't do that to the horse that had meant so much to her. She owed him something for what he'd given her, and before she could think about it, she said softly, "Hi, kiddo. How're you doing?"

She thought he was asleep, but at the sound of her voice, one ear twitched. Encouraged by the slight response, she took a tight grip on the stall bars and tried to say, "I came to see you. I couldn't believe you were sick, not you, the—"

She couldn't go on. He looked so pathetic standing there—*swaying* there—that her voice broke. She couldn't bear seeing him like this. No one should have to suffer so; it wasn't right. She had to find Dr. Vale and demand that something be done.

Biting her lip to hold back tears, she began to turn away. Just then, she heard a nicker—or thought she did. The sound was so faint that she wondered at first if she had imagined it. Quickly, she looked back at Achilles. She was transfixed. For an instant, at least, he had emerged from his awful, pain-filled stupor and had lifted his head. He was gazing straight at her.

"Achilles?" she whispered, unable to believe her eyes.

He nickered weakly again.

It was all the encouragement she needed. She couldn't remember if the veterinarian had told her not to go into the stall with him, but it didn't matter. Her fingers shaking with eagerness, she slid the bolt to the door and went in.

"It's okay, boy," she murmured so she wouldn't startle him. Carefully, she held out her hand as she approached, step by cautious step. "It's me, see? You know me, don't you?"

His neck trembling, he put his head out and nuzzled her palm.

The veterinarian had told her that Achilles wasn't responding to anything. She believed that, having entered a world of his own, he was silently enduring his suffering while waiting for—what? The end? For someone humane enough to relieve him? For... Gene to come?

Gene didn't need an answer. The important thing was that something had finally broken through that wall. When Achilles nuzzled her weakly again, she wound her fingers tightly in his mane and let another flood of tears flow.

"You'll be all right now," she said on a sob. "You'll be all right, I know..."

After a moment, she pulled herself together—or tried to. She couldn't just stand here and *cry,* she told herself. She had to do something constructive. She had forgotten a handkerchief, and she didn't have a tissue, so she used the end of her blouse to wipe her face, then looked around.

The stall floor was bedded almost a foot deep with shavings, and in one corner was a heap of alfalfa that looked untouched. With her hand still in his mane, Gene stretched as far as she could and was able to snatch a few blades of the hay. Holding them enticingly under Achilles's nose, she said softly, "I bet you're hungry. Look what I have for you."

For a few seconds, when he seemed interested enough to sniff the alfalfa, Gene thought she couldn't contain her joy. But when his head dropped again, her spirits did, as well. *He has to eat,* she thought despairingly. *If he doesn't—*

She wouldn't think about it. "Come on," she encouraged, waving the wisps back and forth. "You haven't eaten for days. How are you going to compete if you don't eat? You've got a lot of ground to cover before you go, you know. You're too good to quit on us now."

Tentatively, he took a tiny bite of hay. She held her breath.

The wisp disappeared, and she quickly grabbed another handful and held it out for him. After a tense moment, he took that, too. As she watched him, she felt like cheering. Never, she thought, had she seen a more beautiful sight than this horse chewing!

"You'll make it," she said fiercely, the fingers of her free hand still entwined in his mane. She tightened her grip. "Oh, Achilles, you're going to make it!"

"I'll be darned," someone said just then.

Gene had been so preoccupied with Achilles that she jumped violently at the sound of the voice. When she turned, Dr. Vale was standing outside the stall, staring in frank amazement. The vet glanced from the horse to Gene. "I don't believe what I'm seeing. What did you do?"

Just then, Achilles dropped his head and began to nose around in the hay. Half laughing, half crying, Gene said, "I didn't do anything! He just starting eating."

The vet shook her head. "You can say it, but whatever you did, it worked."

"Yes," said a new voice. "It did."

This time, they both jumped as Shelley emerged from the aisleway shadows. Beside Shelley was Kenny—and James . . . and Ross. Jerking her glance away from Ross, Gene turned to her sister. "I didn't see you. How long have you been standing there?"

"Long enough," Shelley said. She looked at the now-munching Achilles for a long moment, her face expressing a variety of emotions: relief, sadness . . . acceptance. Then she looked at Gene. "If I hadn't seen it, I wouldn't have believed it."

"Neither would I," Ross said. His expression was almost identical to Shelley's. "You brought that horse back to life right before our eyes."

Gene could hardly look at Ross. Even his presence made her feel a physical pain. "I didn't do anything," she said unsteadily. "It was Achilles."

"No," Ross said in a voice that made her meet his eyes, after all, "it was you."

"Whatever it was," James said thankfully, "I'm glad it's happened." He turned to the veterinarian. "Does this mean he's out of the woods?"

Dr. Vale went in to examine the horse, who was nose-deep in the alfalfa, chewing steadily. She took her stethoscope from around her neck and listened in various places for a moment before shaking her head in wonderment.

"We'll have to wait a few days to make sure," she said with another glance at Gene. "But...I think he's going to be okay."

"Hallelujah," Kenny breathed. No one else said anything; he seemed to have spoken for all of them.

Dr. Vale gave Achilles another once-over before she said, "I hate to go, but I have a call. I'll check again when I get back, but you can stay here for a while if you like. The caretaker will lock up when you want to leave. Good night."

She gave Gene another wondering look before she left, but Gene didn't notice. She didn't want to go, but she felt she had to, so she gave Achilles a last, heartfelt pat and said, "Goodbye, sweetheart. I'd better be going, too."

"You don't have to leave, Gene," Shelley said. She reached for Kenny's hand and gripped it tightly.

Gene came out of the stall. "Yes, I do, Shelley. But before I go, there's something I've been wanting to say for quite a while now. I'm going to say it." She took a deep breath. "You were right. For a while, I did confuse Achilles with High Cotton. I didn't realize how much it still hurt to lose that horse, and when it seemed I had a second chance all these years later, I wanted it. I hope you can forgive me. Achilles was yours, and I shouldn't have tried to steal him away from you. I'm so sorry."

"So am I," Shelley said quietly. "But there's nothing to forgive. I knew you and this horse were special the first time I saw the two of you together. I just didn't want to admit it. He was supposed to be *my* ticket to fame, you see, just like High Cotton was going to be yours.''

Gene was so aware of Ross standing there that all she wanted to do was get things straight with her sister and escape. "You don't have to take the blame for me."

"Well, there's enough to go around," Shelley said shakily. "It took me long enough to admit it, but we both know that even though Achilles would work for me, his heart wasn't in it like it was with you. You and he were meant to be together, Gene. Tonight proved it. You did something for him that I could never do."

"You're making too much of it. It was just time—"

"No," Shelley said, holding her eyes. "Like Ross said, it was you." She glanced at Ross, and when he nodded silently, she turned back again. "*You* should be riding Achilles," she said. "You and he are a team. I know he'll take you right to the top, just like High Cotton would have, if . . . if he'd had the chance."

Gene fought to keep back the tears. As they hugged, she said, "Thank you. It means a lot to hear you say that." Then she held her sister away from her. She still hadn't looked at Ross, but she couldn't ignore him any longer. "But the decision isn't ours to make. Achilles belongs to—"

"Achilles belongs to you," Ross said. He'd already looked at James with a silent question, and had his answer when his partner smiled and silently raised his eyes heavenward in thanks. Then James and the others tactfully disappeared, leaving Ross and Gene alone.

These past weeks, Gene had planned what she would say if she saw Ross again—the things she would tell him, the stand she would make. She didn't say any of it. Instead, she said unsteadily, "I know how you feel about my riding Achilles, Ross. You don't have to do this. No matter what you think I did tonight, you don't owe me anything."

"Oh, yes, I do."

When he reached for her hands and held them tight, she told herself to back away—and couldn't. The simple contact between them overpowered all her resistance, and she was pulled toward him, as she always had been. She could no longer deny how empty her life had been these past weeks without him.

"I don't know how I got through this time, Gene," Ross said, his hands tightening over hers. "I tried to call you a hundred times and couldn't. I wanted to stop by and see you, but nothing I could think of to say or do seemed appropriate. How does a man tell the woman he loves that he's been a grade A jerk?"

"You weren't—"

"No, let me say it. I have to. You were right and I was wrong, so wrong. I thought I was safeguarding you, but it was myself I was protecting. I . . . I didn't want you to leave me, to go places I couldn't go with you, so I drove you away on purpose before you could make that choice yourself."

It was so quiet in the barn that she was sure he could hear the hard pounding of her pulse. Her eyes searched his beloved, handsome face, the features she had *always* seen in her dreams whether she had realized it or not, and she said softly, "I could never leave you, Ross, don't you see? You're in me. You're a part of my heart. I've had time to think, too, and as I told Shelley, I realize now that I was chasing the wrong dream."

"It's never wrong to dream."

"It is when you sacrifice what's most important. It's so hard to explain, but I'll try. You see, something in me died when I lost High Cotton. We were a team, he and I. I was only a teenager, but he meant the world to me. I thought nothing would ever mean so much to me again. But then Shelley had her accident, and she asked me to ride, and suddenly, all the competitive feelings I thought I had safely under control started taking over. I became obsessed with the idea of winning—no, not only of winning, but of somehow making it up to High Cotton. I know now that was wrong, Ross. Can you ever forgive me?"

His hands tightened on hers. "We both had things all wrong. But now—"

She didn't hesitate. Steadily, she said, "Now, things will be different. I promise I'll never again take foolish chances. I'll never risk losing your love."

He closed his eyes. He knew she meant it, and when he looked at her again, she could have soared at the expression on his face. His voice choked, he said, "That's all I can ask. You see, I know what it feels like. I still remember the rush, the satisfaction...the joy—"

"Joy?" She shook her head. "You are the one who gives me joy."

He allowed himself a small smile. "I hope so. But in a different way, I know it now. A...a friend of mine helped me to see that. And once I did see it, I thought about how you look when you ride, and what I see in your face, and I know that I don't want to take that away from you. So—" he took a deep breath "—share with me, my love. That's all I ask. I've lost what I did well, but through you, I can experience it all again. I know you won't leave me behind, because if you'll let me, I'll be right there in spirit...."

Gene hadn't known anyone could love this much. Her heart so full she couldn't speak, she threw herself into Ross's arms. Achilles nickered again, as if giving his approval.

Gene and Ross looked at the horse and laughed. Then, as Achilles dropped his head and searched for any wisp of hay he might have missed, their lips met at last in a passionate kiss.

EPILOGUE

THE PACIFIC Three-Day Event was held almost a year to the day after the surgery on Achilles. It was his first major competition, and on that morning in May, Jerry Fazey from the *Tribune* sent a photojournalist to record the event. A small crowd clustered around Kenny's trailer. The drama of Achilles's recovery had been well documented in the sports section of the paper and a continuing series on the horse and his rider had made celebrities of the pair. Fans had come from everywhere to wish them well.

The publicity had also been good for Ross and James. Sales had surpassed even the most optimistic expectations. Trade was so brisk, in fact, that they were opening another outlet in September. The new store would be the first in the growing chain to concentrate on equestrian needs and products.

As for Achilles, he had never looked better. He had regained all his weight and his white coat gleamed in the sun. He seemed to be bursting with health and vitality, and as the starter's five-minute warning came over the loudspeaker, he stamped one foot impatiently. It was as if he understood what was about to happen, and was eager to get going.

In honor of the occasion, James had brought his wife and three daughters. Everyone who knew James was amused to note that in the presence of his family, he wasn't the harassed, harried executive they usually saw, but an assured husband and father who guarded his little brood protectively. He even spoke with authority about the competition that weekend, and proudly told everyone who would listen that Achilles was in first place after the just-completed dressage phase. Next was the cross-country, which he was sure Achilles would win, as well.

Another intriguing sight was that of Malcolm Quincy standing off to one side talking to Ross's ex-wife, Marilyn. They had met last year when he'd come to make arrangements for Outdoor Outfitters to begin selling Roo'sters.

Malcolm had arrived several days before from Australia to help celebrate Achilles's return to competition. With him, he'd brought good news. The home office was so pleased with the response the Roo'sters line had received in all the Outfitters stores that they were planning increased production of several horse-related products that were to be sold exclusively by James and Ross.

Shelley and Kenny had been married six months before. No one believed it when Shelley had laughingly confided that Kenny had only proposed because she ran his business so well that he couldn't afford to lose her, and that she had accepted because *someone* had to balance the books and keep the customers paying. It was obvious to anyone who looked that they were head over heels in love. Their baby was due in

September, and Shelley had already announced that once the child arrived, she'd be back in the saddle again, even if she had to strap the infant to her back to do it. Wisely, Kenny didn't argue, but the fact that she wasn't riding *now* seemed to indicate that he had a little more influence than he admitted to.

Carrying her hard hat and gloves, Gene stepped out of the trailer, ready for the cross-country. When Achilles saw her, he let out a shrill demanding whinny that made people smile. Clearly, according to him, it was time to get started for the best part of the competition.

Gene was just as eager. It had been quite a year for her, filled with more surprises than she could ever have anticipated. With Achilles taking so much of her time in preparation for competition, she'd had to make a few key decisions. One of those had been to resign from her job at Greetings. As she'd told Mason Anderson, she couldn't do justice to both the greeting card company and to the horse. Mason was disappointed, but a few days later, he made Gene an offer she couldn't refuse.

It seemed that the fall of the year was going to be a busy time for everyone. Shelley and Kenny's baby would arrive, the new Roo'sters products would arrive at Outdoor Outfitters and Greetings would introduce an original line of cards called "From the Horse's Mouth," drawn by a new artist named Gene Logan and supervised by a freshly promoted marketing director Wally Tanker. Gene never had found out exactly *how* Mason had seen her caricatures, but she had her suspicions.

The chief suspect joined her, just then, and as she looked up at Ross, she had to smile at his expression. She and Achilles had already taken part in two non-competition horse trials this year, but even though—after one lapse—Ross had never admitted to being nervous, he continued to look a little green around the gills whenever he watched the cross-country.

"You worry too much," she'd chided him gently.

He'd looked deep into her eyes. "I love you," he'd said simply. "Can I help it if I want to keep you safe?"

"I love you, too," she'd told him. "But remember, whenever I'm out there, you're with me all the way."

It was time to start. "Are you going to be okay?" she asked.

"I'll be fine, as long as you come back in one piece." Ross hesitated, then reached into his pocket and pulled out a small velvet box. He said, "I was going to save this until you won the competition, but now seems a perfect time." He opened the box to reveal a spectacular solitaire diamond ring.

Gene gasped. "Oh, Ross! It's beautiful!"

She reached for the box, but he held it away. "Oh, no, you don't," he said with a grin. "You can have it the minute you cross that finish line. You see, I'm not above bribing you to come back to me."

"That's not fair!" she protested, but her eyes sparkled nevertheless.

Instead of answering, Ross pulled her toward him and gave her a fierce kiss. Then he helped her into the saddle. As she gathered the reins, he held up the ring and said, "I'll hold you to this."

"Oh, I'll be back for it," she said confidently. Her face glowing with excitement and love for the man who was willing to risk so much with her, she wheeled Achilles around. "Win or lose, I'll definitely be back!"

* * * * *

Be sure to watch for Risa Kirk's exciting three-book family saga set in Kentucky. These stories will explore the conflicting emotions that often run rampant in powerful families—jealousy, intrigue, betrayal, loyalty, love and pride. And, of course, each story will feature an unforgettable romance.

Follow the fortunes of the Dunleavy family in DONE DRIFTIN', DONE CRYIN' and NEVER DONE DREAMIN'.

Available in the fall of 1995, wherever Harlequin Superromance books are sold.

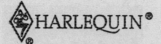

THE WEDDING GAMBLE
Muriel Jensen

Eternity, Massachusetts, was America's wedding
town. Paul Bertrand knew this better than
anyone—he never should have gotten soused at
his friend's rowdy bachelor party. Next morning
when he woke up, he found he'd somehow
managed to say "I do"—to the woman he'd
once jilted! And Christina Bowman had helped
launch so many honeymoons, she knew just
what to do on theirs!

THE WEDDING GAMBLE, available in
September from American Romance, is the
fourth book in Harlequin's new cross-line series,
WEDDINGS, INC.

Be sure to look for the fifth book,
THE VENGEFUL GROOM, by Sara Wood
(Harlequin Presents #1692), coming in October.

This September, discover the fun of falling in love with...

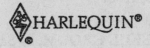
love and laughter

Harlequin is pleased to bring you this exciting new collection of three original short stories by bestselling authors!

ELISE TITLE
BARBARA BRETTON
LASS SMALL

LOVE AND LAUGHTER—sexy, romantic, fun stories guaranteed to tickle your funny bone and fuel your fantasies!

Available in September wherever
Harlequin books are sold.

◆ HARLEQUIN®

This summer, come cruising with Harlequin Books!

PORTS OF CALL

In July, August and September, excitement, danger and, of course, romance can be found in Lynn Leslie's exciting new miniseries PORTS OF CALL. Not only can you cruise the South Pacific, the Caribbean and the Nile, your journey will also take you to Harlequin Superromance®, Harlequin Intrigue® and Harlequin American Romance®.

- ◆ In July, cruise the South Pacific with SINGAPORE FLING, a Harlequin Superromance
- ◆ NIGHT OF THE NILE from Harlequin Intrigue will heat up your August
- ◆ September is the perfect month for CRUISIN' MR. DIAMOND from Harlequin American Romance

So, cruise through the summer with LYNN LESLIE and HARLEQUIN BOOKS!

CRUISE

HARLEQUIN SUPERROMANCE®

The O'Connor Trilogy
by award-winning author KAREN YOUNG

Meet the hard-living, hard-loving O'Connors
in this unforgettable saga

Roses and Rain is the story of journalist Shannon O'Connor.
She has many astonishing gifts, but it takes a near-death
experience and the love of hard-bitten cop Nick Dalton to show
her all she can be. July 1994

Shadows in the Mist is Ryan's story. Wounded in his very soul,
he retreats to a secluded island to heal, only to be followed by
two women. One wants his death, the other his love.
August 1994

The Promise is the story that started it all, a story so powerful
and dramatic that it is our first featured Superromance
Showcase. Laugh and cry with Patrick and Kathleen as they
overcome seemingly insurmountable obstacles and forge their
own destiny in a new land. September 1994

**Harlequin Superromance,
wherever Harlequin books are sold.**

HARLEQUIN SUPERROMANCE®

VERONICA SATTLER!

This September, critically acclaimed author Veronica Sattler comes
to Superromance with her first contemporary romance:

Wild Cherries

Francesca Valera has been schooled in a convent, where nothing
prepared her to deal with her new bodyguard, all-male, all-hunk
Rafe O'Hara. When a plane crash strands them in the Sierra Madre,
her education begins for real. Pursued by her father's enemies, she
becomes a three-way pawn in a very dangerous game. There's only
one man she can trust...or can she?

**Join us for the adventure of your life with Superromance.
Wherever Harlequin books are sold.**

VS-1

HARLEQUIN SUPERROMANCE®

Superromance Showcase is proud to present
award-winning author

Karen Young

The Promise, the last book in the O'Connor Trilogy, is the
story that started it all.

At last you get to meet Kathleen Collins and Patrick O'Connor
in the first flush of youth and passion. Their panoramic story
will take you from the shores of Ireland to New York to
Savannah. Separated by tragedy, each goes on to forge a new
life. But nothing can keep them apart forever—not even
Caroline Ferguson, whose father makes sure she gets
everything she wants....

The Promise. A story so special, it had to be showcased.

Look for *The Promise* this September, wherever
Harlequin Superromance books are sold.

HARLEQUIN®

Don't miss these Harlequin favorites by some of our most
distinguished authors!
And now you can receive a discount by ordering two or more titles!

HT #25525	THE PERFECT HUSBAND by Kristine Rolofson	$2.99	☐
HT #25554	LOVERS' SECRETS by Glenda Sanders	$2.99	☐
HP #11577	THE STONE PRINCESS by Robyn Donald	$2.99	☐
HP #11554	SECRET ADMIRER by Susan Napier	$2.99	☐
HR #03277	THE LADY AND THE TOMCAT by Bethany Campbell	$2.99	☐
HR #03283	FOREIGN AFFAIR by Eva Rutland	$2.99	☐
HS #70529	KEEPING CHRISTMAS by Marisa Carroll	$3.39	☐
HS #70578	THE LAST BUCCANEER by Lynn Erickson	$3.50	☐
HI #22256	THRICE FAMILIAR by Caroline Burnes	$2.99	☐
HI #22238	PRESUMED GUILTY by Tess Gerritsen	$2.99	☐
HAR #16496	OH, YOU BEAUTIFUL DOLL by Judith Arnold	$3.50	☐
HAR #16510	WED AGAIN by Elda Minger	$3.50	☐
HH #28719	RACHEL by Lynda Trent	$3.99	☐
HH #28795	PIECES OF SKY by Marianne Willman	$3.99	☐

Harlequin Promotional Titles

#97122	LINGERING SHADOWS by Penny Jordan	$5.99	☐
	(limited quantities available on certain titles)		

	AMOUNT	$
DEDUCT:	10% DISCOUNT FOR 2+ BOOKS	$
	POSTAGE & HANDLING	$
	($1.00 for one book, 50¢ for each additional)	
	APPLICABLE TAXES*	$_____
	TOTAL PAYABLE	$_____
	(check or money order—please do not send cash)	

To order, complete this form and send it, along with a check or money order for the
total above, payable to Harlequin Books, to: **In the U.S.:** 3010 Walden Avenue,
P.O. Box 9047, Buffalo, NY 14269-9047; **In Canada:** P.O. Box 613, Fort Erie, Ontario,
L2A 5X3.

Name: _____

Address:_____City: _____

State/Prov.: _____ Zip/Postal Code: _____

*New York residents remit applicable sales taxes.
 Canadian residents remit applicable GST and provincial taxes..